AS GOOD
A PLACE
AS ANY

Essential Prose Series 225

Guernica Editions Inc. acknowledges the support of the Canada Council for the Arts and the Ontario Arts Council. The Ontario Arts Council is an agency of the Government of Ontario.
We acknowledge the financial support of the Government of Canada.

AS GOOD A PLACE AS ANY

REBECCA PĂPUCARU

GUERNICA
EDITIONS
TORONTO · CHICAGO · BUFFALO · LANCASTER (U.K.)
2025

Guernica Founder: Antonio D'Alfonso

Michael Mirolla, general editor
Julie Roorda, editor
David Moratto, interior and cover design

Guernica Editions Inc.
1241 Marble Rock Rd., Gananoque, ON K7G 2V4
2250 Military Road, Tonawanda, N.Y. 14150-6000 U.S.A.
www.guernicaeditions.com

Distributors:
Independent Publishers Group (IPG)
600 North Pulaski Road, Chicago IL 60624
University of Toronto Press Distribution (UTP)
5201 Dufferin Street, Toronto (ON), Canada M3H 5T8

First edition.
Printed in Canada.

Legal Deposit—First Quarter
Library of Congress Catalog Card Number: 2024945716
Library and Archives Canada Cataloguing in Publication
Title: As good a place as any / Rebecca Păpucaru.
Names: Păpucaru, Rebecca, author.
Series: Essential prose series ; 225.
Description: Series statement: Essential prose series ; 225
Identifiers: Canadiana (print) 20240460456 | Canadiana (ebook)
20240461770 | ISBN 9781771839396 (softcover) |
ISBN 9781771839402 (EPUB)
Subjects: LCGFT: Novels.
Classification: LCC PS8631.A659 A91 2025 | DDC C813/.6—dc23

Human rights should begin at home.
—ANDRÉS DOMINGUEZ, in Eduardo Galeano's
The Book of Embraces

Contents

ACT ONE:

TORONTO'S GIRL PROBLEM

— 1. —

ON THE NIGHT they left Valparaíso, Paulina's brother Ernesto asked their housekeeper to pack a suitcase for her.

"The smallest one you can find," he told Pilar. Ernesto was already packed; he'd been packing and unpacking since the night General Guzmán had brought him home from Santiago. His old rucksack now held as many clothes and toiletries as would fit, along with a flask of pisco and his copy of Gustavo Gutiérrez's *A Theology of Liberation*. Last night, he'd added a rolled-up *Condorito* comic book, in case Paulina needed some comfort, however small, during their long journey.

On his way to his sister's bedroom, Ernesto met Pilar on the landing.

"I said small."

"It was your mother's," Pilar said, clasping the handle of the brown leather suitcase in both hands.

Ernesto followed her inside Paulina's room, still insisting that she find something smaller, but the old woman pretended not to hear him, sucking her teeth as she opened the top drawer of Paulina's dresser.

"There's still time to shave," she said, digging through the drawer. "Manuel says they are stopping anyone with a beard and long hair."

"No one will stop us."

A truck loaded with bolts of fabric would not draw anyone's attention. It was the same truck Manuel had driven north from his factory in Concepción and no one had stopped him.

"He even drove it after curfew."

"He was lucky," Pilar said, her arms full of Paulina's underthings. "And clean-shaven. At least cut your hair."

"What about Paulina? She looks like a corpse."

Ernesto gestured to his sister stretched out on her bed, staring up at the ceiling.

"I wish I was a corpse," Paulina said.

Never before had Ernesto seen Pilar so angry. Her face turned purple, almost unrecognizable, as she hurled Paulina's underpants at the girl with all her surprising strength. She would have thrown herself on Paulina, too, if Ernesto hadn't stopped her, wrapping his arms around her thick waist.

"She didn't mean it. She's just tired."

Paulina was sitting up, startled, holding one of her slips in both hands. Gently, Ernesto took it from her and turned to Pilar, grinning.

"No one wears petticoats anymore, old woman. It's not the fifties."

"How do you know what girls wear?" Pilar asked him.

In response, Ernesto pulled the nylon slip over his head, the elastic waistband under his armpits.

Paulina couldn't remember the last time she'd seen Pilar or her brother laugh. It was enough to make her laugh, too, Ernesto preening in her slip as he danced a few steps of a cueca, twirling her underpants over his head, teasing Pilar who begged him to stop, did he want her to die laughing?

Only her older brother could charm Pilar into joining him, the two circling the other, using Paulina's underpants for duelling handkerchiefs, laughing as they bumped into each other. For a moment Paulina forgot about Manuel and his truck. She almost expected her father to march up the stairs and tell them to shut up, he had an important patient downstairs, some retired navy admiral in need of dentures.

But her father wasn't coming upstairs. There was no one in the house besides the three of them.

Pilar, out of breath, leaned against the dresser, patting her face with Paulina's underpants. Ernesto continued dancing a few more steps. Paulina was too weak to join in, but from her bed she cheered and clapped, keeping time.

"Better late than never," Ernesto said, taking a bow.

September 18 and 19 were national holidays, sometimes lasting a whole week, people out dancing the cueca in the Plaza Sotomayor until dawn, but this year no one could stay out past eight. Her father would not allow Paulina out that night or any other, even if she promised to be home before curfew. On the first night of the festivities Ernesto had gone to mingle with the small crowds. That year's military parade had been composed of mostly ancient combatants shuffling along Avenida Pedro Montt. Ernesto said it made sense; there were no soldiers available. They were all too busy firing their weapons into the air at all hours, to scare people into staying indoors.

Almost two weeks had passed since that subdued Independence Day, and now they were leaving.

Still grinning, Pilar told Ernesto to go downstairs and see if Manuel needed help. She would go with him, she needed to get something from her room.

Ernesto pulled off Paulina's slip and followed Pilar. As soon as they were gone, Paulina went to her window. The only light came from Manuel's truck, but it was enough for Paulina to see Ernesto approach Manuel in the courtyard, followed by Pilar on the way to her hut at the back. After a few moments she emerged from her hut, carrying something dark and shapeless.

Paulina didn't wait for her footsteps on the stairs before getting back into bed. Pilar could move like a ghost, sneak up on you in weightless silence if she wanted.

"It will keep you warm," Pilar said, the fur coat in both arms, like a sleeping child.

With Ernesto gone, Pilar was back to her usual, stern self, packing Paulina's suitcase, telling her there was no time to dawdle, the sun would be up soon. They needed to leave while it was still dark.

Watching the old woman stroke her dead mother's mouse-grey fur, Paulina recalled the pink eyes and white lashes of Sister Teresa, her old teacher who had albinism and looked like a shrewd mouse. Sister Teresa would help her. When no one was looking, Paulina would slip out of the house and run all the way to her school where Sister Teresa, devoted to her pupils, would be waiting for her; soldiers and helicopters wouldn't keep her from her mission to protect her girls. But Sister Teresa might know about Ernesto, the danger he'd brought home with him to Valparaíso like a bad smell. She might be too afraid to shelter her when Paulina showed up, breathless and with blistered toes, at the barricaded doors of her private school.

Her suitcase packed, Pilar began laying out Paulina's outfit. It was bad enough that Ernesto refused to shave and change out of his jeans. It would do Paulina no favours, showing up at Pudahuel airport dressed like a hippie in the men's overalls and clumsily knit sweaters that Ernesto's girlfriends all wore. The grey wool dress with the lace collar would keep her warm, and she wouldn't need a slip. She would, however, require a bra.

"I'm not wearing that thing. It doesn't fit."

The previous October, just before Paulina turned sixteen, Pilar had brought her to the outdoor flea market. The best shops were shuttered, their owners having joined in the nationwide truckers' strike. The shops that had stayed open had tripled their prices. Ernesto said the Americans were behind the strike, yet another ploy to destabilize the Allende government, to wear the people down with shortages of food and fuel.

None of the few bras on display looked like they would ever fit her, but Pilar said they were not leaving until Paulina bought the one laid out on the vendor's white sheet, next to the alarm clocks and plastic combs. It was the smallest one they'd seen so far, but Paulina could tell it was too big, despite the vendor's wife insisting it was for girls, not women. A training bra, she'd called it. They were not going to find anything better or cheaper, she'd said, and Pilar had agreed.

No matter how much Pilar fiddled with the straps, the cups still gaped and sagged, even the tiny pink rosette stitched between them looked deflated. Yet Pilar insisted that Paulina wear her new bra every day, even to bed. The more she wore it, the more she would "grow into it," as if the shiny, pointy cups could magically inflate her breasts. They would be helped, Pilar believed, by her special herbal tea, the same bitter brew she'd been dosing Paulina with since she'd started her period two years ago.

"Put it on or I'll do it for you," Pilar said, dumping the bra in Paulina's lap.

It didn't matter, Paulina told herself as she pulled off her nightgown. In fact, it might help her, pleading for Sister Teresa's mercy in her best dress and matching wool stockings. She might even offer the nun her mother's fur, and the black satin pumps that were too small for her that Pilar was insisting she wear, in exchange for sanctuary.

Pilar had just picked up Paulina's suitcase when they heard the rock music coming from outside. Pilar couldn't shout down to her son; the neighbours would hear. She would have to leave Paulina alone.

Silently, Paulina finished getting dressed, then grabbed her hairbrush and began detangling her long hair.

"I'll be right back," Pilar said, hurrying out of the room.

Paulina crept to her window, still brushing at the same knot in her hair as she looked down at the courtyard from behind her curtains. The music stopped; she could hear mother and son talking, but she couldn't make out what they were saying. Maybe Manuel was whispering to Pilar that he'd changed his mind. He barely knew Paulina or her brother, why take such a risk for strangers? It couldn't just be for money.

If she didn't move now, it would be too late. Paulina dropped her hairbrush, on her way out the door but then the floor beneath her sloped, dangerously. If she didn't want to faint, she would have to crawl to the door on her hands and knees. What was wrong with her? There was no flu going around, no virus could have spread, not since the coup and the order to stay at home.

No, it was her father's pills that Pilar had been giving her since last night. They made her want to sink back into bed, give in to sleep and warmth, yet somehow Paulina managed to raise herself to her feet, both palms pressed against the wall, steadying herself.

She was leaning against the doorframe, waiting for the dizziness to subside, when Pilar reappeared. They stood staring at each other for a few awful moments, Pilar pressing her thin lips together, Paulina weak and trembling as if she really did have the flu. Then Pilar grabbed the suitcase with one hand, the other gripping Paulina by the elbow, and dragged her downstairs and all the way outside to the courtyard where Manuel and Ernesto were waiting.

Paulina did not scream, she was done screaming. What would be the point? She couldn't slip away, not under Pilar's watch. No, she'd have to wait until she was at the airport for the right moment to run away, she would hitchhike or even walk if she had to, all the way back home to her school. If Sister Teresa wasn't there, then she'd find a way to her house, rumoured to be somewhere near the Polanco funicular. Until then, Paulina would be silent, and wait.

Paulina had never seen her home at this hour. Everything was grey and white, like an overexposed photograph. Manuel's small truck was idling in the courtyard at the back of the house. No vehicle had ever driven over those stones, her father would be furious.

While Ernesto was inspecting the truck bed, Manuel introduced himself to Paulina. In the light of Pilar's flashlight, Paulina could see that Manuel's teeth were a dull, brownish colour, several of his front teeth were chipped. Even for a man in his forties, he had bad teeth. Unlike those of her son, Pilar's teeth were perfect, unreal, gleaming inside her wrinkled brown face. Whenever anyone came to him for a consultation, Dr. de Acosta would call Pilar into his examining room. Some of the most powerful men in the country, generals and politicians, even the great Pablo Neruda, had all peered inside Pilar's mouth while Dr. de Acosta explained how he had reconstructed her teeth. He liked to tell the story of how Pilar had arrived on their doorstep like a gift from God, a divine trial of his dental training. He could have turned Pilar away when she'd shown up looking for work. Instead, he gave her new teeth and a new home after she'd lost both to that year's deadly earthquake, he even let her visit her son in the south between Christmas Day and New Year's Eve. Was this how Pilar thanked her father, by turning Paulina, his only daughter, out of her home?

With Manuel's help, Ernesto climbed up into the truck bed, making space for himself and Paulina amid the bolts of cloth. Pilar gave Paulina another one of the tranquilizers her father had kept locked up for his patients, then pushed her toward Manuel who was kicking at something with his dirty boot.

Pilar watched Paulina with beady eyes, ready to pounce if the girl tried to spit out the pill but Paulina was looking back at her window on the second floor, at the roses General Guzmán, her godfather, had ordered planted outside so that their scent would greet her every morning. In the pre-dawn light, they were a dark grey, not red and pink. She barely felt the pill dissolving under her tongue as she stared.

"Where is he?" she asked her brother, busy arranging the bolts so that they would cover them both, ideally without suffocating them.

She'd asked so many unanswered questions in the past few days, weeks, months that she no longer expected any response, outside of Pilar telling her to be quiet and do what she said.

Bundled in her mother's fur coat, Paulina felt cold all over, she couldn't stop shivering. The sky was grey and pink, a light rain was falling, a spring shower bringing a fresh, green smell that mingled with the smell of exhaust from the truck. Was this what it felt like when death circled you, this heavy feeling in her limbs? Manuel had to pick her up and lay her down next to Ernesto, covering them both with the bolts, so many she couldn't see or hear; they were burying her alive, pinning her down. The truck was starting, it was moving, Ernesto was whispering to her to shut up, he would stuff her mouth if he had to. Had she just spoken? She couldn't tell what was just thought and what was uttered by her mouth.

Paulina's last vision of her childhood home was Pilar's hunched back in the headlights as she turned to go inside. The lawyer would be coming soon about the house, and Pilar was baking him a thousand-layer cake, Paulina's favourite. If she didn't move fast enough, the flies would get into the condensed milk simmering on the stove. Pilar had been so integral to Paulina's life, so present in every moment, sleeping or waking, right up until the end, that Paulina could guess her thoughts, her actions, how just as the truck was leaving Avenida Italia, Pilar was reaching inside her apron pocket. For the rosary, Paulina knew, the one that had belonged to her mother. The old woman's lips moved as quickly as her feet.

~

As if he'd figured out her plan, Ernesto would not let Paulina out of his sight, not for a moment, even waiting for her outside the windowless ladies' room of the airport terminal. If she could only get away from Ernesto, if she could hide somewhere until it was dark and the airport was empty, then she could run to Sister Teresa, to refuge, but Ernesto would not leave her side and there was no time, the plane was boarding. Ernesto kept his arm around her as they boarded, guiding her to her seat like a runaway child. When a stewardess rushed over to show Paulina the brown paper bag the airline provided for the infirm and anxious, Ernesto told her that this was Paulina's first time on a plane, she was just nervous.

"I'm being kidnapped," Paulina said.

The stewardess's smile faded, although she did offer to bring Paulina to the cockpit to meet the pilots once they were on their way; Ernesto, red-faced, said it would not be necessary. The best thing for his sister was sleep.

"Stop drugging me," Paulina said, loudly enough to be heard but no one was looking their way, they were watching the stewardess showing them how to inflate the yellow life vests.

"You won't be happy unless I'm in jail," Ernesto hissed at Paulina.

As he lit a cigarette with a trembling hand Paulina recalled, viscerally, the days before and after the coup, when no one, not her father, not even her godfather, knew where he was. Was he safe in Santiago, or had he been arrested along with the other protesting students? Ernesto in jail; it was unthinkable. Like her father, her brother could be distant, often lost in thought. But he could be kind, even generous. As soon as he finished a book, he pressed it upon someone else, a friend or even Paulina. It was a sin, he said, to throw away a book when someone could be reading it.

The plane began to move. Paulina looked around her in disbelief at the other passengers smoking and drinking and reading magazines as the plane gathered speed until it and the ground parted ways. The blood rushed to her ears, her tongue felt heavy and dry and this time she was grateful for the blank sleepiness that overwhelmed her yet again.

In Buenos Aires, the soldiers' uniforms were a different colour, but their expressions were the same, bored yet alert. Ernesto said the worst was over, they were out of Chile.

"I thought for sure they would stop us," he said, smoking the last cigarette in his pack.

Their visas, stamped by the Canadian consulate, had got them through the checkpoints. Their visas and the time of day; the soldiers had probably been patrolling the airport all night, they were waiting to be relieved, they didn't care if Che Guevara showed up ...

Paulina wasn't listening. She was thinking that Buenos Aires was not that far from home, she could find a kindly truck driver, one who would not rape or murder her, to drive her over the Andes. She stood up, looking for the exit, but Ernesto grabbed her arm, it was time to go, and before she could scream she was being hustled on board another plane. The last plane. There would be no hitchhiking home now. But to be honest, when had she ever hitched a ride in her life?

As the plane was taking off she felt herself begin to cry, soon she was sobbing, her nose ran but she didn't care, snot and tears trickling into her mouth. She calmed down enough to accept the pill that Ernesto promised would be the last, for now. Maybe she would overdose and wake up in Paradise instead of Toronto.

Just before she fell asleep, she felt Ernesto brushing the hair from her face. Were those his tears or hers on her cheek?

Twice during their interminable flight she woke, first to a darkened airplane full of sleeping passengers, then to the sun rising over what her brother said was Toronto.

It had been days since she'd been able to eat a proper meal, her mouth was dry, her stomach tight and hollow, she could barely keep up with Ernesto as he dragged her through the airport. As they stood in line, she began to shake, clutching the sleeve of her brother's denim jacket, about to sink to the floor, her brother holding her up by both elbows. Then an older man in a navy uniform appeared; Ernesto said something in his broken English about visas, but another man was approaching them, pushing a wheelchair.

"Is it the flu?" he asked her brother.

Ernesto shook his head but Paulina allowed both men to help her into the chair. The older man's touch was so kind that she began crying again. She cried so much that when it was their turn the man in the booth quickly inspected their visas before stamping each, not even welcoming them to Canada so eager was he to be rid of them.

Paulina was still crying as Ernesto pushed her toward the exit but soon she stopped, for she was seeing wonders. An entire Chinese family, parents, children, grandparents. A man in a turban, his wife in a golden sari, a red dot daubed on her forehead.

Nathan Weinrib, however, was much less exotic looking than those travellers, even for a Jew. He was shorter than Paulina had expected their sponsor to be. He wore plaid shorts and a short-sleeved shirt, and his toes exposed by his sandals were yellow-brown and hairy, like onions picked too early. An ordinary-looking man, yet somehow handsome, despite his encroaching baldness.

Paulina knew little about Canada except that it was always winter. She imagined the women as a race bred for freezing weather, thick-skinned and obese, possibly descended from seals, yet Mrs. Weinrib was a soft-looking, pinkish blur in a tent-like, yellow dress. She stood behind her husband, a baby in her arms.

"This is Hope," she said, lifting up her baby and pointing it at Paulina and her brother. Hope looked as puzzled as her parents. Clearly, the Weinribs had not expected a refugee in a fur coat being wheeled through the airport.

"So this is the famous Paulina," Nathan Weinrib said in his unmelodious Spanish. He insisted on taking over from Ernesto and pushing Paulina's chair.

Outside it was hot and sunny, as inexplicably hot as summer back home, but Paulina resolved to keep her mother's coat on, like a furry shield, even after she heard Ruth Weinrib, in a Spanish that was even more atrocious than her husband's, say something about how lucky they were, to be greeted by such unseasonably warm weather.

"Can she walk?" Paulina heard Nathan Weinrib ask Ernesto. "I can carry her to the car if you want."

"I can walk," Paulina told him, in English.

Nathan stopped the chair so Paulina could get out, but she got up too quickly, the sun was too strong, she had to grip the armrests with both hands. Even with her eyes closed, she saw the dark spots dancing. Was she going to faint in front of these strangers?

Mrs. Weinrib gave her baby to her husband so she could help Paulina while Ernesto explained in his broken English that his sister was just tired from her first airplane ride. Helpless, Paulina clung to this strange Canadian woman like a tree in a mudslide.

~

While Nathan Weinrib showed Ernesto the renovations he'd made to his basement to turn it into a modest apartment, Paulina took the last of her father's tranquilizers. The pill had the desired effect; without excusing herself, she ducked into her new bedroom and got into the narrow bed with the white wicker frame. Mercifully, she slept for the rest of the day, and into the night, waking only once to eat the packet of cookies Ernesto had left by her bed, beside a *Condorito* comic she read absent-mindedly by the bedside lamp.

The next morning, after a breakfast of more cookies and tea, Nathan took them to a local church that collected donations for refugees, so they could choose weather-appropriate clothes and shoes from the bins, all of it carefully selected and cleaned, he assured them.

As they walked to the church on the big street north of the Weinribs' house, Nathan offered to take special care of Paulina's fur coat.

"In case you find something more practical at the church," he said, in Spanish.

The problem with fur coats was that they attracted moths. His uncle was in the fur business, so Nathan could have her coat stored and cared for, at no cost.

Before she could answer Ernesto said it was an excellent idea.

"You can get it back when we leave," her brother told her, as they descended the steps to the church basement.

"I don't care."

"Yes, you do. Even if it made you look like a bear had eaten you."

Her brother was right, the coat was too big for her. But why did they need to pick through old clothes like beggars when they'd be home before Christmas?

From the outside the church opposite the grocery store looked like any of the houses on the Weinribs' street, no cross or steeple to indicate a house of worship. Nathan said the church was nondenominational, that it wasn't Catholic or Protestant, that everyone was welcome.

"It's like a big tent," he said.

Despite this promising description, the basement of the church was like any other basement, including theirs, damp-smelling and low-ceilinged. At the back, a young woman in a blue vest was sorting through garbage bags. She waved at them, then went back to her work.

Nathan led Paulina to the girls' section, to dig through the bins for as long as she wanted, he said. With his guidance, she chose a puffy silver ski jacket for the winter, and a double-breasted plaid jacket with gold buttons for the cooler weather that Nathan said was just around the corner.

"Try them on," he said.

Both fit her just fine, although the plaid jacket smelled of pencil lead and the zipper on the breast pocket of the ski jacket wouldn't open.

"These should fit you." It was the girl in the blue vest, handing Paulina a pair of silver winter boots. At least the tag was still attached.

"Aren't they cool?"

"Thank you."

"You're lucky," the girl said. "We just got these yesterday. The family's moving to California, so they don't need their winter gear. Are they comfortable?"

Paulina nodded, embarrassed to be scavenging in public, but not Ernesto, who kept grinning at the girl, asking, in his broken English, how she thought he looked in the suede coat he'd dug up.

The boots fit Paulina perfectly, not that it mattered. Paulina would never wear her winter gear. The coup was an aberration, their country was not a banana republic, it had a proud tradition of democracy, even Nathan Weinrib said so, and he was a lawyer. They would be back home before the first snowfall, so there was no point in digging through people's cast-offs, just like there was no point in her brother taking the English lessons he was now signing up for at the church, on the girl's recommendation. Certainly, there was no point in complaining to Nathan that what he called her bedroom was really no such thing. Instead of a door, a curtain of brown beads separated the little nook from the rest of the apartment. The dresser and bed frame, even the little table by her bed were made of wicker and painted white. Paulina thought it looked cheap, but it didn't matter. Nothing mattered, she would go along with all of it, or so she thought, until she saw the robot in her closet.

"It's a water heater," Ernesto said, grinning at her. "Why don't you name it? It will be the pet Pilar never let you have."

"Can't you tell the Jew to move it somewhere else?"

"Don't call him that," Ernesto said sharply. "And don't be stupid. It's not an *estufa*."

Estufas, the portable gas heaters they used back home, were on wheels and could be easily moved from room to room. Yet her brother seemed to think this growling water heater was the mark of an advanced society. The machine was nearly her height, and it hissed and grunted all day and all night. She could hear it even after she closed the door to its room.

At least they didn't have to worry about the cold coming in through the windows. There were only two small windows in their underground home, in the main room opposite the tiny kitchen, which Mrs. Weinrib called "the kitchenette." Her brother's bed was against the wall below these windows, not a real bed but a yellow sofa. It was easy to convert, Mrs. Weinrib said, as she denuded it of its cushions and then, with Ernesto's help, tugged at the seat until it became a small, flat bed. Mrs. Weinrib also insisted they call her Ruth.

"Mrs. Weinrib is my mother-in-law," she said, in English. Her husband must have told her that her Spanish was terrible.

"Of course," said Paulina, unsure why Ruth found this fact so amusing.

Ruth Weinrib boasted of making the white curtains herself, out of muslin to let in more natural light, she said. Not that they needed curtains; the only way anyone could see in would be to walk right up to the windows, then kneel on the ground and peer inside. Even the most dedicated deviant, Ernesto assured Paulina, would not be willing to take that many steps to gratify himself.

Their only view was of the Weinribs' front lawn, green and brown, the same colours as the only real chair in their new home, which Ruth Weinrib called a "love-seat." Instead of cool, clean tiles, the floor was carpeted, rough grey fibres with purplish blotches as if bruised.

While it was pleasantly cool inside their mole's tunnel of a home, it also smelled of damp leaves and even more oddly, raisins. Worse, they didn't have their own bathroom. To reach what Ruth Weinrib called the powder room, they had to exit the apartment by the door connecting the basement to the family's laundry room, walking past the washing machine and what Paulina had believed to be a second washing machine, until Ernesto explained it was a dryer. They were lucky to have one, he said.

"You can't hang clothes out to dry in the winter, they'll freeze solid."

Paulina added shirts and pants frozen like sheets of ice to the horrors of a Canadian winter. She was grateful she wouldn't be there to witness it.

~

One afternoon toward the end of that first, awful week, Ernesto woke Paulina from her third nap of the day to talk about what he called, her bathroom habits.

"You have to start flushing your used paper down the toilet," he said.

Ruth Weinrib had been emptying the basket (also wicker and painted white) and had asked him about the abundant wads of paper she'd found there.

"Why do they have the basket, then?"

"For other garbage. I don't know. Women's things."

He meant menstrual pads but wouldn't say so, no matter how much she prodded him.

"Just flush the toilet paper," he said, red-faced.

Paulina was not to worry; he'd tried it himself and could confirm that Canadian toilets would accept toilet paper and other things, too, like cigarette butts.

There was one more thing. Ruth Weinrib, who was now intimate with her bathroom habits, had offered to take Paulina on a tour of the city. Ernesto wanted her washed, dressed, and ready to go tomorrow afternoon. If they didn't play nice, the Weinribs might choose to shelter another, more pleasant refugee family in their basement. And anyway, Paulina could use a shower. A long one, Ernesto said, pinching his nose and waving his hand like she was the one who'd just farted.

— 2. —

Paulina had always loved the thrill of getting lost in familiar surroundings. That would not be possible in Toronto; according to Ruth, all the major streets formed a neat grid, so that you could never get lost. Bathurst Street and University Avenue ran parallel to the city's main artery, Yonge Street. Bloor, College, Dundas, Queen, and King all ran east and west, also parallel to each other. However, east of Yonge, College became Carlton, Bloor became Danforth. Other than that, the city's layout was so straightforward, even a child could navigate it.

"You can always get oriented," Ruth said. "Wherever you are."

Already Paulina ached for Valparaíso, its hillsides, the brightly coloured wooden houses crowded along narrow, winding streets inaccessible to fire trucks. But the sea was always below, a funicular always nearby to bring Paulina home when the lostness began to feel like danger.

Her father's house was close to the sea, between Valparaíso and Viña del Mar. They were, in fact, closer to Viña del Mar, the orderly suburb famous for its English gardens, but Paulina told everyone she was from Valparaíso, even if her father said otherwise.

Paulina was ashamed to learn that Ruth knew her country better than she did; the Weinribs had studied Spanish in order to explore its most remote regions. Unlike Paulina, they'd travelled the length and breadth of Chile, from the Atacama Desert in the north to Punto Arenas in the south. Also Easter Island and Patagonia, even a sliver of Chilean Antarctica, which they savoured in the afterglow of Allende's victory. Valparaíso had especially captivated Ruth, a former student of medieval art history. The city felt positively medieval, she said, especially those picturesque hills. She'd been distraught when she'd learned that the navy had captured Valparaíso on the morning of September 11, signalling the start of the coup. How distressing it must have been for Paulina, too.

Paulina did not tell Ruth that at first only Pilar had been truly distressed, convinced that an imminent earthquake had silenced her radio. Nor could she tell Ruth that, despite his concerns about Ernesto, her father had welcomed the coup, the restoration of order. Ruth and Nathan would not understand their father's initial support of the junta, Ernesto said.

"You must have been so worried about your brother," Ruth said, as they were walking (exactly southeast, according to the map) toward city hall.

"My godfather took care of him," Paulina said.

On the night of September 11, General Guzmán had gone to Santiago, to track down Ernesto. Paulina had wished that she, too, could go to the capital and escape the silence of their house, broken only by Pilar weeping and praying. True to her godfather's word, however, her brother was back in time for the Fiestas Patrias.

But Paulina couldn't say much to Ruth or anyone about her well-connected godfather or her father. Ernesto had warned her not to tell the nice Canadians that their father had been a friend of the Pinochet family, that he often treated the army's commander-in-chief on his visits home to his native city of Valparaíso. In the aftermath of the coup, Paulina's father would often wish aloud for Pinochet to smile in at least one of the photographs of the junta. If only the world could see the General's beautiful teeth, courtesy of Dr. Leonel de Acosta's talents.

Now Ruth was recalling Allende's farewell address to the country. The student radio station in Toronto had played it, she said. She and Nathan had cried, hearing Allende speak on that poor recording.

In those first, confusing days following the coup, her father had confiscated all the radios, even Pilar's, silencing not just the outside world, but Allende. The man was a Marxist troublemaker, her father often said, although he'd also treated the deposed President, back when Allende was a senator for Valparaíso. The two had even belonged to the same Freemason Lodge. Through this connection, her father had offered to provide Allende's dental records to the media to confirm his death, but he never received a reply. It was as he'd expected, he'd later ranted to Ernesto. Allende's death had been faked. The army would never stoop so low as to assassinate a Chilean president, and Allende hadn't possessed the courage to end his own life. No, his supporters had airlifted him to Cuba, to drink cocktails with his old buddy Castro and plot Marxist conspiracies.

"We kept thinking about Ernesto, wondering if he was alright," Ruth said. "We were so relieved when he called."

They'd arrived at the city hall. Unlike the plazas back home, there were no statues of victorious men on horseback, no palm trees, no gardens. The complex that stood before Paulina was the result of a competition, Ruth said. Bids had come in from all over the world.

"A Finnish architect won. I can't remember his name. It's really modern, don't you think?"

To Paulina, the city hall looked like a concrete spaceship after an emergency landing. Towering above the stranded saucer were two curved towers that looked like they'd been sliced in half. One was notably taller than the other. Paulina wondered if they'd run out of concrete and glass.

All it would take was one earthquake to bring the whole thing down, like the one in the south, the worst on record, when Paulina was barely four years old. The one that had brought Pilar to her. Although a smaller earthquake would also do the job, like the one that had struck Valparaíso two years ago. Their house had survived but they'd had no electricity for days, Pilar had to make a fire in the courtyard to boil water. She wouldn't let Paulina go outside, even when the army arrived, even to see the helicopter bearing President Allende as it flew over them. Still, there was enough to see in the house: long, vertical cracks in their walls, bottles of her father's wine floating in the basement. Even more exciting, a mudslide had disgorged the coffins from a cemetery way up in the hills and one had landed on their street. It was miraculously intact, but her father had agreed with Pilar, Paulina was not to go near it, such things carried disease.

Ruth bought them soft-serve ice cream, vanilla for herself, chocolate for Paulina, from a dark, hairy man inside a truck. They sat on a bench, Ruth going on about the city's efforts to rid itself of its colonial past, her neglected ice cream dribbling down her wrist.

Why would anyone want to erase all traces of their past? In Chile, people were proud of their colonial heritage; indeed, much of downtown Valparaíso had remained unchanged since the nineteenth century. Whenever a Spanish colonial treasure was damaged by fire or earthquake or flood, people like Paulina's father donated large sums toward its reconstruction.

Toronto must seem strange to Paulina compared to Valparaíso, Ruth conceded. It was such a special place, even if the packs of wild dogs had badly frightened her. A funny story, actually.

"We were looking for our hotel up in one of the hills and we turned a corner and entered a sort of plaza, I think. There were steps below us, each step painted a different colour. I was taking a picture of them when I heard dogs barking. There were about half a dozen, their tails were down, they were growling at us, I was terrified. We ran and just like that we ran into the owner of our hotel. Literally, we almost knocked him down. He was very sweet. He took us to the hotel and made us tea. Their little boy was adorable. I worried every time he went outside, that those dogs would tear him apart."

While she didn't resemble a seal, Ruth Weinrib was plain, possibly fat, but it was hard to tell, the way her voluminous skirt concealed her lower half, down to her ankles. She didn't wear make-up or style her greenish-brown hair, letting it hang limply, indifferently, over her rounded shoulders. Back home, appearances mattered. Years later, Paulina would understand how she'd been conditioned to judge other women based on grooming, age, and dress size. Not that she spared herself such judgement: large nose, a mouth that did not respond well to lipstick, actually shrinking when painted. She was short, too, even for a Chilean, and had to stay out of the sun or risk resembling a charred stick pulled from the fire, as Pilar often warned her. There was nothing womanly about her save her eyelashes and her long, dark hair and even that was to be lamented, for it betrayed the mestiza blood she'd inherited from her mother.

Despite Ruth's overall formlessness, her large breasts drew Paulina's envy. At the moment they were full of milk, drawing the attention of men passing by, even those accompanied by wives and children. Beneath her peasant blouse, Ruth was braless, her large, dark nipples were visible beneath the thin white fabric. She reminded Paulina of the pre-Hispanic fertility statue she'd been shown during a school visit to Viña. The guide at the Fonck Museum had held her in gloved hands, gently caressing her round belly and the tiny, intricately chiselled cobs of corn she clasped in her burnt-orange hands. Like that goddess, Ruth Weinrib could probably ensure fertile crops and steady rains with just a wave of her soft, white arms.

Paulina finished her ice cream without tasting it. On the map Ruth had given her, Toronto's fabled grid resembled a board game for the simple-minded, with no challenges, no adventures. Not that it mattered. This brief stay in Toronto would barely merit a mention in her memoirs. Her public would want to know how she'd become a great artist of stage and screen, not what she thought about Toronto's city planning. When her time came Paulina, too, would be full-breasted and fertile, posing for publicity photos with her husband and children, proving she was a real woman, in addition to talented. Yet no matter how hard she tried, Paulina could not see the faces of her husband or any of their offspring, just her own big-nosed teenage face.

Ruth Weinrib, who having toured Chile should have known better, kept insisting that Toronto's history was much more colourful than most people knew, as colourful as that of Valparaíso. In fact, there was one chapter from the city's past that Paulina might find especially fascinating.

At the start of the 20th century, and all the way up to the 1930s, Ruth said, blotting melted ice cream off her sleeve with a tissue, girls had come to Toronto from Great Britain to make new lives. They'd lived in boarding houses, had money of their own. There were many of them, some thought too many, but it was expected that they would eventually give up their jobs and get married. They didn't. Instead, they got better jobs, working in offices instead of factories. Then they did the unforgiveable. They started having fun. The newspapers were full of editorials written by men arguing what to do with them as if they were stray dogs. They called it "Toronto's Girl Problem."

"Plays were even written about them people were so fascinated. Girls without husbands or families in the swinging twenties, doing what they wanted. No one had ever heard of such a thing. The good people of Toronto thought they had to be prostitutes. Which of course they weren't."

Did Ruth expect Paulina to become a Toronto Girl Problem? How could she when she didn't have money of her own? Ernesto had money he said came from their father, but she could only have a small amount at a time, and only for necessities.

At last, Ruth suggested they go home. She was probably bored with Paulina, who had barely spoken. They took the streetcar because Ruth said it looked like it might rain. While she did not care for the clean, odourless city, Paulina did like the red streetcars, admittedly smoother than the blue and silver trolleybuses back home. She also had to admire the Weinribs' street, its many trees and pointy Victorian houses, some with fancy stained-glass windows.

Looking at the brick house with its wide porch you could never guess it contained such a dismal place to live in its bowels. It was as if Nathan Weinrib had buried them alive, but Ernesto said she was being melodramatic, as usual.

"It's only for a few months if that. The junta will call an election and we'll be able to go home. You'll see."

Canada, Ernesto said, was as good a place as any to wait for their country to sort itself out. While they waited, Ernesto would learn English, maybe become a translator back home. He might even continue the sociology studies he'd abandoned because of the coup, starting with a study of the Canadians they encountered. That evening, Ernesto showed Paulina the notebook and pen he'd bought while she was out with Ruth. Paulina opened it that night while he was asleep on the sofa, which he never bothered to transform into a bed. The pages were blank so she filled the first ones with what Ruth had told her about the Toronto Girl Problem. Then she curled up on the floor by the sofa and willed herself to sleep, to dream of those feral girls who had seized this city before her. They rose from the streets in the form of pink seals to suckle Ruth Weinrib's breasts, swollen so large that they eclipsed the moon and the sun.

THAT MORNING PAULINA lied and said she had a stomach-ache.

Two couples, fellow Chilean exiles, had invited her and Ernesto to a picnic. It was Thanksgiving Day, a holiday. The perfect time, Nathan said, to visit the Toronto Islands.

When Ernesto offered to stay behind Paulina switched her story to female troubles and he left her alone as she'd guessed he would. Anyway, the outing would allow him to observe the Canadians; he was anticipating a good cross-section of them aboard the ferry.

Paulina was relieved she wouldn't have to see her brother's new friends again, even if it meant missing the amusement park. She'd felt so awkward around them, an entire afternoon in their company would have been unbearable. Patricio and his wife, Victoria, Victor and his wife, Patricia. Their names were the source of much joking. Nathan had met them at the church where Paulina and Ernesto had chosen their cast-off winter gear. Paulina, too young to have been a part of the student movement that had almost cost them their lives, had nothing to add to their talk of politics, Marxist this,

Communist-Socialist that, Castro and Che, Nixon and
Kissinger. Worse, during yesterday's awkward tea date in
the Weinrib basement, Victoria had offered to make
little Paulina a little tea, using the diminutive forms so
common to Chileans. Paulina had grabbed the first mug
she could find in the cabinet: oversized, gigantic, really,
and the two couples had laughed, Ernesto, too, at the
sight of that large grey mug in Paulina's little hand, the
product of Nathan Weinrib's brief interest in pottery.
While they drank their tea, they even dissected Paulina's
name right in front of her: did Paulina know that Paul
was Latin for small? So Paulina, which was the diminutive of Paula, meant very, very small. Paulina, almost in
tears, excused herself, saying they were out of milk, but
instead of the grocery store she escaped to the fountain-
less, statueless park at the end of the street where she
could cry and watch the squirrels. When she returned,
her bladder bursting, she was relieved to find that her
brother and his new friends were gone.

It was so unfair: both couples were Chileans of
Slavic descent, tall and blond. It was unfair, too, that her
name, like so many girls' names, was really just a male
name in disguise, something that had never occurred to
her before. Maybe she would change her name to an
English name, one that wasn't a version of a male name.
Like Ruth. She would become an Elizabeth, or a Robin,
like the girl at the church. Paulina had gone back on her
own, to rummage some more. The girl's name was
Robin, like Robin Hood, who took from the rich to give
to the poor, except this Robin had directed Paulina to
the cleanest, most recent donations of shoes, T-shirts,
and jeans.

If Robin had asked her, she would have gone with her to the islands. Instead she was stuck in the basement numbly watching TV.

While Paulina was watching a reporter interview a group of dropouts on a downtown street, Ernesto and his new friends were boarding the ferry.

"People call us hippies," said one of the longhaired boys into the microphone.

"Like it's a bad thing," said a girl in oversized sunglasses. The reporter asked if they were on drugs.

At that moment, as the ferry was chugging across Lake Ontario Patricio, moved by his first encounter with open water since leaving home, led the small crowd in shouts of *Viva Allende, Viva Chile,* at first unaware of the three older men watching him. Ernesto observed the scene with growing interest as these men (working-class, he judged) began taunting Patricio. Then one of the men stepped forward, and punched Ernesto in the eye.

Patricio and Victor tried to pull the three men off Ernesto but then one of the men produced a knife. For some reason he didn't use it on Ernesto or anyone else, just waved it at the crowd. As soon as the ferry docked, he and his knife disappeared, along with his pal. Only Douglas Watson stayed behind to face the harbour police.

Douglas Watson shouted at the police that he'd served in the Korean War, he knew all about Communists, he had every right to protest the Chilean invasion of his country. When Patricio challenged him to name their dead and deposed President, Watson snorted and said, Ricky Ricardo. You people, he added, have some explaining to do. Some of the passengers laughed, while others called him a bigot. Not long after noting the social and cultural import of this exchange, Ernesto lost consciousness.

~

In the afternoon Paulina heard Nathan drive off but she didn't think much of it. It was a beautiful day; probably the Weinribs had gone on a picnic. But then Ruth entered without knocking. At first, Paulina believed she'd come to invite her. She was surprised by a rush of pleasure, until she saw Ruth's pale, unsmiling face.

"Something's happened," Ruth said, looking around the basement as if she'd lost something there. "It's Ernesto. You need to come with me."

She'd brought Hope down with her, the baby howling in her arms.

"Is he missing?"

"No, no, he's fine, he's in the hospital. Nathan's gone ahead of us. There's a taxi outside."

Paulina put on the first pair of shoes she could find. Once outside she realized these were her travelling shoes. The black silk pumps were dusty, their decorative bows unravelling, already her toes were aching, but it was too late to change. She got inside the taxi, her ears ringing, Major Street looking more unreal to her than usual as the taxi pulled away from the curb.

If I see a yellow car, Ernesto will live, she told herself, barely daring to look out her window.

"Stop the car," Ruth said, a screaming Hope in her lap.

"Clothes. We should bring him some clothes."

Ruth was right, why hadn't she thought of this? Back in the basement Paulina grabbed whatever she could find, none of it clean, and stuffed it into a paper bag. She was about to leave when she remembered the notebook and pen. If she brought these, then her brother would be well enough to write. She put them in the paper bag and joined Ruth in the taxi. As they were pulling away, she remembered her shoes. She'd forgotten to change them. Seated beside Ruth, she discreetly slipped them off, giving her feet a quick break from so much pain.

Nathan had managed to organize a press conference outside the hospital, Ruth said, he'd called every reporter he knew, asked them to spread the word. He wanted Paulina to speak on her brother's behalf. Did she mind?

"It would really help his case, if we have to go to court."

Paulina agreed she would speak, hoping Nathan would step in and take over. She asked Ruth to tell her everything she knew, but either Ruth didn't know much or she didn't want to tell her. A man had attacked her brother on the ferry, an ambulance had taken him to the hospital, one of his friends had called Nathan from the police station. No, Ernesto was not going to die. But his attacker, a man named Douglas Watson, wanted to press charges against her brother, for assault.

"It's insane," Ruth said. "How are you and your brother supposed to apply for citizenship when this fucking asshole is dragging you into court? Your brother should be the one suing him."

Hope, perhaps worn out from so much screaming, was now asleep, cradled in her mother's arms, tiny fingers curling and uncurling.

"Is it bad?" Paulina asked.

"I don't know. But they've moved him out of intensive care."

The blood was pounding in Paulina's ears as the taxi was pulling up to the looming hospital. They had been here for less than two weeks, and her brother was in the hospital. In this country that was supposed to be a refuge.

Outside a side entrance, the press conference was already underway. Nathan was on the sidewalk facing a small crowd of reporters and their vans parked on the street. Even though it was a holiday, he wore a suit. As soon as he saw Paulina, he rushed toward her and embraced her. Then he turned back to face the reporters, holding Paulina's hand. His was warm, damp with sweat. Nathan asked her if she was okay and Paulina said yes, realizing as she spoke that she'd left the paper bag full of her brother's belongings in the departed taxi. She had remembered her shoes, however. Maybe her brother was right, she was hopelessly self-centred.

"Paulina de Acosta Zapatero," Nathan said to the cameras and microphones. "The victim's sister."

For how long had she dreamed of such a moment? Photographers, reporters, even a television camera, all trained on her. But unlike in her fantasies, she was not backstage at the Municipal Theatre of Santiago, fresh from yet another triumph, or on the set of a Mexican melodrama, her director beside her. Nor was she wearing some historical costume that hugged her voluptuous body. Instead, she had on the T-shirt she'd selected that morning for a day of television watching and fitful snacking. *Capricorns Do It Better*. Robin had said the shirt was especially cool because Paulina was a Gemini, she could tell. Paulina hadn't contradicted her.

The reporters moved closer to her as a single unit; Paulina was sure she would faint or go to the bathroom in her jeans if they asked her a question or took her picture.

"Are you a revolutionary?" someone shouted.

"She's a minor," snapped Nathan.

"So there's an age limit for radicals?"

Laughter. Someone took her photograph and Paulina blinked away the bright spots. She was sweating but only below her chin. Ever since her first period, this sweating in odd places had troubled her. Worse, her mouth was dry and she feared not being able to speak without tripping over her words. But there was no time to be sick, the questions came quickly, all at once.

Holding up a hand, Nathan told the crowd Paulina would answer a few questions, but not too many. She wanted to see her brother.

"She speaks English?" someone called out.

"Paulina attended one of the best schools in Chile. She's fluent in English, French, and German."

"A little German," Paulina said, but no one seemed to hear her. She wondered if the reporters came from different countries, if Nathan expected her to address them in the three languages he'd just ticked off. She could manage fine in English, possibly French, but German had been her worst subject.

"How did you get here?"

"Ruth brought me in a taxi," Paulina said, speaking into the padded microphone someone had shoved in her face.

"He means how you got to Canada," Nathan said. At least no one was laughing at her.

"How do you know Nathan Weinrib?" a different voice asked.

"He is a friend of my brother." Her voice sounded high and childish. It was terrible. Smoking was supposed to deepen your voice but the smell nauseated her and her father had told her it was especially unhealthy for women, it stained their teeth terribly.

"They met in Santiago," Paulina said, or squeaked.

Where were her hands? Was she swinging her arms? No, they were folded behind her back, under her control. Sister Teresa would have been proud.

"Go on," Nathan said, his arm around her.

"They met at a party. My brother did not know Ruth was married. He asked her to dance. He told her he would introduce her to Salvador Allende."

"We met three years ago," Nathan Weinrib said. "When Allende first came to power. Ernesto had just started university."

Nathan pointed to another reporter like a conductor, the press conference was becoming less chaotic, almost syncopated. Paulina felt herself relax, if not bask in the attention.

"Did your brother know Allende?"

At last, a question she could answer, in detail.

"Ernesto met Allende when he was a boy. Allende was a patient of my father. My father is a dentist. He is the best in the country. All the important men come to him."

"What was wrong with Allende's teeth?"

"He had the gum disease. My father drained his gums. This took many hours."

Paulina raised her chin and pushed back her shoulders. There was a chill in the air and she wished she had on her ugly plaid jacket.

"When there was trouble, he called Mr. Nathan in Canada."

Ernesto said sponsorship could take months to arrange, but Nathan Weinrib was a lawyer, specializing in immigration. It said so on the card he'd given him, when they said goodbye. Her brother had put the card in his wallet, along with all the other cards from all the other gringos who had come to Chile to witness the "Chilean Way to Socialism" and been disappointed by how bloodless it was turning out to be, but not Nathan Weinrib, who shared Ernesto's interest in something called, orderly agrarian reform.

"Why did your brother have to leave? Was he a MIRista?"

"I told you before. Ernesto Acosta is not a militant," Nathan said, answering for her.

"Ernesto de Acosta Zapatero," Paulina said, correcting him.

Did these Canadians really believe Ernesto was a radical? Did they picture her brother squatting in the mountains, bare-chested and bearded, crawling through the mud with a mouthful of bullets, ready to shoot and raid villages for supplies, and stoop to whatever else guerrillas did? Was this why Douglas Watson had put her brother in the hospital?

"Ernesto de Acosta Zapatero is here because of flowers."

She was not supposed to tell anyone the specific reasons for her brother's exile. No one needed to know the details, Ernesto had said. They would assume he'd been a supporter of Allende, involved in some radical group at the university, and that would be enough. But if these people believed her brother was a radical Communist agitator, then Canada would be no safer than Chile. In the taxi, Ruth had reassured her that most Canadians did not think like Douglas Watson. But what did Ruth know? She spent her days inside her house with a baby. No, the true story would show the world her brother's kindness, his helpful nature. She had no choice but to tell it.

～

September 13, 1973. Two days after the coup. The university was closed, Paulina told the reporters, so Ernesto had nothing to do, no way to help. He was in his rented room listening to the radio when he heard the call for volunteers at the city morgue. It was the social scientist in him, that was why he'd responded.

"He likes to observe what is happening," she said, so no one would get the idea that Ernesto was a morbid type.

Her brother was at the morgue the next day, put to work immediately by the staff, who were overwhelmed by all the bodies being brought in. Many were unrecognizable but on Ernesto's first and only day, he recognized one, a famous journalist and teacher at his university.

Ernesto rushed out of the morgue to track down the journalist's wife, knowing only that she lived in Ñuñoa near the national stadium. Neighbours brought him to her when they learned that the journalist's body was to be dumped in a mass grave that night. It was his wife's idea, not Ernesto's, to bury him elsewhere. That night, Ernesto and the journalist's neighbours went to the general cemetery and dug out an occupied grave. To their credit they chose the oldest one they could find. They buried the journalist in this grave and Ernesto and a friend dumped its previous occupant in the mass grave. It was dark so he could not see the condition of the coffin, what forty decades had done to it.

"What about the flowers?" someone asked.

Flowers. Ernesto had returned to the cemetery the next day, September 15, to pay his proper respects, but in his hurry had forgotten to bring flowers. He took some from a nearby grave but someone saw him, a longhaired type in jeans stealing flowers from the grave of a general so old he'd served in the War of the Pacific. Ernesto was arrested but he was home a few days later. He'd done nothing wrong, Paulina told them.

"Then why was he arrested? And how was he freed?"

Before Paulina could answer, a woman with a microphone stepped forward.

"Who was the journalist? The man he buried?"

"That's enough for now," Nathan said.

Nathan invited one photographer to accompany them inside to document Ernesto's injuries for his newspaper. As Nathan led them through swinging doors and in and out of elevators, Paulina pretended this was a hospital from a movie, a set, not a real place where people died. As she followed the others down the hallway to her brother's room, she selected the role she would play from now on, the version of herself that she would offer the world: dignified in her suffering, her chin held high and her shoulders squared, much like Alma Siqueiros in her first film, *Love, Not Bread* when she realizes that she must carry on alone on the hacienda without Héctor Torres. Paulina would be brave enough for her and Ernesto both, planning their flight from this terrible country. Even her shoes on the hospital floor sounded tough, confident, each tap a brutal fact unclouded by feeling, although just as they were approaching Ernesto's room, she lost her balance, Ruth catching her just in time.

"You did great," she told Paulina, as she steadied her.

Paulina was still catching her breath when they entered her brother's room, the photographer pushing ahead of them, snapping away, then rushing out of the room, grim-faced.

Paulina approached her brother's bed with small steps, shuffling like a nervous crab, eyes darting, taking in his hospital bed, the nurse watching her anxiously.

Ernesto, unable to sit up, stared at them through half-closed eyes.

"Why the hell did you bring her here?" he asked Nathan, in Spanish.

One of his eyes was shiny and swollen, the lid almost black from bruising, the other bright red with blood where the white should have been.

Only when Ruth hurried her out of the room was Paulina aware she'd been screaming. She could still see her brother's mouth as he was speaking to Nathan, the awful red pulp, the pink saliva.

"What happened to his teeth?"

"His teeth," Paulina repeated, not aware she was shouting.

"My cousin's a dentist," Nathan said in his clunky Spanish.

Paulina looked around for the bathroom, but it was too late. She threw up all over the hospital floor, splashing some onto Nathan's nice lawyer shoes.

— 4. —

DOUGLAS WATSON TOLD reporters that Ernesto had lunged at him without warning like an animal, he'd had no choice but to defend himself. Nathan said he was lying, that Patricio and Victor and their wives had all testified that Douglas Watson had attacked Ernesto first, catching him off-guard, so that he fell to the ground. Ernesto had not spoken a single word to Watson, let alone attacked him. No, something about Ernesto had enraged Douglas Watson but no one could say what that was. Ernesto had long hair and a beard, but so had many of the other men on the ferry that day. Why single out Ernesto for such a beating?

Douglas Watson had twisted Ernesto's arm; it said so in the papers. He'd pinned him down and twisted his arm with both hands while Ernesto screamed. Now Ernesto's right arm was in a sling, and Paulina had to roll his joints for him. At least he was left-handed, so he could manage one-handed tasks, and he didn't need her help going to the bathroom, except for when he came back from the dentist, high on painkillers.

The Canadians were too polite to point out the obvious; not so Victor. The two couples had come by the basement a few days after Ernesto's discharge from the hospital. Ernesto was sleeping in Paulina's nook so they didn't stay long, just long enough for Victor to present his theory to Paulina.

"He is an easy target. Now that he is so fat."

It was embarrassing, but she couldn't argue with Victor's assessment. Since coming to Canada Ernesto had gained weight, and quickly, on top of the weight he'd been gaining back home. Pilar said it was from drinking; too much beer and wine, she'd said. Paulina and her brother were short, just a few pounds made a big difference. Punching Ernesto would have been as easy and satisfying as stomping on a tub full of grapes, Patricio added, unnecessarily but truthfully.

Small, round, and dark—Ernesto was more grape than man. Paulina could not bear to imagine Douglas Watson, a heavy-set middle-aged man glowering at her from the city paper, beating her brother. She wanted to see Watson guillotined in front of the space-ship city hall but Nathan said the last death by hanging in Toronto had been a good ten years ago.

That afternoon Victor and Patricio did all the talking while their wives unpacked the food they'd prepared for Paulina and her brother: empanadas, corn and meat pies, blancmange. Despite their wives' cooking, Victor and Patricio were both lean. The wives, Patricia and Victoria, were sisters, tall and slender like their husbands. Both men had served in the Allende administration and yet, for supposed radicals, looked as ordinary and clean-shaven as policemen. Paulina found it impossible to make conversation with any of them and was glad when they left. But she thanked them for the food.

Paulina was responsible for feeding and medicating her brother. She had to force him to eat, but not to take his pills. Ernesto was not to go over the daily dose of his pain relievers, which in the wrong hands could be abused. The pharmacist had judged Paulina's to be the right hands for the job, but each time her brother pleaded for another pill less than an hour after she'd given him one, she gave in. Ernesto's shoulder, like his face, was still healing. The real concern was the hairline fracture in one of his ribs. That was what was causing him so much pain, the doctor said, not the arm that Douglas Watson had wrenched from its socket and that had had to be popped back in place.

At times Ernesto was lucid enough to tell Paulina of the study he'd made of the hospital staff but mostly he slept. Paulina watched him as much as she could, alert to any sign that he was about to slip away thanks to her generosity as pill provider. At night, she curled up beside him in her narrow bed and tried her best to sleep. His prescription couldn't be renewed but Paulina still worried that he might become addicted to the pills.

When he was conscious, they drank tea and watched the TV programs Ernesto had previously considered evidence of a society numbed by consumerism, now programs he never missed, some internal clock telling him the exact moment to turn on what Nathan called the "idiot box." He watched TV for hours, refusing to answer Paulina's questions about what had happened on the ferry, even when she insisted he disregard Nathan's advice and press charges. Douglas Watson should be in prison for what he'd done, but her brother wouldn't listen, wouldn't even answer her questions, which she thoughtfully saved for the commercials. He wouldn't even open the notebook she'd bought him to replace the one she'd left behind in the taxi.

One night, after taking the last of his painkillers, Ernesto began talking over the evening news, which he usually watched in stony silence, waiting for a report about the junta.

That night, in a low, toneless voice he confessed to Paulina that, before recent events, he'd never been involved in a fight, not even at military school where so many boys were beaten and humiliated. This escape from hazing rituals he owed to Pío Guzmán, their godfather's only child.

"I could never get rid of him when we were boys and then at the academy, I was glad to be his pet. No one dared touched General Guzmán's boy."

"Because of his father?"

"No, because of Pío. He was an animal. They tried once, you know. They came into our bunk one night, but Pío was prepared. He got the littlest one before they could do anything. A pencil right in the ear. A lot of blood can come from an ear, you know. After that, they left us alone. Pío considered me his brother, the little creep. I did all his homework for him. I'm sure he was illiterate, which makes it funny, don't you think? Choosing the pencil for his weapon. He wasn't aiming for the ear, you know. He was really mad at himself. He thought he could have done better."

Paulina waited for her brother to say something about Douglas Watson, how after this first experience of violence he'd had enough of Canada, he was ready to go home, they'd be safer there.

Ernesto leaned back in Ruth's loveseat and closed his eyes.

"Yes," he said, almost smiling, already back in his own, twilight world. "You can get a lot of blood from just one ear."

~

Two weeks after her brother's assault, Nathan Weinrib organized a fundraiser for Paulina and Ernesto, to be held at the home of his wife's cousin. Ruth Weinrib came from a large, powerful family, Ernesto explained, breaking the news about the party to Paulina. This cousin was a well-known local journalist, a columnist and women's liberationist married to a rich art dealer, so the fundraiser would be a silent art auction, the process for which Ernesto explained to Paulina as they walked to the park.

When Paulina balked, Ernesto reminded her that she was now famous, she had a duty to her public. He may have been the victim of a brutal crime but she had emerged as the star of their show. Photographs of her crumpled dark face, partially hidden by her long hair, had appeared in all the city's newspapers. Their editors had preferred her crying face to her brother's pulpy one, some even shrinking the photograph of her brother while enlarging her own. Naturally, people wanted to meet her.

Despite her fears, Ernesto wasn't angry with her for telling his story to the reporters, so long as she kept her mouth shut from now on. His story had only appeared in the papers; it had been eclipsed on all the evening news broadcasts, TV and radio, by a deadly flu outbreak at a nursing home.

She could not refuse her fans, Ernesto said, or Nathan, especially if Douglas Watson took Ernesto to court.

Paulina agreed that they couldn't afford to offend their sponsor and who knew but her newfound fame might lead to her discovery; the Koenigsmans might be friends with Hollywood producers. However, the rich and powerful Mr. Koenigsman, or Mr. Helen as Ernesto called him, would not be attending. He was in New York on business but sent his best wishes and, more importantly, his money, in the form of a tax-deductible donation of some artwork. Since Ernesto was still healing, Nathan would have to be her escort. The party would be this Friday.

"That's in two nights! What am I supposed to say to those people?"

"Let them do the talking," Ernesto said, warily looking around him. "It's their party."

The small, featureless park near their street was empty that weekday afternoon. Ernesto and Paulina sat on a bench, Ernesto waving his good arm at any squirrel that dared to approach them. This abundance of wildlife in a gringo city had surprised them both, the black squirrels that chased each other up and around the trees, the raccoons that toppled the garbage bins in the alley behind the Weinribs' house. Ernesto feared an attack by squirrel and death by rabies, despite Ruth's reassurances that the creatures were harmless. His fear had intensified, however, since the day he'd looked out their window and spotted a family of raccoons waddling across the front lawn in broad daylight.

Paulina found the creatures charming and wondered why the Canadians did not adopt the adorable squirrels for their pets.

"Just smile and nod," Ernesto said as Paulina was helping him up from the bench. It was time to go; the squirrels were spooking him. Ruth had twice brought Paulina to High Park, which was full of squirrels and boasted a man-made lake from which policemen had once fished a human leg. Ruth had brought bread and nuts to feed the animals, and they'd lured a chipmunk, even cuter than the squirrels, out from behind a tree by tossing it sunflower seeds.

"Show them you're grateful," Ernesto said, wincing as he shuffled toward the street.

His jacket was draped over his shoulders like an old woman's shawl, while Paulina's was buttoned up to her chin. The plaid pattern was purple and orange, like the leaves that had started to fall. The trees in Toronto shed more heavily than those back home, Nathan and his neighbours had to rake them into piles on their lawns, bundle them into bags to throw out. How could you just throw out leaves, like old newspapers and bits of string?

Paulina promised to be on her best behaviour at the fundraiser. Ernesto smiled, displaying the new front teeth in his still bruised and slightly swollen face. Paulina had to admit they looked good. If you didn't know better, you would think he'd been born with them.

— 5. —

HELEN KOENIGSMAN LIVED in an apartment on the highest floor of a high-rise building, the tallest building Paulina had ever been invited to enter. This building even had a name, like a small but powerful nation: *The Regency North*. The elevator ride up was so steep it made her ears ring, still sensitive from her first plane ride. Ernesto said it was just her imagination, but Paulina was convinced that travelling such a long distance by air had permanently damaged her eardrums.

For a rich couple, the Koenigsmans did not have much furniture in their apartment, or perhaps they had put it away to make room for dancing. A handwritten sign in the foyer asked guests to remove their footwear which meant Paulina would have to expose her stocking feet to whatever was lurking inside the thick white fibres of the Koenigsmans' carpet.

As she was removing her shoes, some of the guests began circling Paulina and Nathan. A few were in evening dress, but most were dressed casually. Paulina felt self-conscious in her prim grey dress but it was the best she had. At least she had better shoes; Robin had found her a pair of stacked-heel Mary Janes, even buffing and polishing the black leather for her until they looked new.

One male guest had found a compromise between casual and formal attire, in the form of a T-shirt with the image of a bow tie and jacket printed on it, exactly where they would have appeared had he been wearing a tuxedo. Paulina thought this was ingenious and wondered if similar T-shirts existed for women, bodices stencilled on their fronts. If not, they should.

The man in the tuxedo T-shirt introduced himself as Barry Koenigsman and without preamble, offered to take Paulina on his boat, anytime she wanted, for a view of her new home from the lakeshore.

"It's called *The Battleship Koenigsman*. Get it?"

"I get seasick," Paulina said.

Before Barry could respond, perhaps to point out she was lying, Nathan, handsome in blue turtleneck and jeans, told Barry that Douglas Watson was dropping all charges against Ernesto. He'd waited until the party to tell Paulina, so they could celebrate in style.

"Good," Barry said, smiling down at Paulina. "Last thing you need is a trial."

Paulina returned his smile. It was wrong but she was disappointed by the news. She'd been imagining herself in a courtroom, even dreamed at night of standing in the witness box, one hand on a Bible, the other dramatically raised. She was not sure what she would have said but it would have been enough to make Douglas Watson beg for his life. Still, it was a relief. A criminal record would have weakened their case to stay in the country as refugees. *Nathan wants me to stay out of trouble*, her brother would say, whenever he smoked the grass Nathan smuggled him downstairs, which was most nights.

Barry drifted away, replaced by other guests. Doing her best to act gracious, Paulina accepted their compliments of her English, her charming accent. As not much was required of her, she began to relax, enough to consider the table of food in the distance, until someone pulled Nathan away and Paulina had to face the guests and their questions alone, each one more puzzling than the last. Did Paulina think the junta would keep the copper mines nationalized? Before she could attempt a non-answer, another question stumped her. How many prisoners were being held in the national stadium? The place could hold at least 90,000 people, but could there really be that many political prisoners in the whole country? And what about the thousands murdered so far, did her brother know any of them? Did she?

"Murdered?"

Where was Nathan? She felt sick, she had to get away from these people, they were bearing down on her.

Someone grabbed her by the arm.

"Come have a look at the art."

Her saviour was a tall woman in a strapless green dress. Wordlessly, Paulina followed her to the opposite end of the room, to the artwork to be auctioned off for her benefit. Propped against one wall were paintings of various sizes, the smaller ones perched on easels.

"I'm sorry about all the questions," the woman said. "They should know better, haranguing you like that, but they're just worried. You read these things in the papers and you don't know if they're true."

"That's okay." They're not true, Paulina wanted to say. They can't be.

The woman smiled at her.

"This one is my favourite," she said, pointing to one large canvas, completely white, save for a small square of red in the centre. The card below read: *Blondes Have More Fun. Barry Koenigsman, 1968.*

"I'm Helen," the woman said.

Paulina wondered if, in addition to shoes, Helen Koenigsman also forbade bras, or maybe none of the women in Ruth's family bothered with them, no matter how generously they were endowed.

During the chaotic final months of Allende's presidency, Paulina had believed that the fracturing of her country had pushed her to grow up and out of her sickness, cooling her childish crushes on the older girls at school. Yet now in this cold country her fever had returned.

"Which one do you like best?"

For a moment, Paulina assumed Helen was asking her to make an impossible choice between left and right breast. Realizing her mistake, she pointed to the red square in the centre of the white canvas. Helen smiled. Her approval made Paulina's scalp tingle and her gums throb.

"There's someone you need to meet," Helen said.

Helen led her to a white leather sofa, and a seat between herself and a woman she introduced as Valerie Thomas. The sofa was wide enough to prevent any brushing of legs but Paulina's hairline tingled all the same. All their limbs may as well have been intertwined, breasts and hips touching, for all Paulina's shivering body knew.

The contrast between Valerie, delicate and Black, and Helen, tall and white, entranced Paulina, who was certain that even their bones must be radically different, Valerie's small and fragile, Helen's large and dense. All the rush of her initial attraction to Helen now shifted to Valerie, as easily as water poured out from one vessel and into another.

~

Years later, Paulina would cringe at the memory of this encounter but not because of her attraction to Valerie. Chilean society was homogeneous, Ernesto had explained to her one night during his recovery. The majority of its people were of mestizo heritage, half-bloods. People of purely European origin formed its upper class and another minority, the Indians, formed its lower class.

Paulina had always known where she belonged in this hierarchy: to the white upper class, despite a nearly invisible drop of mestiza blood.

Canada, her brother had explained, was not so easy to categorize. Paulina must be prepared to encounter a greater variety of races. It would be interesting, he said, to observe her reactions when she encountered someone different from herself.

And so, first reaction upon meeting Valerie Thomas: the sensation of seeing in the flesh a person or place she had only seen in movies. Valerie Thomas was beautiful enough to be an actress. She wore a sweater made up of little white balls all stitched together. The contrast between these fuzzy white balls and her short, neat Afro fascinated Paulina, as did her glossy, orange lips.

"Great party, eh?" Valerie smiled at Paulina, revealing small white teeth as lovely as the rest of her.

Paulina agreed that it was a great party. If only she could tear off her high-necked grey dress, better suited to a little girl than a grown woman. Ashamed, she gazed down at her feet, then at Valerie's; there was a small hole in Valerie's sock through which her great toe was visible, its nail painted the same orange as her lips. It was somehow both touching and titillating, this bit of slovenliness.

Paulina did her best to follow the conversation between the two women, which seemed to concern her education. What education? Their mysterious phrases had to refer to someone else.

Self-directed learning. No grades. Instead of teachers, facilitators. Accordance with ministry standards. Waiting lists a mile long. The board had pre-approved her, what an honour.

Smiling, Valerie turned to Paulina.

"Education is like a boat," she told her. "And the student is captain."

Helen agreed. Paulina would begin steering her boat next Monday at an experimental public school within walking distance of her house. It was somewhat late in the semester but Helen assured her that Valerie would "bring her up to speed."

A lump was forming in Paulina's stomach as if she'd been force-fed hot wax.

Helen turned to Valerie.

"What exactly does it stand for again? ASPIRE? You'd think I'd know by now, I'm on the board."

Helen winked at Paulina. Paulina returned her gaze to Valerie's orange toenail.

"I'll write it down." Valerie reached for her purse.

"We're very lucky to have Valerie," Helen told Paulina. "She just graduated from McGill."

Valerie passed the scrap of paper to Helen, who gave it to Paulina, who read the words written there in perfect cursive: *Academic Success: Peer-based, Integrated, Reflective Education.* Paulina returned the paper to Helen as if it were on fire. Underneath these meaningless words, Valerie had drawn a circle containing two dots and a curving line meant to be a smile. Paulina was sure if she looked at it any longer she would cry or scream or both.

"Does my brother agree?" she asked Helen.

Ernesto would never agree to this. No need to go to school, no need for her brother to work. They would be home in a matter of weeks. That was what they both wanted, Paulina reminded herself. That was what all the exiles wanted. Victor and Patricio had boasted of not buying furniture for their small apartment beyond what they needed. Like Paulina and her brother, they had mismatched plates and cups and bedding. There was no need, they'd said, but Paulina had noticed Patricia and Victoria exchanging looks. They probably want babies, she'd realized, but could not have them until they were back home. A lot of women, Ernesto told her when they were alone, refused to give birth until they were back on Chilean soil.

Helen stubbed out her cigarette in the ashtray, which up till then Paulina had mistaken for a sculpture up for auction. It was made of brass and stood on one leg beside the sofa, like a one-legged, flightless bird.

Helen placed a hand on Paulina's knee, setting off a pulse between her legs, like a butterfly was trapped between her thighs, furiously beating its wings.

"Ernesto said at your old school, the girls weren't very nice, they picked on your best friend Marcela. You won't have that problem at ASPIRE. Ruthie can walk you over Monday morning if you want but I told her it's not far, you'll probably want to walk by yourself."

Paulina stared at Helen's hand still on her knee, at the ring on one of the long, white fingers. The stone was a deep red colour, like a drop of blood.

"Everyone is really nice at ASPIRE," Valerie said.

Paulina looked down at her own feet this time. What was she doing, exposing her stocking feet to strangers?

"No," she said. She rose from the sofa, her legs trembling instead of pulsing.

Luckily, the auction was underway, the people who had been interrogating her less than an hour ago were now busy at a long table, writing down their bids on the cards provided. In the hallway, she put on her shoes, then retrieved her plaid jacket from a closet that was about the size of her basement bedroom. She was on her way out the door when she collided with Valerie.

"I have to leave." She sounded rushed and breathy, like Marcela when she was having an asthma attack.

Valerie smiled at her.

"I could use some fresh air," she said, putting on her coat, tan suede, long and belted. The white fleece lining its collar framed her face, drawing attention to her pointed chin. The toes of her boots poked out from under her chic, flared pants.

"I can drive you home," she said. "Unless you have a ride?"

They were waiting for the elevator, the sweat was pooling at the small of Paulina's back. Was she being rude? She should say something to Valerie but what could she possibly say? I love you, let's run away together?

At last, Valerie leaned forward and pressed the button. "No place to go but down," she said, grinning.

— 6. —

IT WAS RAINING, a light, odourless rain. This country had no rain smell, no night smell, no morning smell. An odourless country of basement-dwelling slugs, or so Paulina had thought, but now there was Valerie. And she was going to drive her home.

Valerie removed a small umbrella from her purse and invited Paulina to get under it. Paulina could hear Valerie's breathing, soft and steady, as they walked to her car. Paulina's chest ached so much she wondered if she had bronchitis again. Back home, she'd been ill with it for weeks. Pilar had said it was her fault for standing in front of the fridge barefoot like a half-breed. While she was bedridden, her godfather had brought her a book in English, *Little Women*. Her father was on a trip, where or why she couldn't remember. General Guzmán had sat on the edge of her bed, unafraid of contamination, and told her to sign her name in her book. When she was all grown up, she could show her children how she wrote her name when she was a child.

Where was her book now? Was it still on the shelf by her bed with her other books, and the seashells that she'd kept in such perfect condition, and her scrapbook, in which she'd pasted pictures of Alma Siqueiros? What was she doing here, sharing an umbrella with this beautiful woman, who was a head taller than her and smelled of talcum powder?

"Are you nervous about school?" Valerie asked her, as they were walking toward her car.

"I cannot go."

"But why not?"

"My father will not like it."

"I thought your father . . ."

"Yes," Paulina said.

Her father was dead but that didn't mean he'd want her going to a public school.

"I'm so sorry. What about your mother?"

"My mother died after I was born."

When Paulina was old enough to ask about her mother, her father had explained that, because Dolores had caught the measles so late in her pregnancy, Paulina had not suffered the usual birth defects. She'd been infected late enough to spare Paulina, but not herself.

On the anniversary of her mother's death, Pilar would bring out the photographs for Paulina and now she saw them in a flash: Dolores on the day of her wedding, a dark-eyed young woman in a simple white dress, standing by her new husband who was more than a decade older. Dolores in the garden wearing her fur coat, this time smiling, if uneasily, showing off her husband's gift. If not for Pilar, Paulina would never have known what her mother had looked like. After her death, her father had given Pilar the fur coat and the suitcase, dumping the photographs and Dolores's rosary in the pile earmarked for charity or burning, whichever the housekeeper decided. Pilar had saved the photographs for Paulina, the rosary for herself.

"I'm so sorry."

Valerie unlocked the passenger door of her boxy red car for Paulina.

"Helen says your father was a dentist?" she asked, starting the car.

"Yes. The best in the country."

"That explains your teeth. They're really beautiful. Perfect, even."

"Thank you."

Her father had chosen dentistry because, as he'd often said, a skilled dentist was always in demand. It would not matter if he was a poor orphaned Basque who'd fled Spain after the Civil War, arriving in Chile a sickly teenager aboard a ship named, Paulina had recently learned from Nathan, after a Canadian city. It would not matter if he rented a room above a grocery store and worked as a dockhand while he studied. It would not matter if he was a lapsed Catholic who'd deserted Franco's forces, so long as he worked fast and did not gossip, even when generals and senators fainted at the sight of his tools. He would never again know hunger, nor would his family, not with the rates he charged, although he always refused Neruda's money; the poet, then Chilean consul in France, had personally stamped his permit to board *The Winnipeg*.

"So where do you live?" Valerie asked, while they were stopped at a red light.

Paulina opened her mouth, then closed it as she realized that she did not know her current address. Up until then, it had not seemed important.

"I don't know the address," she said, looking out the window, as if for a sign.

"I could take you back to Helen's?"

Paulina shook her head. Her mouth was dry; she was in danger of sinking into a blank panic.

"Minor Street." She spoke the name so loudly that she startled them both. "I live on the Minor Street."

"What Minor Street? Where is it?"

"Not Minor Street, no. Major Street. I live on the Major Street. Major."

"In the Annex, right? Below Bloor?"

"Yes," Paulina said. Major Street, how could she have forgotten? She was the orphaned minor who lived on Major Street. She didn't know the number but she told Valerie she would recognize the house as soon as she saw it, which she did.

"I love these beautiful old Victorians," Valerie said, pulling up to the Weinrib house.

Did Valerie know that Paulina lived in the basement like a sack of onions? Had Helen or Nathan told her? Could she smell it on her?

Like any normal, well-mannered Chilean Paulina leaned forward to kiss Valerie goodbye on both cheeks, without incident and successfully ignoring, or so she thought, the warmth and scent of Valerie's skin, the feel of her lips as they brushed her cheeks in turn.

It wasn't until she was about to open the passenger door that Paulina saw her hand on Valerie's knee.

She couldn't move, not her hand, not her body. All she could do was look down at her traitorous hand, waiting for Valerie to slap it off her leg. Instead, she reached over Paulina to open the glove compartment, her elbow brushing against Paulina's thigh. Discreetly, Paulina retracted her hand.

"So you won't lose it," Valerie said, writing her phone number on the palm of Paulina's hand with the pen from her glove compartment.

Paulina's hand tingled, she could smell Valerie's hair she was so close. It smelled salty, like the ocean.

"Call me," Valerie said, releasing Paulina's hand. "If you're ever in trouble or just need to talk. But I hope to see you Monday. ASPIRE is a wonderful place, I know you'll love it."

Paulina stood on the pavement, stunned, as Valerie drove off, revealing a man on the other side of Major Street. He had a small white dog with him. The dog was straining at the leash, squatting on the curb, then jumping up and kicking his back legs toward General Guzmán who, smiling at Paulina like she was a stranger, bent down to pick up the dog's shit, his hand inside a plastic bag.

Before Paulina could shout or run, a dark car pulled up and her godfather got inside.

When she finally moved, she felt like a stone statue cracking and crumbling. She had no reason to be ashamed, she wanted to shout after General Guzmán in the retreating dark car. She'd done nothing wrong, simply accepted a ride. From the outside, she and Valerie would have looked like two friends, heads lowered, one holding the other's hand, offering comfort. The more she thought about it the more innocent it became.

Paulina unlocked the door to the Weinribs' basement, vowing that the next time she saw the General she would explain everything and he would understand. He would have to; the man was her godfather, he'd renounced the devil for her.

— 7. —

ERNESTO WOULDN'T LET her go back to bed, insisting she make them tea while he sat at the kitchen table and hassled her.

"They were about to call the police. We owe these people everything."

Ruth, in a panic, had come downstairs to rouse him from bed; Nathan was on the phone, saying Paulina had disappeared from the party. Ernesto had just gone upstairs and picked up the phone, when Helen told Nathan she'd overheard Valerie Thomas offer to drive his sister home.

"What were you thinking?"

"I didn't do anything wrong," Paulina said, staring at the kettle on the compact stove.

"Don't wander off like that. People are watching us."

Paulina turned to face her brother.

"Who is watching us?"

"Everyone."

"General Guzmán?"

"Don't be stupid."

"I saw him," Paulina said, taking the whistling kettle off the stove.

"What do you mean, you saw him?"

As she poured their tea Paulina told her brother about their godfather's appearance, leaving out the part about him picking up his dog's poop.

"It's just your imagination," Ernesto said, spooning sugar into his mug.

"No, it was him, I know it."

"You just think it was. I see people all the time."

"Who do you see?"

"Friends. People from school. It doesn't matter, it's not real."

If her brother saw old acquaintances, it was because of the marijuana he smoked. Her vision had been different. She was absolutely sure it was her godfather. As for the marijuana, she wished Nathan would stop supplying Ernesto with the drug, even if Ernesto said it helped him with the pain. Lately, Paulina had started rolling his joints for him in advance, leaving them in a plastic bag on the kitchen table. Ernesto was right: she was good at it. At first, she'd considered taking a puff, just to see, but she lost all interest the night Ernesto wet himself after finishing his nightly joint. Paulina had watched in disbelief as the dark stain spread across the front of his jeans while her brother, oblivious, dozed off on the sofa.

"Why do I have to go to this school if we are going home soon?"

Part of her wanted to go if it meant seeing Valerie again, while part of her didn't for the same reason.

"There will be questions if you don't go."

"What questions?"

Her father had told her not to worry about her education. Until the junta reopened the schools she would learn to cook and manage a household; she could do that much. Not that Pilar had let her touch anything during those long hours together in the kitchen. Paulina was to learn by watching. Watching and eating because her father was right, who would ever marry such a stick of a girl?

Ernesto heaved himself up from the table and went toward the sofa, returning with a copy of *La Tercera*, of all things. Nathan's contact at the Canadian consulate in Chile had sent it to him, he said. They weren't going to show her, they didn't want her to worry, but after tonight, Paulina needed to understand the importance of not drawing the wrong kind of attention.

On the front page of the paper was Ernesto's bruised and bloodied face, magnified as to be almost unrecognizable. Paulina read the headline in disbelief; what had happened to her brother was an example of the kind of greeting Chileans like him could expect abroad.

The reporter, a man named Otto Rubio, claimed that, according to his sources, the body Ernesto had discovered and given such a fine burial was actually that of a depraved MIRista, a left-wing terrorist and enemy of the Republic of Chile wanted for rape, robbery, and murder, the grave he and his fellow degenerates had robbed the final resting place, not of some old general, but a young soldier, a fine man recently murdered while defending their country and its Christian values from radicals like her brother.

Ernesto de Acosta was not just a Communist but a thief and a defiler, of graves and dead bodies. Douglas Watson was a hero for defending his country from Communist invasion, and from perverts like her brother, who'd done vile things to the dead soldier's body, too vile to describe in a family newspaper. Despite his sister's impassioned defense, the man was a pervert and a fairy, a *maricón*, his passport rightfully stamped with an L, identifying him as *persona non grata*, unwelcome in his native country.

At the bottom of the page was a white box with a red dot inside, reminding Paulina of Barry Koenigsman's painting. Simply by gazing at this dot readers could transmit their prayers that Ernesto de Acosta release his sister from his sick grip and let her come home.

There was no picture of her.

"But I told the truth, it's not my fault if they changed it. Newspapers are full of lies, Papa always says so. No one will believe it."

Ernesto took the paper from her and threw it on the floor.

"Ruth is going to invite a girl to the house, she goes to your new school. A girl your age. So from now on you do what I say and I won't ask you about that telephone number on your hand."

Despite her disappearance, or perhaps because of it, the fundraiser had been a success, her brother said.

"When do we get the money?"

"It's not that simple. Nathan will set up a special account for us. Did you think he was going to come downstairs with bags full of cash?"

"No," Paulina said. She'd been thinking just that, but the money, for reasons her brother said he didn't feel like explaining, would have to be frozen for some time.

They finished their tea in silence, Paulina wondering not for the first time how well she knew her brother, now her legal guardian. She'd been nine years old when their father sent Ernesto, then fourteen, to the military academy in Santiago. After graduating, he'd stayed in the capital for university. For the past seven years, they'd only seen each other when he came home for the holidays. Even after the big earthquake, he'd stayed in Santiago because it wasn't safe to travel.

But they'd been close, in their own way. Paulina always looked forward to the summer break, when Ernesto would be home just before Christmas, to stay with them until school started again in March. Not that he was around that much, but he always came home for dinner. When it was just Paulina, her father barely spoke to her or Pilar, preferring to read his medical journals while he ate, which was unfair, even Ernesto agreed; why did he get to read at the table while she was forbidden from doing so?

Things were always better when her brother was there. It felt like decades ago, the three of them eating together, Paulina listening to her father and Ernesto argue over her brother's grades, his clothes, his hair, his friends. They were always arguing, but it was better than silence.

~

Lying in bed that night, Paulina went over the events that had brought her to this strange country, something she did most nights, otherwise she risked waking up in a sweaty panic, not knowing where she was or how she'd got there. It was hard to remember the exact details, like the date of her brother's return from Santiago, their departure from Chile. She got them mixed up with the date of her father's death. It wasn't because the dates were so close together, Ernesto said. It was because she'd been in a state of emotional shock, she still was. That was why she'd seen their godfather walking a dog on Major Street. That, and because Pilar wasn't around to dose her with her father's pills.

So that she wouldn't forget she wrote down all the dates in the notebook she'd bought for her brother, which he never used.

On September 23, their father died. The funeral was scheduled for September 29, the day after they left. Their godfather was taking care of it. Ernesto said that when it was safe for them to come home, they would visit his grave. Pilar said her father would understand. He would also understand why she, and not Ernesto, would deal with their father's lawyer about the house. She and Ernesto had worked it all out. The house would not be sold, it would be there for them when they came back, because her father had left it to them in his will. Pilar would take care of it while they were gone. General Guzmán would understand, she said. Paulina was not to worry.

On September 23, Pilar found their father slumped at his desk. In a panic, she'd called General Guzmán. Their godfather had been to their house many times since he'd brought Ernesto back to them. He came right away, rushing into her father's study with his doctor, who was also their family doctor. When they came out of the room and closed the door behind them, Paulina knew he was gone. Pilar brought her into the kitchen, to wait for the doctor to come talk to her.

Her father had died of a stroke, Dr. Rozental told Paulina. He always spoke to her like a grown-up, kind but forthright. Her father's death had been sudden but not surprising. At sixty-two, he was not a young man, his health had been declining, he'd been worn down by work and worry. The uncertainty and chaos of the past three years had been too much for him.

Her godfather was the same age as her father but he had not been worn down by life, his hair was dark, not grey. Ernesto said he wore a wig, probably made from the hides of the poor animals he hunted, but Paulina didn't believe him.

Pilar brought her upstairs. Her father was with God, she said. That was why Paulina wasn't crying.

She never saw her father again. Her godfather ordered Pilar to lock the door to his study. It was hard to believe he wasn't behind the door, at his desk, working.

On September 23, the day her father died, General Guzmán's dark hair was neatly combed and shiny, like always. Paulina could still feel the weight of his hand on her shoulder as he promised to take care of her. Her and her brother. Ernesto was not home. Where had he gone? Paulina had no idea. Since returning from Santiago with their godfather, he was rarely at home, not even for meals; their father did not like that. Ernesto would never tell him where he went; her father would get angry, didn't he know it was dangerous? When he was home they would disappear into the study, Pilar would hear them arguing. It frightened her, so she would go upstairs to her room. What were they fighting about? Why couldn't her father just be happy Ernesto was back?

Her godfather said that all that worrying about her brother had killed her father, and Ernesto hadn't even been there when he'd died. It was shameful, he said. But he would keep his promise to protect Ernesto, he loved him like a son.

When she heard her brother climbing the stairs late that night, Paulina rushed out of her room to tell him what had happened. She was still ashamed of herself for crying, saying he'd killed their father with unnecessary worry. Ernesto had been unmoved, until she told him how the General had offered to move them into his own house. Then he ran from her, Paulina running after, out the back door and across the courtyard to the small hut. As soon as Pilar opened her door Ernesto asked the old woman if her son still had that truck and if so, would he like to make some money. Then he told them both his story, the story of the morgue, and the flowers.

Her brother was in trouble because of flowers. Even the General could not help him anymore, so serious was his trouble. Ernesto said that the people looking for him would harm Paulina if they could not get to him.

That night, back in the house, her brother had called Nathan Weinrib in Canada, desperate. Nathan had promised to call the consulate first thing the next morning. He would get Ernesto and his sister out of the country. He had a friend there who could speed things along.

General Guzmán had gone to Santiago. He would be back for the funeral. It was better for him if he didn't know, her brother said. Otherwise, he'd be in danger, too. This was why she was in this room without a door or a window in a strange country, afraid to close her eyes. Because of flowers.

Paulina sat up in her narrow bed, holding a pillow to her chest. For the first time, she couldn't draw a neat line between those events, and where she was now. Seeing General Guzmán had broken it.

It couldn't be just flowers that had brought her so far from home. There was a deeper reason, but what? Her brother's life was beyond her comprehension.

Ernesto always said she had a big mouth. He did not trust her enough to tell her the whole story. He'd done something serious, she knew that much. Probably by accident, but whatever it was, it was even more serious than she could imagine. Not murder, of course, but something almost as bad.

Paulina lay back down. She would wait until Ernesto had fully recovered before asking him to tell her the truth, and not just about himself, but about the stadium, the supposed thousands of people murdered by her country's army. It had to be a lie, like the lies in that newspaper, but why would anyone invent such horrors? Next time one of these Canadians asked, she would tell them that General Guzmán would never allow it, and he was a powerful man in her country. Powerful and good; he gave Paulina chocolate and books when he came to visit. He had a dead tooth that her father had removed and replaced with a fake one, perfectly white. He had not charged the General for the procedure because of his service to their country. Her godfather was a military man, honourable and trustworthy; when the time came, her father said, he would return the favour.

— 8. —

THAT SUNDAY, PAULINA knocked on the Weinribs' front door, prepared to apologize for her disappearance from the party, but it was Ruth who apologized to her.

"Lorraine seems to be running late," she said, taking Paulina's jacket. "I'm so sorry."

In a yellow sweater and long black skirt, bumblebee colours, Ruth Weinrib buzzed around her living room laying out what she called little treats. There were cookies and squares, all different shades of beige and brown. Paulina thought Ruth seemed far too excited for the visit, or maybe she was just glad to be free of her baby, who was with Nathan at the park, she said. So Paulina wouldn't have to see him, not yet. Or Hope.

Whenever Hope was with Ruth and Paulina, she cried and fussed, probably sensing Paulina's lack of maternal instinct. Back home, all her girlfriends had been eager to become mothers. When Paulina had confessed to Marcela, the least popular and most teased of their group, that she wasn't sure if she even wanted children, Marcela had told her to go see a doctor. Any girl who didn't want to be a mother had to be sick.

Marcela, like the other girls, cooed over babies whenever they spotted them during their afterschool sorties downtown. Paulina went along with it but to her babies were boring or terrifying, sometimes both. They either bawled or stared back, glassy-eyed, from inside their carriages. Some of her friends had baby cousins or siblings; they were already practised mothers. Like Inez. Once, Inez had brought her older sister's baby with her to the park. While they were oohing over it, it had suddenly turned purple. Quickly and calmly, Inez had put her finger inside her nephew's mouth, excavating a tiny plastic button. She'd done this as if fishing an olive from a jar. Paulina had almost fainted.

No, she would never be interested in Hope; she would never even pretend to be interested even as Hope became noticeably bigger and reached the usual milestones. This lack of interest had hardened into a shell concealing Paulina's soft, oozing secret: she was, as Marcela had said, not a normal woman. Unnatural. Marcela was fat and breathed through her mouth, but at least she'd been normal, she'd wanted what all the other girls had wanted.

Seated on the sofa facing the big windows looking out onto the street, Paulina stared at the plants on the windowsill, wondering how they would fare in her sunless apartment below. The Weinribs had hardwood floors, not carpet, and photos of the small Weinrib family were everywhere, propped up on the bookshelves, hanging from the walls. They also displayed souvenirs from their time in Chile, arranged on a shelf: unglazed dishes and cups from Pomaire. A ceremonial gourd and straw for drinking maté. A large rosary of lapis lazuli beads hanging from a nail. All gathering dust, forgotten, never put to use.

It was sunny outside but with a slight chill underneath the warmth. Ruth poured tea and asked for Paulina's thoughts on Canadian autumn.

"The leaves are nice."

It was the right answer. Ruth loved what she called, "fall foliage."

"When I was little, I used to go out into the yard and gather up the prettiest leaves and bring them to Miss Ross. She was my English teacher. She showed me how to dry the leaves and press them in a book. If you'd like, I can show you how to do it. It could be a nice souvenir of your time in Canada."

With a pang, Paulina recalled a school trip to the botanical garden in Viña, Sister Teresa pointing out the trees that were native to the south. In March, the delicate almond-shaped leaves of the coigüe trees turned a vibrant orange. When no one was looking, Paulina pocketed a few leaves to bring home to Pilar. The most beautiful trees in their country were in the south, Pilar said. She was going to take Paulina home with her, for a whole summer, when she and her brother came back from Canada. Paulina's father was gone, he couldn't forbid her from travelling with their housekeeper to her native village.

It was nearly eleven-thirty when the doorbell rang. Lorraine Morris, who was supposed to help Paulina adapt to her new school, did not apologize. She didn't look like the type who apologized, she didn't even smile when Ruth introduced them.

Lorraine gave Ruth her denim jacket like she was her housekeeper. She was wearing rust-coloured, corduroy overalls over a white and blue striped T-shirt. Without asking, she helped herself to a square and a cookie, then sat cross-legged on the floor within arm's reach of more treats.

Her big hands were pale and freckled like her face. Even her lips were freckled. Paulina couldn't look away. She was as fascinating, in her own way, as Sister Teresa, with her oversized, lumbering body, her long chin and frizzy brown hair.

Ruth joined Lorraine on the floor, crossed-legged like her guest. Paulina remained seated on the sofa, the better to observe Lorraine, now staring at Ruth's coffee table.

"Ronnie has that exact table," she said, breaking her silence.

If a fish could talk, it would sound like Lorraine. One of those slow-moving fish that lived on the muddy bottoms of lakes and rivers.

"Who's Ronnie?" Ruth asked.

"My mother. She has that table."

"I don't think so," Ruth said, smiling at her.

"You're wrong. It's exactly like this one."

"That can't be. We made this ourselves last summer. It's maple."

Ruth, still smiling, refilled her tea, sipping it from a small cup without handles. Lorraine had refused a cup of the pale-yellow tea. Paulina didn't blame her; it tasted like unsweetened liquorice and Ruth hadn't put out any sugar.

Like Pilar, Ruth made her own tea blends; a jar of dried leaves and bits of bark sat on Paulina's kitchen counter in the basement, untouched. Paulina wondered if, like Pilar, Ruth also kept a special jar in her pantry.

Pilar had shown Paulina the jar of crimson leaves and silvery buds the day of her first period. In case Paulina got in trouble, she'd said, like Pilar had when she was her age.

Like Marcela.

"That's my mother's table," Lorraine said, stretching out her legs so that they were under the disputed table.

Ruth explained again how she and Nathan had made the table, how when they'd finished sanding the wood it had looked too smooth and perfect so they'd taken it outside to beat it with chains and stub out cigarettes on it before applying the final varnish. The result was a table that had character, it was unique. One of a kind, Ruth said.

Lorraine reached for another square. Paulina still had not eaten anything. She was considering a biscuit when Lorraine spoke again.

"Your husband must have made one for my mother. I bet they had an affair."

Red patches appeared on Ruth's throat. Paulina stared at Lorraine, half-repulsed, half-impressed. Who cared how many Black women Paulina lured away from parties? Lorraine was way worse than Paulina could ever be, clearly a juvenile delinquent like the ones in the late-night movies on TV. Lorraine even wiped her mouth the same way they did, using the back of her hand instead of a napkin.

Then Lorraine forever endeared herself to Paulina by picking up one of Hope's toys, a large plastic ring, from off the floor.

"What's this?" she asked Ruth.

"That's Hope's teething ring. She's always sucking on it."

Lorraine dropped the bright yellow toy on the floor as if it had burned her, wiping her hand on her thigh. Paulina laughed. She couldn't help it.

Now Lorraine turned her attention to Paulina, the whole reason she'd come to Ruth's house in the first place, just as Ruth got up to answer the ringing phone.

"What's that on your hand?"

Paulina, blushing, thrust her hand between the sofa cushions.

"A phone number." She'd tried again that morning to wash off the numbers but they were still faintly visible, like squiggly blue veins.

"Whose number? A boy?"

"No."

"From a friend? What's her name?"

"Miss Valerie," Paulina said, her voice weak.

Before she knew it Lorraine was on her feet, staring down at her.

"Valerie Thomas the teacher?"

Paulina nodded, thrusting her telltale hand further inside the sofa.

"We need to talk," Lorraine said, her face red, her freckles darkening. "Somewhere private."

Ruth returned from her phone call.

"Why don't you take Lorraine downstairs?" she suggested, already gathering up the tea things. The party was over, or perhaps it was just beginning, judging by Lorraine's grin.

~

Paulina led Lorraine across the Weinribs' lawn to her subterranean front door, past the tree hiding the entrance to her apartment, not looking behind her, not wanting to see Lorraine's reaction to the five concrete steps leading down to her door, to the jumble of paint cans and extension cords beside the stairs. Nathan had promised to throw all this out so that she and Ernesto could plant flowers or otherwise beautify their home but Ernesto said it was too much bother, they'd be going home soon.

There was no shame in poverty, Alma Siqueiros had reassured Héctor Torres in the final scene of *Orphaned by Love*, when she met him at his boarding house near the silver mines of Bolivia. Alma had then proceeded, with feminine discretion, to tidy his shabby room. Paulina did her best to do the same, gathering the plates and cups full of her brother's cigarette butts from off the table and the floor, bringing them to the sink where she began to wash and carefully dry each item. Pilar said storing damp dishes brought cockroaches.

"I never met anyone my age with her own place. You're lucky. Ronnie won't even let me make tea. She won't let me near the stove, not after the rice incident. New pots and pans cost money, she says."

"Why do you call her Ronnie?"

"Because it's short for Veronica. And because she hates when I call her that. She can go suck an egg."

"Did she really have an affair with Nathan Weinrib?"

"I just said that to mess with her. Don't you ever do that, just say things to mess with people's heads?"

"No."

"You should. It's fun."

Paulina agreed to try it sometime. She was waiting for Lorraine to sit down. The top of her frizzy head almost grazed the ceiling. Why wouldn't she sit down? Was the kitchen chair dirty? Should she wipe it down? Worse, was she expecting Paulina to cook for her? The small electric stove was still a novelty, as was cooking for herself, so Paulina and her brother lived on canned soups and packaged biscuits, dreaming aloud of Pilar's corn and meat pies, their surfaces crusted with bronzed sugar. Many mornings Paulina woke up smelling Pilar's casseroles, or tasting her pancakes sandwiched with caramelized milk.

Pilar would be ashamed if she saw Paulina offering a guest only tea and maple cream biscuits, but it was all she had. Paulina hoped it would be enough; Lorraine seemed like someone who needed regular feeding, or she would get cranky.

Putting the kettle on the stove, Paulina wondered if tea was a bad idea, unless Lorraine's bladder was as sturdy as the rest of her. Otherwise she might tell everyone that the new girl at school didn't have a bathtub, just a scummy shower stall.

At last, Lorraine was sitting at the table, but she'd noticed the half door built into the kitchen wall. Paulina had forgotten about it. Lorraine was staring at the large, sliding bolt, a plank of wood painted white like the door and the wall. Ernesto had once forced it open, revealing the alleyway between the Weinribs' house and their neighbour's. After that, he'd instructed Paulina to keep it locked, unless they needed to make a quick exit. She'd assumed he'd been joking, but now she wasn't so sure.

"Holy Toledo," Lorraine said, reaching over the table to jiggle the bolt. "Where does this lead to? The Red Queen?"

Paulina set down the tea and leaf-shaped biscuits, aware she was blushing again.

"Alice in Wonderland. Get it? Do you have that where you're from? Off with her head?"

"Yes," Paulina said, pushing the sugar toward Lorraine. When was she going to talk about Valerie? What did she know about her?

"Got any milk?"

Her dentist father had forbidden Paulina from adding too much sugar to her tea, Chileans had terrible sweet tooths, he said. But milk? Milk was for coffee, not tea. There was milk in the fridge but this was for breakfast cereal. How easy it had been to give up their usual breakfast of bread and jam. What was the point anyway when no one in Canada had heard of quince cheese or rolls baked into satisfying spirals to be unravelled and crammed with jelly as you ate? In Canada, she and Ernesto had developed a taste for Froot Loops, eating it for lunch and dinner some days, slurping up the pastel-coloured milk from their bowls.

Lorraine liked her tea with a Chilean amount of sugar, and just as much milk. She sipped and poured and stirred until it was just right, then tackled the biscuits, prying one open with both hands, scraping out the maple cream with her large front teeth.

Paulina couldn't look away, even if it was rude. It was like watching a giant squirrel gnawing on an acorn.

"These are the best," Lorraine said, reaching for a second. "Ronnie only buys the store-brand, and they don't make these. We have store-brand soda and store-brand oatmeal cookies because of the divorce. She won't let me drink coffee or tea until I'm eighteen because she says it interferes with 'vitamin absorption.' She got that from the stupid housewife magazine she still gets even though she doesn't have a house anymore and she's not a wife either. She had to sell the house after the divorce."

"Divorce?"

"They split up last year. My dad moved back to the States now that the draft's over. He's a draft dodger. Last Christmas I had to freeze my ass off in New Hampshire. This year, Ronnie says we're going somewhere warm."

Lorraine said her father refusing to fight in the Vietnam War was the only good thing he'd ever done. But she didn't want Paulina feeling bad for her.

"I'm not one of those sad kids of divorce."

"In my country you cannot divorce."

"Really? Even if the guy's an asshole, you have to stay with him? What if he beats you?"

"Only the very rich can divorce. They pay for *la nulidad*."

"What's that?"

"I don't know in English, but I think it means the marriage does not happen."

"Poof, it's gone? That's wild."

Lorraine began taking apart another biscuit, while Paulina sat with her hands in her lap, her tea and biscuits untouched, waiting for Lorraine to say something about Valerie.

At last, Lorraine's mouth opened, revealing half-chewed morsels that looked like clumps of wet sand.

"What?" Paulina asked. She was sweating, this time at her hairline.

"I said, I'm officially bored. When does your brother get home? You live with your brother, right?"

Now that he was better, Ernesto was spending most of his time with Victor and Patricio. Paulina wondered if he was having an affair with one of their wives. Maybe she could accuse him of that, to "mess with his head."

"He is home late," Paulina said. "He is with friends."

"He's your guardian, right? The guy who got his face all mashed up?"

"You saw the newspapers?"

Had Lorraine seen her face inside a newspaper box on the street, or did she get the paper delivered to her home? Nathan had brought Paulina to Bloor Street to see herself behind glass, loaned her the coins required to free herself. Paulina was afraid someone would notice her buying a newspaper with her face on it, but no one did. The Weinribs also had all the papers delivered to their house, passing them on to Ernesto when they were done with them, but on the day she made her debut, Paulina got them first.

"You're prettier in person," Lorraine said, staring at her with the same intensity as she'd stared at Ruth's coffee table. "I guess cause you're not crying. What does your brother look like when he's not all mashed up? Ronnie thinks he must be really handsome. One of those Latin lover types. So he's not coming home soon?"

"No."

"Oh. I brought a little gift for you guys. Still, waste not, want not, like Ronnie says. We need at least six hours."

For what? Were they going to work? Did Lorraine take in sewing or washing? Like Pilar had in those chaotic weeks before the coup? Her father had been furious when he'd found out. Pilar turning his house into a laundry—didn't he pay her enough? Pilar had been silent, staring at the floor as he'd yelled at her, the same floor she scrubbed every morning on her knees. Pilar was lucky he didn't turn her out of his house. That was the same week Pilar had brought out the cream for his after-dinner coffee, placing the bottle, cold and damp, directly on the table. Her father had not said a word, just stared at Pilar until she realized her mistake. When she returned with the warmed cream in its porcelain jug, her eyes were red and her father had been nice again, thanking her, even saying she could leave the dishes if she wanted for later, and watch TV in her room.

Grinning, Lorraine reached into the pocket stitched onto the front of her overalls, opening her hand to reveal two capsules, a purple one and a pink one.

"It's not as scary as people say. It's great for talking. You get the best talks on speed, real personal, intense jazz you'd normally never say."

Paulina wondered if Lorraine really needed a drug to, as people said on TV, "spill her beans." There could be no spilling of hers, however. Under the influence of this powerful drug, who knew what Paulina might tell Lorraine about her father, General Guzmán, her brother, her thoughts on Valerie's face or Helen's breasts? She couldn't take drugs even if she wanted to. People were watching her. Ernesto said so.

Lorraine gave her the smaller, pink pill. For her first trip, Paulina should go easy.

"Up the queen."

After washing down her capsule with the rest of her tea, Lorraine trudged over to Ernesto's unmade sofa, to lie on her back on top of his sheets and blankets, her eyes closed, her pudgy arms crossed over her round breasts, like a vampire in a coffin.

Paulina's capsule was still on her tongue, in danger of dissolving. She took the tea things to the sink and, her back to Lorraine, spat the drug into her hand. Then she saw the jar of Ruth's herbal tea on the small wedge of countertop by the sink. Quickly, she unscrewed the jar and dropped the capsule inside.

"It's starting," Lorraine said from the sofa bed. "Wow."

"Wow," Paulina echoed from the kitchen sink.

"Can you come talk to me?"

Paulina crouched on the floor by the sofa. She was considering what to say when Lorraine sat up and pointed to her hand. Before Paulina knew it, Lorraine's large, freckled hand had grabbed hers.

"Your hand is so tiny," she said. "I could swallow your whole pinkie."

Paulina feared she might, but Lorraine did something far worse. She traced the faint numbers inscribed on Paulina's palm with a pudgy finger, those numbers Paulina knew by heart.

"Tell me what happened, exactly," Lorraine said, sitting up and leaning forward so that her face was close to Paulina's, her grip tightening.

"Nothing." Paulina blushed, trying to pull back from Lorraine, but the girl had both her hands now. Did she not know her own strength? People on drugs could become dangerous, even violent. Sister Teresa had said so. Her father, too. He worried about Ernesto taking drugs.

"Be a good girl and tell me everything. You'll feel better if you do."

Lorraine released Paulina's hands, crossing one leg over the other repeatedly. The tone of her voice had changed, too; it was cold, robotic but rushed, so that it was hard to understand her.

"Tell Dr. Judy. You can't keep secrets from Dr. Judy. Lorraine tries to keep secrets but Dr. Judy squeezes them out like popping a pimple."

Paulina didn't know if she was supposed to address Lorraine or Dr. Judy, only that she had to say something or Lorraine would pop her, too.

"Like I say, nothing. She takes me home, we are at my house, we say goodnight, I kiss her ..."

Lorraine leaned forward, her hands clasped in her lap.

"You kissed her?"

"Yes," Paulina said, remembering how she'd kissed Valerie on both cheeks. Lorraine did not need to know about her straying hand.

"And she gave you her number?"

Paulina nodded.

Lorraine began pacing round the room, somehow managing to collide with what little furniture there was, stomping so much that Paulina feared the entire apartment would come down, first the walls, then the ceiling, until they were both outside, the sole survivors of Lorraine's manmade earthquake, the entire Weinrib household crushing them.

Finally, Lorraine stopped moving, standing in the middle of the small room, looking down at Paulina.

"Are you a lez?" she asked.

"I don't know what that is."

"Then say it. Say lez, I dare you. Say it one hundred times."

Paulina was on her eighth lez when Lorraine stopped her.

"It's hot in here. Why is it so hot in here?"

Before Paulina could offer to open one of the small windows, Lorraine began taking off her overalls, starting with the buttons.

"Let's trade clothes," she said.

The corduroy overalls were too warm, she said. And her T-shirt. Warm and itchy.

"I've got ants in my pants."

"How did they get there?" Paulina asked, but Lorraine had her back turned to her.

"No peeking," Lorraine said.

Paulina turned around, to give Lorraine more privacy.

"Your turn," Lorraine said, kicking her clothes over to Paulina.

Paulina turned to face her, then turned back around, Lorraine's clothes in her arms. She could still see Lorraine's pink underwear, her substantial, lace-trimmed white bra, her pudgy, freckled thighs.

Heart pounding, Paulina stripped down to her bra and underpants. At least she had a nice bra now. On Robin's recommendation she'd gone to Honest Ed's, a gaudy discount department store that looked like a cross between a fire station and a casino and took up an entire city block on Bloor Street. According to her calculations, the five bras she bought cost about the same as the one she'd bought back home, although this might have been because they were marked, Factory Irregulars; an Irregular herself, they fit her perfectly. They were lacy and silky, although the mushroom colour was a drawback. Pilar said padded bras were for streetwalkers, but Paulina couldn't stop staring at herself in the powder-room mirror, turning sideways to see the subtle, uplifting effect.

How Lorraine was going to be cooler in Paulina's turtleneck sweater she didn't know, but she wasn't going to argue with her. As she was putting on Lorraine's overalls and T-shirt, she could hear Lorraine behind her, grunting and sighing.

Lorraine's clothes smelled like the unsweetened yogurt Ruth sometimes left for them, outside their door.

"What are you, a midget?"

Paulina turned around. Lorraine was trying to pull her jeans up over her hips. She was wearing Paulina's sweater, her breasts straining against the fabric.

Somehow Lorraine managed to pull on Paulina's jeans, but she couldn't zip them up. The flared hems grazed her knees, she looked like a giant in doll's clothing. Not that Paulina must have looked any better; the straps of Lorraine's overalls kept sliding off her shoulders.

Paulina tried not to laugh, shaking from the effort, tears sliding down her cheeks, but it was impossible, and Lorraine was laughing, too, they were laughing at each other. Paulina was still laughing when Lorraine grabbed her and kissed her on the mouth, a hard, dry kiss.

Before Paulina could say anything Lorraine was taking mincing steps to her front door, her hips constrained by Paulina's jeans.

"I'm not a lez," she shouted back at Paulina.

Opening her front door just enough to see, Paulina watched as Lorraine teetered along her street, Paulina's jeans sliding down her backside, in the direction of Bloor Street.

Someone hooted at her and Paulina shut her door. For a long while she sat in the loveseat, shaking, still wearing Lorraine's clothes, wishing it wasn't true, that Lorraine's rough, drug-induced kiss had been her first.

— 9. —

IN CHILE, PAULINA had belonged to a select group of girlfriends, four sets of best friends: Inez and Flor, Ana and Ivonne, Raquel and Eva. Paulina and Marcela. Her father had cleaned and straightened the teeth of all the girls, except for Marcela, who had a pronounced overbite and whistled when she talked.

Paulina attended the elaborate parties the girls' families had thrown for all seven girls when they turned fifteen, but none of them seemed to care that Paulina never had her own quinceañera. Maybe they'd been too caught up in their own festivities, or maybe they didn't see the point. After all, Paulina had no mother to choose her dress and plan the menu. Her father had his own reasons for not throwing her a lavish celebration of her fifteenth year; so long as Allende occupied La Moneda he was saving his money. Who knew when that Marxist might try to expropriate his home and business. Bribing politicians, especially Marxists, was expensive. When Allende was gone she could have a party.

Fortunately, this didn't change Paulina's standing in the group. She was still expected at the beach on Friday afternoons, to celebrate the end of the school week with the boys from the boys' school. In gratitude for overlooking her social failure, Paulina allowed the girls to pair her with Néstor, a distant cousin of hers on her mother's side. Néstor had a long neck like a goose and eyes too close together in his long, narrow face. Paulina pretended to find him irresistible, ignoring his Adam's apple and squeaky voice, the way his thick eyebrows broke off into individual hairs above his nose. She even squealed approvingly when he pinched her, his signal that he was about to playfully chase her in and out of the water, then dunk her head until she came up, gasping.

One afternoon, instead of chasing her into the water Néstor grabbed hold of Paulina, his lips dangerously close to hers, on the verge of making contact.

Paulina stomped on his foot. Néstor, howling, released her and she ran fully clothed into the sea, swimming toward the horizon, her school uniform stuck to her body. Néstor, believing she was drowning, waded in, doggy paddling until he caught up with her. Paulina had no choice but to drag him, wheezing and coughing, back to shore. She left him gasping on the beach, not looking behind her as she picked up her school bag and began the long walk home, not a word to anyone, then or after.

The girls thought this lovers' spat, as they called it, adorable. Now when Néstor approached her, arms outstretched, ready to pinch and splash, Paulina made herself as solid as her neighbour's cat whenever she tried to pick the tabby up and bring him to her house. She resolved each time to allow him to carry her off in his skinny arms, to be grateful at last to belong, be normal. Yet each time he approached, she stiffened and he retreated. The girls laughed and begged them to patch it up but Paulina couldn't bring herself to even look at him. What a relief when Néstor's father sent him to military school, not Ernesto's academy in Santiago, but to a Bolivian institute notorious for its harsh discipline. Still, she'd tried to love him, at one point keeping a rubber band around her wrist to snap against her skin whenever she was repulsed by his eyebrows or fermenting apple smell. But the purple welts were in vain. If anything, she hated him even more.

Even more important than a boyfriend was a best friend. Just as she'd allowed herself to be paired with Néstor, so she allowed the girls to pair her with Marcela. Best friendship seemed to require strenuous displays of feeling, love and animosity, taunts and apologies. Yet Paulina remained indifferent to Marcela, never once goading her into a fight although she knew the routine. First, you wrote down every confidence your best friend had ever shared with you, in a long note you passed around in class behind her back, the first move in a campaign to sway everyone to your side. A period of ostracization followed during which you pretended your former best friend didn't exist. Finally, you let the other girls engineer a tearful reconciliation, the two of you embracing as if nothing ugly had ever happened, everyone crying, even Inez, the toughest girl in class.

No, this was one performance Paulina knew she couldn't pull off. She could fake a lot, but not that kind of feeling, not for Marcela.

Each morning the headmistress measured their skirts before they could enter the imposing stone building, originally a hospital built by English adventurers who'd come to Chile in the previous century to make nitrate fortunes. One morning when Paulina's was deemed the shortest, a first for her, she made a scene, protesting that as the shortest girl in the class her skirt length, which would have been scandalous on a taller girl, was acceptable on her. For this outburst she was punished, ordered to stay behind after school and help Sister Teresa care for the class plants.

"*Plus roi que le roi*," Sister Teresa said, as they were watering her violets. "Do you know what that means? Because you are least like those girls, you feel you have to exceed them. You dress like them, you act like them. You've even changed your voice, did you know? Of course, you don't."

Paulina could never know how she sounded to others because of bone conduction, which was what happened when her voice bounced and pinged against her bones as it was leaving her head. It was the same for everyone. None of us, Sister Teresa said, ever hears our true voice. Least of all Paulina.

— 10. —

PAULINA WAS SO nervous about seeing Lorraine again she agreed to let Nathan drive her to school on his way to the office.

She'd barely slept the night before, but Ernesto didn't care that she was tired or that her stomach hurt, she was going to school. If she didn't, he'd make Nathan her legal guardian.

Nathan and Ruth had both attended the University of Toronto, and on the drive Nathan pointed out the nicest parts of the campus to her. She was lucky, he said, to be attending a school on campus. Of course, it was temporary, until ASPIRE found a permanent home.

"The founders had Cambridge and Oxford in mind," Nathan said. He'd been to both, and there was no comparison, but give it another hundred years and it might be as impressive.

He made the campus sound like his coffee table, in need of aging and roughing up but to Paulina it was green and sprawling and romantic, unlike that cement fist of a city hall. Instead of concrete and glass, there was stone and well-kept lawns, stained glass and spires. Why couldn't the whole city look like this?

Nathan dropped her off at a tall brick building on the outskirts of the campus. The university was expanding, he explained, buying up buildings like this one on College Street. Work was starting next year, the large offices would be divided up into student apartments.

"I've got a friend, Mitch, he's a real estate lawyer."

Paulina nodded. She could have listened all day to Nathan talk about Mitch, his dealings with the university as it gobbled up real estate in all directions from its genteel, green heart. He'd been nice enough not to mention the party or her going home with Valerie, whose phone number had finally faded from Paulina's palm. If only Valerie, too, could fade, into memory, then fantasy. Paulina had enjoyed some of her best, most intense and pleasurable infatuations with girls she'd only seen once or twice, on the trolleybus or at the cinema. So long as these crushes remained in her imagination, she was safe. But now she was going to see Valerie five days a week. Valerie and Lorraine.

"It'll be fine," Nathan said, leaning over and opening the passenger door for her.

After he drove off, Paulina stood before the glass doors. She was considering what might happen if she just walked away, maybe passed the school day hiding out in a park or a library, when Lorraine appeared behind her, reflected in the glass.

"Hey," she said. "Having second thoughts?"

Paulina turned around. Lorraine was smiling at her.

"Are we late?"

"You can't be late at ASPIRE. It's not like there's a bell or anything. I'm going to the store to get some chips, if you want to come?"

"Okay."

They walked west on College Street, then down a side street to a store with a sign that read, Player's.

"Wait here," Lorraine said. "You want anything?"

"No, thank you."

Paulina was about to sit on one of the plastic crates on the sidewalk, when Lorraine came rushing out. She'd only been gone a few minutes.

"Let's move," she said.

Back on College Street, Lorraine unbuttoned her jean jacket, revealing a pack of chips.

"I got you this," she said, opening her knapsack. "It's a Crunchie bar. Ever had one?"

"My father says candy is bad for your teeth."

"You can have one, it won't hurt you. Let's take a load off."

Lorraine's teeth looked fine, if a bit horsey. Paulina tore into the candy bar as they were walking back toward the nice part of campus. She was doing her best to chew the hard, sticky toffee under the chocolate coating, still working on her first bite when they reached a circular green lawn the size of a small lake, ringed by ivy-covered Victorian brick mansions.

Taking a load off meant sitting on the grass, eating stolen snacks. They weren't alone; other, older students were sprawled out, too, some sleeping, others reading, singly or in small groups, on blankets or their jackets. A radio was playing, the rock music competing with the guitar a young man was strumming for a girl wrapped in a blanket. To Paulina it was like a scene from one of those American movies about college life.

Someone had left a towel behind, and they shared it. Paulina's thin-soled tennis shoes were wet from walking on the dewy lawn, the sky was overcast, it was cold, too, and the towel was damp.

It was the best time she'd had in Toronto so far. It got even better when Lorraine started tossing chips at the pigeons strutting on the grass nearby.

"Do you know what ASPIRE stands for?" she asked, offering Paulina a swig from the bottle of cola she'd pulled out of her bag.

"I don't remember."

"No one does. It's just a crazy idea some hippies had. It's not like a regular school, you know, with classrooms and a gym and a cafeteria. It's just some rooms on the third floor."

This was Lorraine's second year at ASPIRE. There were only a few students, she told Paulina, all about the same age. The school didn't accept younger students. They weren't mature enough.

"There's Rita and Chuck and Yvette, she doesn't talk to anyone, except Brian."

"Are they your friends?"

"My friends are on my old street. Where we lived before the divorce."

Lorraine said that the best part of ASPIRE was that there were no classes. It was just you and your facilitator.

"Rita and Brian and me have Albert, and Chuck and Yvette have Valerie. There's a schedule. I have Albert this morning, then he has Rita and then Brian."

When you weren't with your facilitator, you were expected to work on your own.

"No goofing off," Lorraine said.

"It's self-directed," Paulina said, repeating what she'd heard Helen Koenigsman say.

"Right. That means you have a project. It can be whatever you want, and you don't have to write it, you can just talk about it. Like, I'm doing a project on suffragettes. You know, the women who fought for the vote? So I meet with Albert in the morning, and he gives me things to read, and we rap about it for a while."

"Who is Albert?"

"My facilitator. You call them by their first name. They're not there to teach you or anything. They don't give you tests or grades, just things to read and exercises to do. If you want your diploma, you have to take a test."

Lorraine said that even though it was a bit of a freak show, she liked ASPIRE much better than her old school.

"The teachers were idiots, they were always making mistakes, like Mrs. Berger, she kept mixing up 'adverse' and 'averse' and she was my English teacher."

Whenever Lorraine corrected one of her idiot teachers she got sent to the principal. Eventually, Mr. Stringer told her mother that Lorraine would be expelled if she didn't stop being disruptive and interfering with her fellow students' education.

"So I stopped going to school," Lorraine said, ripping open a second bag of chips. "It's rude to interfere."

Skipping school was called truancy, and it was that that got Lorraine expelled. If not for her father she'd be attending some lousy public school.

To get into ASPIRE, you had to pass an interview. But not Lorraine. She had connections.

"My dad knows someone on the board." Another draft dodger, she said, married to a Canadian woman.

"I guess it was the same for you? They just let you in."

"I guess."

It was a relief, not being the only special case at school.

Lorraine, grinning, picked up the empty wrapper from off the grass.

"What's wrong, you didn't like your Crunchie?"

"No, it was delicious."

"I'm just messing with you. They make these right here in Toronto. Albert took me to the factory. The whole neighbourhood smells like chocolate. It's really old, almost a hundred years. A lot of girls used to work there. Girls our age."

These must have been some of the Toronto Girl Problems Ruth had told her about.

"Imagine working in a candy factory," Lorraine said, a fistful of chips in her mouth.

Paulina agreed it would be a trip. Speaking of trips, Lorraine said.

"Those pills were in my dad's rain jacket, he's a real pill head. He left it behind the last time he visited, he's always forgetting stuff. It wasn't cool, giving them to you. They could have been anything."

"It's okay."

"We were both really tripping. I don't remember much."

"Me neither."

Lorraine took a paper bag out of her knapsack.

"Here," she said, not looking at Paulina. "Ronnie washed them for you."

"Thank you. I don't have yours."

"That's cool. You can bring it tomorrow, and you don't have to wash them or anything. Can you get my jacket from Ruth?"

Paulina said she would. Not only that, but she'd also wash and dry Lorraine's clothes. Ruth had showed her how to use the machines while her brother was convalescing.

How had Lorraine made it home, did she remember kissing her, did it mean anything, but Paulina couldn't ask her. Lorraine's face was bright pink, even her freckles looked darker.

"We should get going. It's probably going to rain."

As they were leaving the park, Lorraine offered Paulina the last chip.

"It's a wish chip," she said. "See, it looks like two stuck together? You eat it and make a wish."

There was so much to wish for it seemed like tempting fate, but she did as Lorraine instructed, taking the chip without touching it with her thumb, trying to look solemn while she chewed and Lorraine finished her Coke.

"What did you wish for?" Lorraine asked.

"For you to steal me more chips and Crunchies."

Lorraine snorted, so hard that soda came out of her nose. They were still laughing when they got to the glass doors of ASPIRE.

～

Paulina's acting career began, appropriately, with a lie, a modest one, that she told Valerie on her first day at ASPIRE.

She was sitting by herself in the nondescript room Lorraine called the lounge, waiting for Valerie. Lorraine and her facilitator Albert had retreated to a nearby round table strewn with newspapers, coffee mugs, and an open package of cookies. No wonder he was a facilitator; Albert didn't look like a teacher, not with that beard, a bushy red affair that put Ernesto's to shame. Paulina was grateful that Valerie was her facilitator. Her table was clean and tidy, just a small, flowering plant in a plastic pot beside a pack of orange pencils.

"I'm so glad you're here," Valerie said when she joined Paulina at the table.

"I'm sorry I am late," Paulina said. She was sweating in her usual, unusual places: the crease of one elbow, the hairline just above her left ear, as she desperately tried not to stare at the outline of Valerie's breasts, visible beneath her silky blouse. Its delicate print of black birds in flight also troubled her, particularly the way one wing pointed directly to the spot below Valerie's left nipple.

"Don't worry about it. It's your first day. Did Lorraine show you around?"

"Yes."

"Feeling good?"

"Yes."

The candy and soda had lifted her fatigue, as had the coffee Lorraine had poured her from the pot in the corner kitchen of the lounge.

"Are you sure? You look a bit tired. Would you like some more coffee?"

"No, thank you."

"That sweater is lovely on you. Blue is your colour."

Robin's-egg blue, Robin had said. As in the bird, not me. From now on it would be Paulina's lucky colour, and sweater.

"Let's get started. This is for you."

Paulina assumed the workbook with the green cover and lined pages would be for her homework, but she was wrong.

"I want you to write in this every day," Valerie said. "You don't have to show it to me. It's for you to write whatever you want."

"Like a diary?"

"Yes, it could be a diary, or you might want to write stories, or poems."

Valerie gave her another book, a real one this time.

"Helen told me your brother says you want to be in the theatre. *Uncle Vanya*. It's a classic. I think you'd be a wonderful Sonya."

Pilar must have told Ernesto. Paulina's scalp shivered with pleasure. She always got teary-eyed whenever she felt she had someone's full, approving attention.

"I was in a play," she said, taking the book, hoping Valerie hadn't noticed her shining, wet eyes.

"What play?"

Her dream of becoming an actress had always seemed so absurd that she'd never told anyone except Pilar, who'd laughed and said that until she had Elizabeth Taylor's breasts, she could forget it. Even Sister Teresa, who'd been so encouraging, seemed to think of acting as a way to acquire the social graces, not a career choice for a girl of good social standing.

"Lorca," Paulina said. "*Blood Wedding*. I played the Bride."

"Then that's what we'll do," Valerie said. "Your independent project will be on the theatre."

Paulina would learn English and history from reading plays. She would become a scholar, in addition to already being an actress.

Paulina couldn't contradict her, not when Valerie was smiling at her, the same hopeful, encouraging smile Sister Teresa had once bestowed on her.

~ 11. ~

SISTER TERESA LOVED the theatre. Plays and poetry were the jewels of the Spanish language, she said, although her real passion was Latin. On her first day in their classroom, she explained to the girls that the word *albino* came from *albus*, Latin for white. A rumour soon spread that she'd been chased from her former school because the students there had thought she was a witch, that she'd come to Valparaíso because it was an important port city; its citizens, *porteños*, were sophisticated, used to seeing all kinds of people from all over the world on their streets. Pablo Neruda even had a house in town.

She was everyone's favourite teacher, until the day she announced that they would each have to recite a poem before the entire class, according to her detailed instructions, which she made them write down. First, they were not to change a single word of the poem she would choose for them, and if they forgot a word, she would stop them and make them start over again from the beginning. While reciting, they were to stand tall, shoulders back, gaze directed not at the floor or the ceiling or at their fellow students, but toward an imaginary horizon. They were to keep their hands folded behind their backs, not hanging by their sides like dead weights or worse, fluttering like birds. As for emotion, they were to speak with real but restrained feeling. Just as giggling was forbidden, so too were tears.

The girl who delivered the best recitation would receive a prize. Hands shot up, but Sister Teresa just smiled and said it would be a surprise.

The best way to learn was by example, she said. They were to watch her closely as she recited a poem by Gabriela Mistral, the country's greatest woman poet and the humblest of Nobel Prize winners, an unmarried, childless schoolteacher who had devoted her life to her craft and her pupils.

No one could look away while Sister Teresa recited the poem, not even those stupid girls who were still convinced she was a pink-eyed witch, so powerful was her voice, the pull of her emotions, just under the surface but deep: *And what ever happened / to the poor dead girls / so cleverly kidnapped / from their April days / those who rose and submerged / like dolphins in the waves?*

Sister Teresa had chosen this poem, she explained, to warn them that their girlhood would end before they knew it, and so too their April days. Domestic responsibilities would submerge them all, a flash of their former insouciance occasionally emerging like the sheen of a dolphin breaking the waves, only to disappear again. Insouciance was their word of the day.

Paulina was hooked. If she could summon Sister Teresa's power, her April days would never end. When Sister Teresa chose Mistral's poem for her to recite, it felt fated.

The nausea that gripped Paulina on the morning of her recitation retreated as soon as she felt herself slipping into another persona, another voice, that of the great, unconventional Mistral. No one laughed, and even Inez looked impressed. So she wasn't surprised when Sister Teresa placed a copy of Lorca's *Blood Wedding* on her desk.

"I've found my Bride," she said.

Paulina couldn't bring herself to thank her, much less raise her head. It had been so easy for her to evoke emotion in herself and in others that she felt like she had cheated somehow.

The other roles were yet to be cast, although there were rumours that Inez, the tallest girl in class, was to play Paulina's lover, Leonardo. Besides the Bride, Sister Teresa wanted Paulina to play one of the woodcutters and, if no one else was suitable, the Moon. Three roles!

She could relate to the Bride's wish to court death rather than become someone's wife, by running off with Leonardo. That the Bride lived alone with her Spanish father, her mother long dead, only strengthened Paulina's identification with the part. It was a shame it took so long for the Bride to show up, but when she did she gave several charged, poetic speeches. As the woodcutter, Paulina would get to stomp around, wielding an axe. Best of all, the Moon had the longest, most dramatic speech in the play, warning the runaway lovers that it would pour its light through the forest, so that they couldn't hide from their sins.

Rehearsals were to begin on the afternoon of Monday, September 10, 1973. First, however, Sister Teresa would explain her choice of Lorca's tale of neighbour turned against neighbour, of a rural village so governed by violence that even a simple wedding became a blood-soaked affair.

Paulina was looking forward to her speeches, especially the one in which she pronounced herself "a shame to clean women." But even as Sister Teresa was distributing copies of the play to the rest of the class, Paulina knew, they all knew, that they'd never get the chance to enact the grown-up passions of Lorca's tragedy.

Now, maybe, Paulina would have her chance.

~

"We eat candy apples and popcorn for lunch, Lorraine and I, they're cheap. We buy them from street vendors. Mrs. Weinrib leaves food for us outside our door. Ernesto says there is no point in his getting a job because we will be home soon. On the night of October 31, children come to your door and ask for candy. If you do not have candy, they throw rotten eggs at your house. I did not go outside even though it was my birthday. Ruth baked me a chocolate cake and Ernesto bought me a calendar so I can count the days to when I turn eighteen."

Paulina couldn't bring herself to look at Valerie, to see the disappointment she felt radiating from her like steam, so she fixed her gaze on the television set in the corner of the lounge, to the handwritten sign taped to the screen. *I am furniture, not art.* Albert's guitar was propped up against the TV. To calm herself, she read the stickers below the strings: *This guitar climbed Mount Washington. Expo 67. Vive le Québec libre!*

"I'm sorry I missed your birthday," Valerie said.

"That's okay. It was weeks ago."

It hadn't been much of a celebration. So why choose that dismal, rainy day for the subject of her monologue? She'd written more, about longing to be eighteen and free of her brother, to get a job and save enough money to go home and get her godfather to fix everything so that Ernesto could come home, too. Then she would come back to Toronto, where she and Lorraine would rent an apartment. Paulina would become a famous actress; Lorraine said a lot of American movies were filmed in Toronto. Hollywood North, they called it. But all that sounded stupid when she read it back, so she'd crossed out sentences and more sentences until all that was left was this stupid paragraph about food and her birthday.

Valerie was smiling at her from her spot on the rug, sitting with her legs tucked under her. Lorraine said that Albert's girlfriend had led last year's class in making the small, square rug; against a shaggy orange background, two children, brown silhouettes, held misshapen, nubby hands.

"Is it bad?" Or phony, she wanted to ask. That was what Lorraine called anything really bad.

Valerie's smile faded.

"It's not quite what I'd expected," she said. "But it sounds more like the start of a story. How did you feel when you were writing it?"

She hadn't felt anything but a desire to please Valerie, but Paulina could tell that wasn't the right answer. Unable to respond, she shifted her gaze to the ceiling, to one of the many plants hanging there. They were spider plants, Valerie had told her last week. It was a hardy plant, she'd said, it could flourish anywhere. She'd snipped off one of the plantlets that hung from its branches, put it and some soil in a plastic pot for Paulina to take home but in the basement the tips of its slender green and white leaves were turning brown. Paulina brought the plant back to school. If Valerie had noticed, she was keeping it to herself.

"Dig a little deeper," Valerie said. "Was it hard having a birthday so far from home? Do you want to go home soon like your brother? How does it feel to be seventeen? What do you think will happen when you turn eighteen?"

"I will be an adult."

Paulina's face burned, she couldn't look at Valerie. She may as well have asked her to run away with her.

"That's true," Valerie said, her smile brighter. "How are you liking school so far? It must be very different from back home."

"I like it. No one measures our skirts."

Valerie laughed.

"You seem like the kind of person who doesn't like a lot of rules."

Paulina had never thought of herself that way, but Valerie was right. She liked being able to come and go as she pleased, to read whatever interested her, to be treated like an adult with opinions and ideas. So did Lorraine, her best and only friend. After a brief introduction, the other students had avoided Paulina, as they were already avoiding Lorraine. Lorraine said they were anti-social freaks, they were jealous because she and Paulina had connections.

Valerie said she was less concerned about Paulina's material than she was about her delivery. Paulina needed to develop her confidence.

"How about next time we start with the basics?"

You have to walk before you can fly, she said. Paulina would take her first steps tomorrow afternoon, during their next session.

~

The man at the post office looked at Paulina's envelope, then at her.

"I never got this business of street name first, then the number. You think they'd make it standard everywhere."

Paulina smiled. She had to be nice; this man could pretend to post her letter, then fish it out and blow his nose in it. Pilar would never read it then.

"Will there be a problem?" she asked.

"Not on our end," the man said, stamping her envelope like a judge bringing down his gavel.

⁓ 12. ⁓

VALERIE HAD FOUND a book for them at the library: *Loosen Up! Warm-Ups, Games, and Exercises for Beginning Actors.*

"Let's try the tongue twisters first," she said.

These exercises would help Paulina to speak more clearly, to control her breath and modulate her accent. Not that there was anything wrong with her accent. It wasn't that strong and anyway, at her age, she would never lose it completely. But learning to control it would give Paulina range.

"What's range?"

"It means you can play more roles."

People might judge her because of her accent, ignore her true potential. Something like this had happened to Valerie's parents even though, like everyone in Guyana, they spoke English, English and Creole. Valerie's parents had been so worried about their daughters succeeding in Canada that they'd forbidden them from speaking Creole outside the house.

"You're from Guyana?"

"My parents are, and my older sister, but I was born here."

Did that make Valerie South American? Like her? What did Paulina know about Guyana? In school, she'd been taught that it was the only English-speaking South American country. The capital was Georgetown.

It turned out Valerie's family was from Georgetown, one of the few families accepted into Canada. Her mother had been a schoolteacher, her father an engineer, but in Canada they both struggled to find work. Her parents worked whatever jobs they could find, until they had enough money to open a small convenience store in Pickering. As for Valerie's older sister, she was back in Guyana with her husband.

Valerie didn't have a husband; she didn't have a wedding ring. Lorraine said she didn't think Valerie had a boyfriend, either, or they would have met him. The facilitators always brought their boyfriends and girlfriends to school. To gawk at the freaks, Lorraine said. She'd told Paulina this while they were eating lunch in the lounge. They ate lunch together every day and while they ate, Paulina helped Lorraine find pictures in old magazines for Lorraine's "trippy" collages: babies' heads on top of businessmen's bodies, a bikinied torso beneath a dog's head. They didn't talk much but when they did, it was to speculate about Valerie—where she lived, if she had pets, what brand of lipstick did she wear. They'd tried calling her once from a pay phone, but Paulina must have forgotten the number, because a man kept answering, shouting at them that he didn't know any Valerie.

Valerie wasn't a lez, Lorraine said. Paulina still didn't know what that word meant, and there was no one she felt she could ask, so she simply agreed that no, Valerie was definitely not a lez.

Lorraine couldn't know what Valerie had just told her, about being from Guyana. She tried to hide it but Paulina could tell that Lorraine was jealous of her for having Valerie all to herself, of Valerie taking such a special interest in her. Lorraine already made fun of Paulina for wanting to be an actress. Who did she think she was, Tatum O'Neal?

It would be her secret, their special bond. Valerie's people were South American, like Paulina. Valerie understood her, she could "feel her," because she knew what it meant to leave your country and have to start all over again.

~

That first afternoon, Paulina got through eight repetitions of *Peggy Babcock* but stumbled over, *a regal rural ruler. Green glass grass gleams* almost brought her to tears, but Valerie said she just needed practice.

All that week and into the next, Paulina practised her tongue twisters whenever she was alone, which was more than she liked, thanks to Patricio and Victor. Eventually, she mastered the hardest one, the one that even Valerie sometimes messed up: *Green glass grass gleams*.

Satisfied by Paulina's progress, Valerie said it was time to leave the tongue twisters behind and focus on perfecting her pronunciation. One afternoon, she invited Paulina to study her mouth as she spoke, starting with the "th" sound that she said was giving Paulina so much trouble.

Paulina stood a foot or so before Valerie ("Come closer, Paulina, I don't bite") and watched her full lips part, purse, then pull apart. Valerie's pink tongue danced for her, brushing against the roof of her mouth, darting out like the snout of a mouse sniffing the air, flicking against her lower teeth as she slowly enunciated the words that evaded Paulina's lips and tongue ("teeth, ship, joke, ask, fifth"). Each word became a caress, stripped of all meaning, reduced to raw sounds that reverberated throughout Paulina's body. Imitating the exaggerated movements of Valerie's lips and tongue felt as intimate as kissing. Losing her accent became Paulina's obsession.

Over time, she learned the precise movements of her own tongue, the tension of her lips and jaw as she spoke, how even tiny changes could alter the sounds she made. She even showed off for Lorraine, who wasn't impressed, not even by a dozen flawless renditions of, *Green glass grass gleams*.

"You'd sound better without that feather up your ass," she said.

Lorraine was just jealous. Paulina had Valerie and her praise all to herself. She was excelling, exceeding everyone's expectations, while Albert had written on Lorraine's mid-semester evaluation, *you're right where you need to be*. Lorraine had shown it to Paulina, proud of her accomplishment, and Paulina had felt sorry for her. Who wanted to be where they needed to be, when you could be where you dreamed of going?

— 13. —

ONLY ONCE DID Paulina doubt that Valerie really understood her. Before the Christmas break, Valerie suggested Paulina start watching the evening news in her quest to improve her articulation. All the students at ASPIRE were invited to read the papers; Albert led a Current Events group that Lorraine said was a real snooze.

Didn't Valerie know that Paulina and her brother never missed the news? This was on top of reading newspapers, and not just the local ones, but the American ones Nathan bought for her brother. Paulina wished Valerie could see her and her brother seated at the kitchen table, watching their small TV, the local news about fires and sports, the commercials for men's razors and instant coffee and cigarettes, watching and waiting until, as Ernesto would joke grimly, it was their turn in the spotlight.

Ernesto would flinch at the images of the junta on their small screen, the four men in their uniforms saluting, followed by other images, of men and women lying prone on the pavement, machine guns pointed at them.

During his recovery, Ernesto had stopped going to the church for English classes, so Paulina had to translate for him, both the news on TV and in the papers. It wasn't easy. There were a lot of words she didn't use much, in either language: gunfire, purge, firing squad. Random killings: that had been a difficult one. How could taking a life be random?

"Is it true?" Paulina would ask, scanning the flickering images in vain for her godfather. Had the junta really executed two thousand just because they'd supported Allende?

"I don't know," Ernesto would say, again and again. *I don't know, stop asking me.*

Paulina wanted to call their godfather and ask, but Ernesto said he wasn't in the country, the junta had sent him abroad, to reassure their allies that Chile wasn't becoming a bloodthirsty dictatorship and anyway, it would cost hundreds of dollars to call, and Nathan would get angry. That was also why she couldn't call Pilar.

People had died, Ernesto admitted. How many, he didn't know. No one might ever know.

It couldn't be true, what they were seeing and reading. That was why General Guzmán had appeared to her, the night she'd met Valerie. He'd had a message for her, about what was really happening, but then that car had come along and taken him away.

Or maybe her brother was right, it had just been her imagination. Paulina saw Valerie everywhere, in the grocery store, the record store, the used clothing stall in Kensington Market that Lorraine brought her to because she'd heard that rich kids went there to sell their clothes for drug money but it was all just ratty old jeans and T-shirts. Paulina would see Valerie and then she would turn around and it would be some other woman.

There was one person she could ask, one person who would tell her the truth. Pilar. In her letters Paulina could ask her all the questions she wanted. Not that she did. She didn't want to upset her. But if Pilar didn't write back soon, she might start asking.

~

Paulina only had to translate their news for Ernesto. The rest he just watched, staring indifferently at the images of tanks rolling through deserts, men in suits speaking into microphones behind long tables, addressing other men seated before them at other long tables. The tracking of storms across the Great Lakes, bringing the first real snow of the winter. None of it interested her brother.

One night while Ernesto rolled himself a joint, Paulina watched the rest of the news, in case there was something about Chile but instead they were talking about the United States, this time, about the upcoming one-year anniversary of the Supreme Court's ruling that women could have abortions.

Roe and Wade sounded like one of the folk groups her brother listened to on the portable record player Nathan had given them. Paulina imagined a married couple, the woman in a Victorian nightgown mooning over her harp, but no, the reporter was saying it was a case that had given women the constitutional right to an abortion. Abortion: the word sounded so close to the Spanish, *aborto*. In Chile, the word was whispered at school. It was a sin, it was murder. It was not discussed, calmly and factually, on TV, but here was this clean-shaven man saying that some people were insisting it was time for Canada to do what the Americans had done.

A woman appeared on the screen, introduced to viewers as "Jane." Her face was shadowed and in profile, like the Queen on the back of a tarnished Canadian nickel.

The woman, whose identity had to be protected, began recounting in a hushed voice how her family doctor had reluctantly agreed to her request for an abortion, how he'd sent her to a hospital in the nearest city to plead her case before three doctors. Jane had borrowed money from her mother for the bus fare to Edmonton and a stay in a hotel, taken unpaid leave from her job, only for the all-male therapeutic abortion council, as they were called, to deny her request. Two of the doctors had said that her health was not at risk, while the third, more sympathetic doctor had argued that what constituted risk to the mother wasn't clearly defined by the law, so he couldn't say one way or the other.

It sounded like Jane was crying as she told the reporter that she could barely afford the three children she already had. What was she supposed to do now?

"It's not what the nuns told you at school," Ernesto said as another woman, not in shadow and old enough to be a grandmother, screeched that abortion was murder. She held up a picture of a fake-looking baby with blood coming out of its mouth.

"They don't cut women open and pull out their screaming babies."

"I know," Paulina said, her face flushed. Had Ernesto guessed that her sexual education had been an extended game of broken telephone with girlfriends? Pilar hadn't been much help, either, with her herbs and warnings of what happened to girls who didn't wait until they were married.

Girls like Marcela.

"It's safe, when a doctor does it," Ernesto said. "And it's not a baby, not yet."

"How do you know all that?"

Ernesto got up and turned off the TV just as a priest appeared, brow furrowed.

"If you want to go on the pill, I can help you." Like "therapeutic" abortion, the pill was no longer a crime, some doctors were even willing to prescribe it to single women, too. It was the most effective form of birth control, a miracle, really.

"But if you want it before you turn eighteen, you'll have to say you have menstrual problems."

"I don't have menstrual problems."

"What about when you couldn't come to the islands because of your period?"

"I don't need a pill."

"Why are you getting so angry? I'm just trying to help."

"I'm not angry," Paulina said, storming off to her nook.

If Ernesto cared about other things beside Chile, he might know that the same law that had decriminalized abortion and the pill a few years back had also decriminalized homosexual acts between adults, Albert had said so during a Friday morning meeting of his Current Events group, which she'd started attending. Lorraine saw Dr. Judy on Friday mornings to talk about her parents' divorce, but even without her there, Paulina didn't dare speak, let alone ask about the gay liberation protest Albert and his friends had attended in August, the first of its kind in the city. Albert was quick to tell them that he himself was not gay, he had just attended out of curiosity.

Paulina was also curious, curious and desperate for someone she could talk to about what she'd read in the papers, about all of it, what was happening in her country and in this one, too.

Green glass grass gleams. Green glass grass gleams. Green glass grass gleams. Paulina repeated it to herself in bed that night but it didn't stop the dream from coming. It was always the same; she was alone in Manuel's truck, peeking out from under a bolt of fabric, the truck going in circles, past her house, her school, Plaza Sotomayor, Bellavista Hill, all of it flattened out, the sea and the hills so that she could take it all in at once, but it was dark, a thick grey mist clung to everything, it was getting harder and harder to see. That was when she realized no one was driving the truck, it was just going in circles, it would crash. She had to stop it, but how when she didn't know how to drive? Maybe she could turn off the ignition, stop the truck and get out, find her way home, but she couldn't move, she was trapped.

She was trapped because she was dead. This was what happened when you died, what had happened to all those people reported to have died in her country. You went round and round in circles, helpless, past the places and people you'd loved when you were alive, but you couldn't stop, couldn't get off the truck and go to them. Everything and everyone you'd loved remained in the distance, half-obscured by a thick grey fog as heavy as smoke, as cold as snow.

— 14. —

THE NEXT DAY school was cancelled. Paulina found out when Lorraine, bundled up as to be almost unrecognizable, knocked on her door late that morning.

Paulina was glad to see her. That morning, Ernesto had told her that they would not be home for Christmas. They might not be home for awhile, he said. Hearing him say it aloud made her realize that she'd known this for weeks now. Ernesto said it was for the best; she could finish school. Then they would go home.

If she was home now, she wouldn't be going to the movies with Lorraine during the day, and not just any movie. A horror movie, Lorraine said.

"It's so scary they've got a nurse in the lobby in case you faint or go into shock. Does Ernesto want to come?"

"He's in the bathroom."

"So we'll wait."

"He's going to a friend's house," Paulina said, putting on her coat.

No fan of winter, Ernesto was staying home. Paulina thought he was missing out; the whole world was hushed and white, the streets nearly deserted, just a few people out, shovelling sidewalks and driveways. Lorraine said it was too cold and icy to walk, they would take the subway downtown. They'd never taken the subway together before. Paulina was relieved that she'd finally overcome her fear of underground transportation. Ernesto had reassured her that, because Toronto was not prone to earthquakes, she would not be buried alive under rubble. Living in the Weinribs' basement was subterranean enough for her, but Ernesto insisted they ride the Bloor-Danforth line together, from east to west, at least once. Paulina had liked it so much that sometimes she rode the subway alone, staring out the window at the whooshing darkness, or at people's houses or buildings when the train emerged out of the tunnel. If she wasn't so afraid of perverts exposing themselves to her, a real problem according to Lorraine, she could have ridden the subway for hours, in the timeless, formless space it provided, onto which she could project different versions of herself, her future.

That morning the subway was so packed she and Lorraine had to stand all the way from Spadina to Bloor station, surrounded by screaming children and their parents. One man bumped his sled against Lorraine's behind, but she just laughed.

"I think I'm pregnant," she said, as they were getting off the train.

The nurse at the movie theatre turned out to be a bored-looking old woman in a nurse's cap. A stupid gimmick, said Lorraine. Unlike the subway, the theatre was nearly empty, just a few teenagers in the back, and an old man drinking beer.

Lorraine liked to sit in the front row, the better to direct her comments, usually critical, at the screen. It hurt Paulina's eyes but Lorraine said it was the only way to really appreciate a movie.

"That blood is fake," she said, pointing to the screen. "They make it out of corn syrup. That's why they're drinking so much of it and not barfing."

It was still gross. Lorraine teased Paulina for covering her eyes as the actors licked blood from off the floor and the walls. She was glad when the film reached its gory conclusion.

On their way out, she and Lorraine passed the nurse, now reading a newspaper and smoking a cigarette.

"How's business?" Lorraine asked her.

"Booming," the woman said, not looking up from her paper.

"Don't ever go to that theatre alone," Lorraine said, as they hurried up an eerily deserted section of Yonge Street, on their way to the subway.

"Why not?"

"There's a man who'll sit next to you with his hat on his lap and when he lifts that hat I guarantee you won't like what you see. Or maybe you will?"

"That's disgusting."

"He was there, you know. Sitting right behind us. Didn't you hear his heavy breathing?"

Lorraine pulled Paulina's earmuff away from her ear. She pressed her cold mouth against her ear and panted. Paulina squealed, jumping away from Lorraine, almost colliding with a man in a long fur coat. She was afraid the man would be angry, but he just grinned at her.

As he was walking away, Lorraine whispered into Paulina's exposed ear that the man she'd nearly assaulted was a pimp, that he wanted Paulina to work for him. Paulina put her earmuffs back on, clamping both hands over them, pretending not to hear her.

"He pays really well," Lorraine said. "Six weeks' vacation and full benefits. Dental even."

"So why don't you work for him?"

"How do you know I'm not?"

"Because you're too lazy."

"Says you."

The subway ride in the other direction was much quieter. Between Bay and Spadina, they even had the car to themselves, except for an old man slumped over in his seat. It looked like he was sleeping. His bare hands rested in his lap, over his crotch.

"I know him," Lorraine said. "A real pervert. Just watch, he'll have his fly down in no time."

"How do you know so many perverts?"

Lorraine's honking laugh filled the car. "Because I'm a girl, stupid. Hasn't it happened to you? Some man waving his dick at you on the street?"

"Of course not," Paulina said, as they were getting off the train. The old man was still asleep.

"No dirty phone calls?"

"Never."

"What about getting your bum pinched on the bus? Or boys lifting your skirt at school, or twisting your titties? What about a good old-fashioned game of grab-ass with your gym teacher?"

"I told you, no," said Paulina, her cheeks hot.

"Aren't you the lucky one."

As they were climbing the stairs out of the subway, Lorraine slapped Paulina's bottom, laughing when she squealed. People turned to look at them, but Lorraine didn't care.

"Welcome to the club," she said.

～

Dear Pilar, Merry Christmas! Lorraine invited me to her home for Christmas dinner but Ernesto made us spend the holiday with the Weinribs, who don't have Christmas because they are Jewish. There was turkey and apple pie that was mostly apple with the peel still on. The Weinribs gave us gift certificates for a local record store. Ernesto gave the Weinribs a gift certificate for a local bookstore that he said was from both of us. After dinner Ernesto said we should go for a walk. Every house we passed was full of people eating, laughing, and exchanging presents. Real ones, not just slips of paper.

I am now wearing my winter jacket. It is silver and puffy, and I have matching silver boots that have never been worn. An old woman on our street fell on the ice and now she is in the hospital. Another neighbour's lock froze and he came to get help from the Weinribs because he could not get inside his own house. So this is winter in Canada and everyone makes jokes about whether I will survive it but I don't see what is so funny about freezing to death. I would take the worst flood over such cold. I wish you would write please. I miss you, Paulita.

— 15. —

THEY WENT FOR another walk on New Year's Eve, just before midnight. The Weinribs had invited them to a party but Ernesto had declined. He'd had enough of being paraded in front of Nathan's friends as the Chilean exile, the failed revolutionary hero.

Paulina was relieved when he told her it would be just the two of them. Christmas dinner had been awkward enough. And in Toronto they didn't have fireworks in the bay to watch, just TV.

"Remember how Pilar would jump when they started?"

Ernesto smiled, his hands under his armpits. This time he'd forgotten his gloves. He often left the house forgetting something, a glove, a hat, a scarf, but refused to go back. Next time I'll remember, he'd say, but he never did. Lately, he was always forgetting things, even what day of the week it was. Paulina wondered if all the marijuana he smoked was to blame.

"The junta won't allow fireworks this year," Ernesto said, rubbing his hands together. "People are already too shell-shocked."

The cold was making Paulina's eyes tear up. Ernesto joked that maybe she was allergic to Canadian winter.

"Ha ha."

Without his gloves, Ernesto's hands were red, raw-looking, like meat in a freezer. He shoved them in his pockets, bowed his head against the wind. They were on another street that ran parallel to theirs, with the same Victorian houses, the same snow-covered trees and cars.

"A few more blocks," Ernesto said. "It will make a man out of you."

At the military academy, the drill sergeants used to make them walk for hours in the cold and the rain, following them in a jeep, their windows rolled up. Some of them were so old that a case of the sniffles would have killed them.

"Real tough guys. I used to see them in Papa's waiting room, shitting themselves. Even Guzmán, all puffed up even though he'd turned green. They'd leave, pumped up like war heroes, high on whatever drugs Papa gave them. A commander at my school was like that. He was so grateful to Papa for keeping him in painkillers, he put me in charge of the library when I asked him. That library was my refuge. Pío and his buddies never went there. Too busy dreaming up hazing rituals. Like the broomstick they used to put a boy in hospital. The General made sure they didn't expel Pío that time. Our commanders, they encouraged us to brutalize each other. They said it would make us men."

Lately, Ernesto had been talking to Paulina like she wasn't even there, delivering monologues that would have impressed Valerie. Even the cold couldn't stop him.

Ernesto had hated coming home for the holidays, seeing those same men gathered at their father's table, gorging themselves on Basque delicacies, the seafood dishes and cream-filled cakes he forced Pilar to make without any help.

"He treated her like crap," Ernesto said, wiping his nose with his scarf. "Not letting her go home until after Christmas, and then she had to come back to do it all again for New Year's Eve. He exploited her."

It was true, Pilar was so busy preparing their holiday feasts that Paulina barely saw her. As soon as she was done cleaning up on New Year's Day she was gone again, to squeeze in a few more days with her son. But at least her father let her go. Inez's maid lived with them, too, but never took a day off. Where would she go, Inez once said.

Those holiday feasts were just for their father to show off. That was why he invited his patients, many of them retired commanders from Ernesto's academy. Old widowers whose grown children were on skiing holidays in Portillo. Ernesto was always expected home for the holidays, including their father's New Year's Eve party. Even General Guzmán didn't expect his own son to attend. He would tease Ernesto about not going out and raising hell like his Pío. No one dared mention Mrs. Guzmán celebrating the holidays in that special clinic outside Santiago. Ernesto said it would make anyone crazy, bringing a thug like Pío into the world.

"But it wasn't so bad," Paulina said. "We had fun. Like when we went swimming?"

Night swimming was their secret New Year's Eve ritual. Late at night, after the guests had gone home and their father was in bed, Ernesto would drive them to the beach. The last time, there had been a thunderstorm.

Paulina had been afraid of the lightening, but Ernesto had insisted they go. At first, she'd stayed close to the shore, but soon she followed her brother's lead, swimming farther out. It was raining so hard she couldn't tell the rainwater from the seawater; it was thrilling, but frightening, too. And she couldn't leave Ernesto alone, not the way he was treading water with his head thrown back, his mouth open as if he wanted the rain to fill him, drown him. Paulina swam right up to him, panting, begging him to get out of the water. Only if you race me, he'd said, and she'd swum alongside him toward the shore, this time letting him win.

"I would have swum to Peru to get away from those men. Papa's beloved generals. They are the ones in charge of our country now. Cowards and hypocrites and degenerates."

Paulina wanted to ask if General Guzmán was one of these degenerates, but the wind picked up speed, taking her breath away. Her eyes were watering, snow was collecting on her eyelashes. Another minute in this weather and they would die.

"Let's go back, Ernesto."

"One more block."

"That's what you said before this one."

"One more and we'll go back."

"I can't!"

"Walk backwards," Ernesto shouted to her, over the wind, now blowing so hard it was hissing at them.

"This is stupid," Paulina yelled back. But the wind was so strong she could no longer keep her eyes open. She followed Ernesto's lead, turning around, feeling silly and helpless as side by side they walked backwards.

"Long strides, that's the way to do it. Use your arms for balance. Like this." Ernesto held his arms out, level with his shoulders.

"Now move your arms like this."

He circled his arms like propellers. Paulina did the same.

"See? Better, isn't it?" Her brother's face was red from shouting instructions at her like a drill sergeant.

It was better, not that she'd admit it. Ernesto began skipping like a lunatic as he made circles with his arms, going faster and faster.

"Are you crazy? You're going to fall."

He was healed, yet Ernesto still seemed vulnerable, even more so because of the extra weight he'd gained. He'd had to go back to the church a few times for new clothes, to accommodate what Patricio called his "beer baby."

"Hey!"

Paulina turned around. A man and a woman stood before her, the man raising his arms as if to protect himself from a wild dog, the woman cowering behind him.

"They're nuts," the woman said, her words directed at Paulina. Her coat was open, as if she'd just thrown it on. There was a large gap between her two front teeth, black smudges under her eyes. If Lorraine had been there, she would have whispered in Paulina's ear: *hooker*.

Ernesto caught up to Paulina just as she was delivering what she considered the perfect insult.

"It is a free country," she said. One of Lorraine's favourite expressions. And true when compared to her own.

"Why don't you go back to yours?" The man nearly spit the words at her, his face red. His black coat reached his boots, hiding his frame so that she couldn't tell if he was big or small. This man was more afraid of the cold than she was.

"Why don't you go back to yours?" Paulina repeated, another of Lorraine's tricks. When a man on Yonge Street called Paulina an uptight bitch because she wouldn't smile for him, Lorraine had repeated his insult back to him, shutting him up.

"Fucking spics."

"You are the spic," Paulina volleyed back. Whatever a spic was this man was probably an even bigger one than she or Ernesto.

Until then Ernesto had been silent as if waiting for his cue. Now he stepped forward and punched the man in the face, producing a terrible cracking sound. The man fell backwards onto the sidewalk. The woman screamed and crouched over him. Ernesto stood over them both, face red, panting. The man was groaning. Blood was streaming from his nose into his mouth. He coughed and spat. The woman turned to face Paulina and her brother, her cheeks streaked with mascara.

"I'll tell the police. You'll go to jail for this. Fucking spics!"

"Will she really call the police?" Paulina asked as Ernesto grabbed her arm and dragged her away. Where inside that soft, vulnerable body had he found the strength not only to beat another man, but to run from the scene of his crime? Her brother still attracted so much pity, from Nathan, from Ruth, from the women he sometimes brought back to their apartment when he thought Paulina was sleeping. His smile, the sadness in his eyes, his softness; Ernesto could never be a fighter.

Yet as she ran against the wind Paulina exulted in the fresh memory of his blow, imagining the same fist splintering Douglas Watson's hateful face, the faces of all their enemies, here and at home.

"Nathan will take care of it," Ernesto said, catching his breath now that they were home. "Do you know what spic means?"

"Something bad?"

"It's an insult. He'll think again before saying that word."

Inside their apartment Ernesto sat at their kitchen table, clutching a bag of frozen peas in his left hand, drinking a beer. He didn't say anything when Paulina helped herself to a bottle.

— 16. —

ON THEIR FIRST day back after Christmas break, Lorraine showed Paulina her tan lines. The demonstration took place at lunchtime, in a locked stall of the ladies' bathroom. Lorraine had worked on her tan every moment she could, until the old man had appeared one day as she was walking from the beach to the hotel. At first she hadn't cared, he was just some old man, let him follow her. Then he'd started to shout at her in Spanish, running after her, all the way back to the resort, but he knew better than to go inside.

Lorraine's mother was so upset that she got the manager, who got a security guard. The four of them went back to the beach so Lorraine could identify the man, Lorraine sure he'd be long gone but nope, there he was. Up close, his skin was scarred, bad acne maybe. He'd taken off his shirt but not his skimpy, grubby jean shorts. His baseball cap had the logo of the Montreal Expos on it. Lorraine wondered if he'd gone to Montreal to get it, also whether his balls would pop out of his shorts. Her second question was answered in the affirmative when the manager and the security guard began dragging him off the beach. Even while he struggled, the old man did not forget Lorraine, calling out to her from over his shoulder. If only Paulina had been there to translate; what he'd said had to have been really filthy, judging by the manager's face.

"What happened to him?"

"The police came and took him away. Julio says there's lots of old perverts who come to the beach even though they're not allowed. You're only allowed in the resort if you work there but people sneak in."

Lorraine had met Julio toward the end of her holiday. She was in bed, her mother asleep beside her, when she realized she'd left her retainer on her dinner plate. Lorraine had recently started wearing the device to correct her misaligned and overcrowded teeth. She hated it, often leaving it behind at school or in Paulina's apartment. It had cost her a mother an arm and a leg, she had to find it.

Panicked, Lorraine got dressed and left the room while her mother slept, to look for her arm-and-a-leg retainer. The resort was made up of bungalows like theirs, with a bedroom, a sitting room, and a bathroom. It was all very nice but there were a lot of ants in the bathroom. There was a dining hall, a swimming pool, and another building with a disco inside. Lorraine was on the path to the dining hall when a man stopped her. He seemed nice so she told him about her missing retainer. He spoke some English, at least enough to understand that she'd left something of great value on her dinner plate. He offered to help her, taking her arm. He said his name was Julio.

Julio led her to a large bin behind the dining hall. Without hesitation or squeamishness, he began digging through the garbage, as if he did this every night. While up to his elbows in trash he sang to Lorraine, a love song, he said. But Julio could not find her retainer. Lorraine started to cry. Her mother was always yelling at her to be careful not to lose the device. Ronnie worked part-time at a bank and it was only because Lorraine's great-uncle had died and left them a little money that they could go on vacation after her mother had paid off the retainer.

Julio took Lorraine, still crying, to a sort of shack close to the beach. There were people sitting at a table and she recognized some of them as the waiters from the dining hall. Julio spoke to them in Spanish, presumably asking if they'd seen Lorraine's retainer, but no one seemed to care. They were more interested in fiddling with their radio. Miami, Miami, Julio said, pointing to it. At first it was just static but then they could hear the DJs.

A Bread song came on, Lorraine's favourite. Julio danced her around the shack and she forgot all about her retainer. When the song was over he kissed her, in front of everyone, no tongue, but he didn't need to use his tongue, not with those lips. It was, Lorraine said, her first kiss.

So Lorraine really had forgotten all about their kiss, still Paulina's first. Or maybe it didn't count, because she'd been "tripping."

Paulina, sensing an important shift in the story, returned her attention to Lorraine, seated on the toilet lid, tearing strips of paper from the roll. Julio had been so nice to her, she kept saying. He was so handsome. He was a little put out when he realized she was a virgin but not for long. Afterwards they'd exchanged addresses.

It sounded about as romantic as Paulina and her brother exchanging Christmas gift certificates with the

Weinribs. Wasn't Julio supposed to declare his love and propose to her? Why wasn't Lorraine crying tears of womanly shame and joy, like Alma Siqueiros in *War Widows*, when she lost her virginity to her soldier fiancé? Instead, Lorraine looked serious, even a bit grown-up, as she told Paulina how she'd promised to get Julio out of Cuba, but she needed her help.

"You're crazy," Paulina said, her back against the stall door. Did Lorraine expect them to storm the island and kidnap the man?

"Cuba is a Communist country, he can never leave."

"What do you know? Ronnie knows a woman at the bank, she married a Cuban she met in Varadero. He was working at a resort, too."

"Why do you want to marry him? Do you love him? Does he love you?"

Lorraine led Paulina out of the stall to the sinks, opening all the faucets before speaking. Sometimes office workers came into the ladies' room, clutching their handbags when they saw an ASPIRE student.

"My period didn't come," Lorraine told Paulina, over the rushing water.

"You are pregnant?"

"I don't know. I think so. That's why you have to help me. Write him a letter in Spanish. Convince him to come here and marry me."

"He won't come here, Castro won't let him."

"Why are you being such a drag? Just because you've never been in love? Because you're a lezzy?"

I am in love, Paulina wanted to say. Instead, she insisted she wasn't a lezzy, adding, a beat too late for the full impact, "You are the lezzy."

Lezzy was a variant of lez, which Paulina had finally figured out meant lesbian, *lesbiana*, a word her girlfriends used to whisper about their teachers, including Sister Teresa; in either language, it made Paulina feel like she was trapped inside an itchy sweater. Lorraine enjoyed pointing out women in public she thought might be lezzies. Her choices followed no discernible logic: sometimes the women were shorthaired and masculine-looking but not always. Usually the women were young but old women could be lezzies, too. Paulina had learned to play the lezzy game, to laugh, especially when the lezzy was old enough to be the grandmother she'd barely known, her mother's mother, who lived somewhere near the Peruvian border.

Lorraine made it clear: Paulina either wrote the letter or risked being labelled a life-long lezzy. Yet despite this threat hanging over her, Paulina enjoyed composing the letter, using her best Spanish to encourage Julio to risk his life and make an honest woman of Lorraine. In case he needed further enticing, she described all the wonderful freedoms awaiting him in Toronto, beginning with Hostess potato chips that came in many strange and wonderful flavours, like ketchup and barbecue, with always enough wish chips to wish on. These he could crunch while sitting through two movies in a row, sometimes more because no one checked your ticket or even asked your age, at least not at the movie theatre on Yonge Street. Then there was the new tower currently under construction. Paulina was not sure what its purpose was so she invented one: protecting the city from military coups. And absorbing lightning. However, Julio was not to worry, there were no earthquakes or other natural disasters in Toronto, unless you counted winter. There were cheap pizzerias and restaurants that offered steak dinners, everything included, at bargain prices. Julio could go into a drugstore to buy tampons and roll-on deodorant and no one would notice or care. There was a cream you applied to your legs and underarms that melted the dark hairs away, not that he would need that, or the tampons, but the cream was miraculous, nonetheless.

There were Chinese families, and men in turbans, and girls with short hair, and boys with long hair, and drunks who hollered on the street. There was every kind of person imaginable in Toronto and you could pretend to be anyone you wanted. Once she had seen two men holding hands in a parking lot, but she didn't put that in the letter.

Re-reading her letter, Paulina thought Julio would be a fool not to risk it. Toronto, too, had its dark corners, its alleyways, even a ravine where Lorraine said they could hide if they were ever falsely accused of murder. You can do whatever you want here, Paulina wrote Julio in their shared language, and no one will care. In Chile, if she dared go to the movies alone one dull afternoon, by the time the film was over the priest, whose cousin manned the box office, would have informed her father of her transgression. In Chile, no one had a truly private life but in Canada, there was privacy, even in public spaces. No, something better than privacy. Anonymity. Paulina underlined the word three times. Then, in a postscript, she told Julio that he needn't feel burdened by Lorraine's condition; if the doctors let her, Lorraine could have an abortion, and they could wait for the right time to start their family.

Paulina went with Lorraine to post the letter. Lorraine kept trying to peer down the chute, to make sure the letter was inside but it was too dark, so she walked in circles around the mailbox, worried that the letter had somehow fallen to the ground, until Paulina stopped her by using one of Lorraine's favourite expressions: *get a grip*. She brought her to their favourite pizzeria, where Lorraine got her period while they were waiting for their food.

Weeks passed with no response from Julio.

"If he really loves you, he will find a way."

"How, when he can't leave his Commie shithole country?"

Eventually, Lorraine stopped talking about Julio and began a brief yet passionate anti-Communist phase that culminated in an improvised lunchtime presentation on the evils of the Soviet Union, impressing Albert, who made her president of his Current Events club.

Borrowing money from her bank, Lorraine's mother bought her a new retainer, still believing Lorraine's story that one of the resort employees had stolen it. You can't trust those Spanish types, Ronnie said. Next winter they were going to Florida.

~

One night not long after Paulina had learned that Lorraine's mother didn't trust Spanish speakers, the police came to the Weinrib house, to follow up, they said, on a complaint about a violent assault carried out by a Spanish-speaking male.

Over Nathan's objections the police brought Ernesto to their station, just to answer a few questions, they said. Nathan insisted on going, leaving Paulina alone with Ruth, who made them a pot of fennel tea, to soothe Paulina's nerves, she said. Not that there was any cause for worry; Ernesto was innocent, he would be back soon. Paulina wished she could tell Ruth what had really happened, but her brother had told her not to tell anyone, so she drank her tea, finally understanding what it meant when people said their stomach was in knots.

She was half-asleep on the Weinribs' sofa when Ernesto came back. Everything was fine, she heard him telling Ruth in Spanish, it was just a mix-up. Nathan wasn't with him; he was still at the station, filing a complaint against the cops for harassment.

That night for the first time, Ernesto locked the door to their apartment.

"Did you say anything to Ruth?"

"No. What happened? Did they arrest you? Did they hit you?"

Ernesto got a beer from the fridge and drank half of it while standing at the sink. He hadn't been touched by anyone, he told Paulina. Just humiliated. The cops had ordered him to stand in a row with four other men, a Mexican and three Cubans. It was ridiculous, they were all different heights and builds. The woman and her boyfriend were on the other side of the two-way mirror so he couldn't see them, but he'd watched enough TV to know what was happening. He was in a line-up.

At the station, Nathan had warned Ernesto that if the woman picked him out he would do his best to defend him, but a charge of violent assault could lead to deportation, for him and for Paulina. Nathan did not ask Ernesto whether he'd attacked the man.

"Who did she pick?"

"The Mexican. I could tell by the way they kept asking him to come forward."

It made sense, Ernesto said. He was the darkest of them all.

Drinking tea with Ruth, pretending to listen to her talk about her plans to go back to school, Paulina had gone over the question she would have to ask her brother if he ever came back to her.

"Did you hit Douglas Watson first?"

It was meant to be a question, but it sounded more like a statement.

"I didn't hit him," Ernesto said. He got another beer from the fridge and returned to the table.

"I barely pushed him."

Paulina's throat tightened, as if preventing her from asking more, but she couldn't help herself.

"Why did you push him?"

"The same reason I punched that asshole on New Year's Eve. People need to be educated, freed from their prejudices. Sometimes it's the only way they'll learn."

That was why he hadn't pressed charges against Douglas Watson. He'd started the fight. Watson had called them spics and Ernesto had reacted with violence. That was her brother, not the soft, lazy man he pretended to be. Underneath the padding he'd acquired in Canada lurked a guerrilla.

"So every time someone calls you a name you hit them?"

"Not necessarily. But I'll do something to make them regret it."

"And what will happen to us?"

"Nothing. We have Nathan. He takes good care of us. He knows a few things about being called names."

They were not spics; Ernesto was determined to teach anyone who mistook them for one a lesson. Paulina was to have faith that the man upstairs—not God, of course, he meant Nathan Weinrib—would keep them out of trouble.

"But what will happen to the Mexican?"

"Don't worry about him. The cops told Nathan he's been brought in before, for exposing himself to girls. This is the best thing that could happen to him. If no one stops him his behaviour will escalate. That's how deviance works, small steps, the deviant pushing more and more against social norms. This arrest will save him."

Something about this theory troubled Paulina but she pushed it away, as forcefully as Ernesto had pushed Douglas Watson aboard that ferry. Which was exactly what he'd deserved.

~

The scowling man at the post office said that the holidays were always a busy time of year. Anyway, it wasn't the fault of Canada Post. We can deliver letters to anywhere in the world, he said, but we're not responsible for what goes on in less advanced countries.

— 17. —

"WE'RE NOT SAYING you're a bad influence on each other. We're just suggesting that you cool it a bit. Spend less time together."

Albert was smiling but they knew they were in trouble. That afternoon Paulina had interrupted Lorraine's session because, she told Albert, she had an important message for her. Of course, said Albert, I hope nothing's wrong? Paulina knew she was putting on a good show; Lorraine looked so serious, even anxious. Still maintaining her demeanour (doctor with bad news) Paulina bent over and whispered, *lezzy*, into Lorraine's ear. Lorraine leapt up, pulling her hair with both hands, screaming and laughing. When they wouldn't calm down, Albert went to find Valerie. They all needed to have a talk, he said.

If not for Valerie's presence Paulina was sure Lorraine would have had a lot to say to Albert, most of it swear words.

"Other kids have been complaining. They say you two are out of control."

"There was the egg incident," Valerie said. She was wearing her blouse with its pattern of birds in flight, the first two buttons undone, revealing her delicate collarbone. Paulina could not bear to look directly at her, not with so much blood rushing to her face, sweat erupting somewhere unexpected and embarrassing. She could tell Valerie didn't want to be there, either, in the narrow room that served as the facilitators' office, let alone remind everyone of the egg incident, as she was doing now.

At least Valerie didn't know that Paulina had stolen the egg. It had been so easy: open the carton, take an egg out, slide it into her jacket pocket. As they were leaving, Paulina wondered aloud why people even paid for eggs when they were so easy to steal. Lorraine agreed that people were chumps. It hadn't occurred to Paulina that maybe Lorraine, more practiced, should steal the egg. *Those people*, that's what Lorraine's mother had said. Maybe she was right. Illicit activity had not been so hard for her, not at all. It was thrilling, even. Like starting fights must be for Ernesto.

Walking back to school Paulina wondered if Lorraine thought she was poor, that she had to steal eggs to feed herself. Maybe she should tell Lorraine that Ernesto always left money out for her, her share of what he got from the Canadian government. She had more than enough for books, subway tokens, lunches and snacks. Not that she needed to buy much food; Ruth still left bags of groceries and containers of cooked food outside their door. What else could she need? It was Lorraine who had a problem, sneaking into movie theatres and swiping cigarette butts from Albert's ashtray. Yet, she'd asked Paulina to swipe the egg.

It had been worth it, at first. In the school kitchen Lorraine had cracked the pilfered egg into a coffee cup, using her hands to separate the white from the yolk, as Ronnie had taught her. They didn't need the yolk so she slipped it into another cup, leaving it on the counter in case anyone wanted it.

"Ronnie says it's a sin to waste food."

Eyes closed, they dipped their fingers into the cup of egg white. Lorraine had read somewhere that this was what sperm felt like. Paulina thought it strange that Lorraine, who had had sex with a man, could still be so childish about things like that.

From the outside it must have looked like a religious ritual, the way they dipped and dipped, eyes closed, threatening to anoint each other with egg white until they lost interest, forgetting about the cups of raw egg until some idiot students, thinking they were clean, had used them for coffee. Valerie and Albert were especially angry because one of those idiots had been Chuck, who stuttered and twitched and was supposedly allergic to eggs.

They would have denied everything but then Rita Wong claimed to have seen them in the kitchen. They'd never hated anyone so much, they told each other, as they now hated Rita Wong. They hated everything about her, including the fact that she had a Chinese mother and a white father. The day after she'd betrayed them, Lorraine had made Rita cry by shouting, "Pick a race!" at her when they passed her in the hall. Paulina said she knew all about half-bloods, Chile was full of them, so they started calling Rita "Rita the Mestiza." Paulina did not mention that on her mother's side, she, too, was a half-blood, but it didn't matter because Lorraine preferred "lezzy" so they stuck to that.

To Paulina, Rita Wong was a real lezzy, with her dirty sneakers, her thick bangs, her braces and acne. Lez, lezzy; these terms had broken free from their mother, "lesbian," like the shoots snipped from Valerie's spider plant, to be applied to anyone they found disgusting. Even Chuck qualified. Only a lez would be allergic to eggs.

It was strange, how pleasurable it felt to be repulsed.

"Straighten up and fly right," Albert was saying.

"What does that even mean?"

"It means we don't want you to get expelled," Valerie told Lorraine. "And yes, we can expel students."

Lorraine muttered that she was sorry, sorry for making Rita cry, sorry for everything. Then she started to cry.

"Please don't tell my dad," she said.

Paulina had never seen Lorraine cry before, not even over Julio. Her whole body shook, but she did not make a sound. Albert and Valerie looked as alarmed as Paulina felt.

Valerie gave Lorraine a box of tissues, assuring her she wasn't being expelled, it was just a warning. Lorraine's body became still and, in a meek voice Paulina had never before heard from her, she asked to be excused.

Out in the hallway, Lorraine pressed her mouth, still damp from crying, against Paulina's ear.

"Lezzies."

They ran down the hallway, Paulina laughing so hard she couldn't breathe.

~

Paulina was afraid that Valerie would still be angry at her but the next time they met, she was radiant. She had excellent news, she said. Sir Jerome Mason, Canada's most respected actor and director, had contacted the school in search of a young actress for a part in his upcoming, unnamed play, and Valerie had suggested Paulina.

They had three days to prepare her audition for the great man of Canadian theatre. Valerie said it would be enough if they worked hard. And she had the perfect part for Paulina, sure to impress Sir Jerome, who wasn't really a knight, she said. It was just a nickname, bestowed on him affectionately by his fellow actors.

It seemed impossible. Three days to become Sonya from *Uncle Vanya*, to convey the full range of her loneliness, her broken heart, her determination. But Valerie had once heard a radio interview with Sir Jerome in which he'd said *Uncle Vanya* was his favourite play. Maybe it was the perfect Sonya he was looking for and if so, it was fate, because they'd already read and discussed the play.

They began rehearsing Sonya's monologue that day. Paulina just needed to tap into Sonya's motivations, Valerie said. Where her head was at.

"Her father and stepmother are gone, her uncle's too miserable to help her, the doctor doesn't love her, he won't marry her. She'll have to take care of the estate herself. Her only reward is death, that's what she's saying. Death after a lifetime of work, alongside her uncle. It's about as bleak as it gets."

Not to Paulina. Sonya's infatuation with the doctor may have been pathetic, but it wasn't indecent. Indecent and criminal, as homosexuality still was in Chile. Sonya, a sad sack but no deviant, was not in love with Yelena, her glamorous stepmother. So far as Paulina knew, there were no plays about women pining for other women, in Russia or elsewhere.

Valerie was not a deviant, not a criminal, which was why she did not love Paulina. Each time Paulina delivered her speech, in her bed at night, in the shower, waiting for the kettle to boil, she felt her despair harden into Sonya's resignation. Work, all she had was work. Her chest ached, her eyes pricked with tears, as she spoke Sonya's words. Valerie was impressed.

"It's all there, right under the surface. All the emotions you need. You just need to tap in, pull it out."

The theatre would be Paulina's Russian farm; she would devote herself to it until she died, alone but not unloved. Her audience would give her the love she craved, without question or conditions.

For months, Paulina had been living her life in English, the language had forced its way into her dreams. Thinking and living in this foreign language was keeping her safe, from herself, her feelings, from what was happening back home. Becoming Sonya was taking her even farther away. If Sir Jerome Mason chose her, and why wouldn't he, she could spend the rest of her life inhabiting other people. Even better, rehearsals were scheduled to start just before the semester ended. Leaving school early meant she wouldn't have to see Lorraine, who'd been avoiding her lately, after telling her that their plan to sneak into Rochdale College and spy on the nude sun worshippers on the roof was off. Paulina had been hoping they might squeeze in a trip to the Polish neighbourhood where Valerie supposedly lived, but Lorraine said she was too busy for goofing off. It was probably for the best; what if Valerie saw her skulking around her neighbourhood? In the end, it was just another rejection for her to channel into her performance. She was almost grateful for it.

— 18. —

STANDING BEFORE THE great man so that he could inspect her, Paulina finally understood the meaning of that curious expression, "sizing someone up." Sir Jerome seemed to be weighing her with his gaze, taking off a few points here, adding a few points there. She stood before him, trembling, yes, but sizing him up in return, like the plain yet clever Sonya would do.

Sir Jerome's head looked too large for his body, as if grafted on. Perhaps to compensate for his baldness, his eyebrows were a tangle of white and yellow hairs. His smile, however, revealed two rows of perfectly white teeth. Dentures, most likely. Her father's speciality.

Judging by his smile, Paulina must have earned his approval. Whatever had turned to jelly in her stomach had stopped its sloshing. She was ready to lose herself in Sonya. She was Sonya. Her love, like Sonya's, was unrequited. All she had was her work and the uncle she'd just saved from suicide. Paulina wasn't even nervous, so eager was she to exult in her and Sonya's shared sorrows.

Valerie had decided that Paulina would deliver the first part of her speech on her knees, gradually rising to her feet as Sonya took strength from her suffering, like a tree growing out of the ground. She'd loaned Paulina her white peasant dress, not that Sonya was a peasant, but she shouldn't look too contemporary. It was too short on her, she'd said, but perfect on Paulina. So perfect that Paulina should keep it.

"What will I have the pleasure of hearing?" Sir Jerome asked Valerie.

"Paulina wanted to do Sonya's monologue from *Uncle Vanya*," Valerie said, beaming at her.

Sir Jerome shifted in the plastic chair provided for him, turning his great head to Paulina.

"There is something of Marion Cartwright in you, has anyone ever told you that?"

Paulina said no, no one had ever told her that. She hoped Marion Cartwright, whoever she was, was a great star, like Sir Jerome.

"No, they wouldn't," Sir Jerome said, back to sizing Paulina up. "Marion wasn't the ingénue type like you. Came into this world a matron but at least she left it before becoming a crone. Died in a boating accident before her fortieth birthday. I haven't thought of Big Marion in ages. I cast her in *A Winter's Tale* at the National. She was marvellous."

Big Marion? Was this a compliment? Should she thank Sir Jerome, or offer her condolences on the passing of Big Marion, who at least had been marvellous? Thankfully, Sir Jerome spared her the trouble by telling Paulina he was ready for what he called, her Sonya.

"I don't know how much more of this chair my prostate can take."

Sonya's were the last words of the play and Paulina had been looking forward to clearly enunciating each one, especially now that she'd succeeded in taming her accent. We. Shall. Rest! she recited silently, preparing to launch into her monologue.

Her face was raised to the ceiling, she was about to deliver the first words of her speech when Sir Jerome Mason rose from his chair, to stand over her like the great tree she was supposed to become.

"I can get you a better chair," Valerie said, but he ignored her.

It had rained all day (everyone apologized to Paulina for the dismal Canadian spring) but at last the sun had come out. The light coming through the windows was strong enough to reveal one of the great man's eyebrow hairs, much longer than its fellows. It curled up and out, like the antennae of some insect that could detect phony acting.

Sir Jerome smiled down at Paulina as he removed his tweed jacket, wrapping her in it as if he'd just pulled her out of a river. His rich mid-Atlantic accent filled the lounge.

"Your mother died after bringing you into the world. Your father is dead or so they want you to believe. You are betrayed by your protector, kidnapped by pirates, then sold to a brothel in a strange land. You are fourteen."

Paulina had been certain that Sir Jerome was speaking about her until the part about the pirates and the brothel. What was a brothel?

"A house of ill-repute. A whorehouse, a bordello, where women are kept for the pleasure of men."

"I am seventeen," Paulina told the great man, her voice shaky, no longer in her control. She looked to Valerie, waiting for her to correct the bit about Paulina being a prostitute, but Valerie looked as shocked as Paulina. Didn't Sir Jerome want to find out if she could act?

Sir Jerome circled Paulina several times with intimidating strides. Paulina was afraid to move, to breathe. The scene reminded her of an exorcism she'd once witnessed on the docks of Valparaíso. Did Sir Jerome believe a devil had possessed her? Had he come not to discover her, as she'd so desperately wished, but to exorcise her?

"Marina, child of the sea. One of Shakespeare's great innocents. I thought it might be nice, a real virgin playing the part, but they turned out to be hard to find, even in the private schools. Especially in the private schools. I called every high school, my dear, searching for you. The drama teachers thrust forth their prodigies, self-conscious, arrogant girls pushing out their chests at me. That was why I kept the play, the role, such a secret. I didn't want to see girls old beyond their years trying on the innocence and purity of Marina like a pair of jeans. I had never even heard of your school until I met your teacher outside Bathurst Station. She very kindly gave me a pamphlet about Angela Davis and I told her that I'd been the first to cast a Black actor in a Shakespearean production in this country. We had a long chat, didn't we, Miss Thomas?"

Why had Valerie not told her the whole truth, about Sir Jerome running into her outside Bathurst Station while he was looking for virgins? Was Valerie dating Sir Jerome? No, Valerie would never be attracted to a man old enough to be her grandfather. It was impossible, unnatural.

Sir Jerome helped Paulina, his jacket still draped over her shoulders like a cape, to her feet. She did feel like she'd washed up on a strange shore, shivering despite the warmth of the room. Marina, she thought. I'm going to be Marina, in a play by William Shakespeare, directed by a man Valerie says is the most important actor in Canadian theatre. Yet without his sports jacket Sir Jerome seemed to shrink, to disappear inside his crumpled blue shirt and sagging tweed pants. His wrists were thin, his hands were spotted. Valerie would never let those hands touch her.

"It's only fair to warn you, my dear. Some of the old farts I've cast might chase you around the theatre on all fives. But don't fret, they prefer warm milk by the fire to the beast with two backs. At least George who plays your father is under thirty, as is Denise, who plays your mother. And June Fairfield, who will play your nurse and the queen who wishes you dead and the madam who tries to make a whore of you, is one of Canada's greats. You'll learn more from her than from any of us, so watch her closely. Oh, for fuck's sake, can't you see we're talking?"

Albert was at the door, Rita and Lorraine behind him. Timidly, he informed them that he'd booked the lounge for a music class.

"Your sitting in a circle and chanting like Moonies can wait, I'm sure."

Sir Jerome shut the door on them, then turned back to Paulina.

"Table read is next Saturday at ten. Ricky, our stage manager, will drop off the script for you tonight, and your call sheet. Don't worry about learning your lines.

Some actors are line-perfect at the first read, acting their little hearts out. I like the blank slates better. Valerie says she's been teaching you Shakespeare? How does she manage, Miss Thomas?"

"Exceptionally well," Valerie said, smiling at Paulina, her eyes wet. "We've read *Othello* and *The Merchant of Venice*."

It was true. Valerie had helped her, buying her copies of the plays that had the original version and another, modern one, so that Paulina could go back and forth between the two. Paulina would ask Valerie to get her a similar copy of *Pericles, Prince of Tyre*.

Sir Jerome removed his jacket from Paulina's shoulders, carefully, as if unveiling a sculpture. Paulina, trembling, was afraid to move and break the spell.

"There are some smutty jokes in your bordello scenes that you won't understand. Better to keep it that way. And that charming little accent of yours, we'll keep that, too. I like you a little foreign."

Paulina stood in the centre of the room, still trembling. Marina, she was thinking. Child not of man, but of the sea. No one else can play her but me.

~

"Why pick her?" Lorraine asked. "She's a midget and her voice is all squeaky, like a strangled mouse."

"It's just because everyone feels sorry for her," Rita Wong said.

"No, it's because she's a troublemaker. We had a meeting with Valerie and Albert. They want to get rid of her."

Fuck you, Paulina thought, but what she said surprised even herself. The perfect line, delivered without haste or heat as she pushed open the door to her toilet stall.

"I am officially bored with you lezzies."

They stared at her, open-mouthed, as she left the washroom, imitating Sir Jerome's great strides. Fuck them both, indeed. Her real life had just begun.

INTERLUDE

— 1. —

"The theatre's so distressingly modern. So clean and well lit. Doesn't smell like anything, let alone grease paint."

"No dark corners to hide in, either."

"Sir Jerome's becoming a hippie. That's why he's doing it on campus."

"Such a short run, too. Just ten nights."

"Will you be wearing your rug for this one, Hal?"

"Bugger off."

"All the men in my family died with a full head of hair."

"If only it had been theirs."

"Jerome's an old fool. All his savings sunk into this ship."

"The blonde is a real find. Great tits."

"But who'll believe she's the little boy's mother?"

"Did anyone understand a word she said?"

"Cast for publicity. She and her brother were in the papers, the brother's some commie hippie who got the snot kicked out of him on the island ferry. She's an orphan. Sir Jerry likes the refugee angle, a real-life Marina. She's terrible, but who knows? It might work."

"She does look like something the sea spat out. Why did she show up wearing her nightgown?"

"It's the style these days. They all want to look like Victorian virgins while acting like trollops."

"At least there's a pub nearby."

"Full of students and dropouts."

"Beggars can't be choosers. Gentlemen?"

"We'd better grab a seat by the gents. Hal's prostate is on its last legs."

Paulina had been hovering outside the ladies' room around the corner from the elevators. As soon as she was sure the old men were gone, she hurried back inside the theatre. Sir Jerome was still seated at the long table set up on the stage, where the cast had read through the play for the first time. The stage manager, or Little Ricky as the old men had called him, sat next to Sir Jerome, both men bent over a large, open binder.

"Am I terrible?" Paulina heard herself whine.

Little Ricky gave Paulina one of the many clean handkerchiefs he carried with him for such occasions. His pink face took on even more colour.

"Ricky has never really adjusted to the throbbing emotions of actors," Sir Jerome said. "You'd never guess it but he's just turned fifty. The theatre keeps him young. He's been with me since I opened the National Theatre in Ottawa."

As if to confirm his advanced age, Little Ricky ran a pale, chubby hand through his greying hair. During the table read he'd barely spoken, only opening his mouth to read the stage directions in a soft voice. The older actors kept shouting at him to speak up, for Christ's sake. Whenever Sir Jerome spoke, however, Little Ricky closed his eyes and smiled as if his favourite song had just come on the radio.

"Am I terrible?"

She thought she'd done well. Except for Denise Francis and George Woods, no one else knew their lines. Yes, she'd stumbled a bit in the bordello scenes, missing a few cues, but that was because of the way the six old actors had stared at her, eyes twinkling, mouths slack.

Sir Jerome raised himself up from the table, taking both of Paulina's hands in his dry, spotted ones.

"My dear," he said. "You are Marina. Leave the rest to me."

Paulina left the theatre feeling reassured. Somewhat. The old men were right about Sir Jerome's choice of venue. The theatre was on the top floor of yet another ugly building swallowed up by the university, at the opposite end of the campus from ASPIRE. The space, reserved for avant-garde student productions, was far from the grand theatre Paulina had envisioned for her debut. But there were compensations, starting with the cast.

During the table read, Paulina had sat opposite Denise. George Woods, dark-eyed and dark-haired, did look like he could be her father, but Denise Francis was tall, blonde, beautiful, a fashion model and at twenty-one, only four years older than Paulina. How her chest had ached as she and Denise read the lines from their only scene together, when mother and daughter were reunited at long last. Such beautiful if confusing words. As soon as she got home Paulina would read the play again, the ordinary, unadorned version Valerie had bought her as a congratulatory gift, not the script Little Ricky had given her. Her Modern English translation was her other, sordid secret.

— 2. —

As promised, Sir Jerome brought his slapstick to the first rehearsal.

"The whip," Oliver said when he saw it. His mottled cheeks darkened with pleasure.

The slapstick, Sir Jerome told them, went back to the third century BCE. Not his, of course. His came from the Stratford Festival, summer of 1953.

"Two flat pieces of wood, hinged at one end, that when slapped together ..."

"Don't hog it," Oliver said, reaching for it with a trembling hand. He had several small cuts on his chin, presumably from shaving. Paulina didn't think he should be trusted with the slapstick. But he only wanted to examine the wood, he said. What kind was it? No one knew.

The older actors were disappointed to learn that they would not get to use the slapstick. Only June would wield it when, as the Bawd, she took Paulina over her knee and spanked her. Little Ricky had scheduled the first rehearsal of this scene for late in the afternoon when the old men were either at the pub or in their shared dressing room, napping. Yet somehow they were all present and very much awake when June took Paulina over her knee.

"Think of the queen," she whispered to Paulina as she took up the slapstick.

"Which one?" Paulina asked, kneeling beside June's chair.

Preserve your person, Sir Jerome had told her. This was her motivation. At least the slapstick did not make contact with any part of Paulina, just as June had promised. But the old men shifted in their seats all the same.

Paulina was grateful for Denise in the front row providing moral support, her book on her lap. Whenever Paulina and June rehearsed the scene, Denise was there, to shame the old perverts with her presence, she said. And her book. When not needed on stage she liked to sit near the Benny Hills, as she called them, and read her book. The Benny Hills stared at the cover of *Against Rape* as they might an open grave. Once Denise had gone to the bathroom, leaving her book on her seat, and Paulina had seen Edgar, the second oldest of the group, pick up the book the way one might a dead rat by its tail.

The Benny Hills all smoked, even on stage, but the first time Denise lit a cigarette during the table read they had all exchanged glances and Alfred, who Paulina would later see light a cigarette with one that he was still smoking, sucked his teeth, loudly and moistly. The Benny Hills also gave June equally disapproving looks when she smoked, even though she was their age. They complained, too, about the heat and humidity inside the theatre, clamouring for air-conditioning or they would melt, but it was mid-June, too early for it to be turned on.

"Imagine them melted like candles," Denise had whispered to Paulina, and they'd both laughed.

June never complained about the heat or her blocking or the lack of good restaurants nearby. She was aging beautifully, Denise said, and Paulina agreed. Unlike the Benny Hills, June's greying hair was always combed, she never smelled fusty, and she ate with her mouth closed. Denise said she had excellent bone structure, which was all that mattered. Paulina agreed again, she agreed with everything Denise said, especially that the Benny Hills were old perverts, they belonged to another era and the sooner they died out the better. They were old friends of Sir Jerome's and Denise said he had cast them out of pity. Every time Harold spoke his line, "To sing a song that old was sung," Denise would smile at Paulina and Paulina would smile back, even though she did feel a bit sorry for the Benny Hills. Yes, their jokes were stupid (sexist, Denise said) but sometimes Paulina would see Oliver sitting alone backstage, staring into space as if lost in his own world, the way her father had sometimes done, and feel sad for him. But then Oliver would pop his head into their dressing room to ask the girls, as he called them, if they knew what martinis and women's breasts had in common?

"One is not enough and three is too many," Denise said, not looking away from her reflection in the make-up mirror.

"She thinks she's Constance Talmadge now that her picture's in the paper," Oliver said.

"Who the hell is that?" Denise shouted at his slowly departing back.

Pericles, Prince of Tyre was Denise's first production after being discovered by a talent agent on the Yonge Street mall, that strip of the world's longest street kept

closed to traffic and popular, not just with truant teenagers like Paulina and Lorraine, but also talent agents
who sat on benches and stopped anyone who looked
promising. You had to be careful, Denise told Paulina,
but this guy was the real deal. Professional. Before her
casting in *Pericles*, he'd booked her a job modelling for
the magazine that came with the weekend edition of the
newspaper. In a series of colour photographs Denise illus-
trated the dangers of driving while female. Women were
not to drive with the roof down or the windows open
because long flowing hair obscured the driver's vision. A
photograph of Denise behind the wheel accompanied
this warning, her face partially obscured by her long
blonde hair. Women were also not to wear wide-brimmed
hats or platform shoes or apply lipstick while driving and
there were photographs of Denise doing all these things
and worse. Paulina kept the magazine under her bed.

The photographs had appeared at the end of the first
week of rehearsals, causing a sensation among the Benny
Hills. Sir Jerome had not said anything about them, although the article mentioned that the model, Denise
Francis, was an actress who would soon appear in the
first play directed by Sir Jerome Mason since leaving the
National Theatre.

Only Paulina, June, and George knew the truth about
Denise's casting. After leaving Ottawa, and in need of
funds for his new production, Sir Jerome had offered his
services as acting coach to a few, select agents. Both
George and Denise had the same talent agent who'd sent
them to Sir Jerome.

June said that a man of Sir Jerome's stature coaching
unknowns wasn't unheard of, but they had to keep it

from the Benny Hills, they were vicious, they gossiped like old women. Indeed, Paulina had once overheard them speculating about how Denise had really earned her part, Edgar declaring that he would never have cast her, Denise wasn't his type. Women with such large breasts looked ridiculous, he said.

"You know the old saying?" he croaked, just as Paulina was walking past them in the corridor, where they'd gathered to gossip.

"More than a mouthful is a waste," she said, repeating Alfred's witticism from that morning. Then she hurried away to the safety of the dressing room, to Denise and June and George.

GEORGE WOODS HAD longed to be an actor since boyhood but his father expected him to take over the family business. He compromised by managing the books for his father's shoe store a few times a month, when he wasn't on the road. Last month he'd gone on tour with the latest hit musical imported from Broadway, singing in the chorus in medium-sized towns throughout the province. He was away so often that his mother had begun using his bedroom to dry sausages.

George Woods shared these confidences with Paulina during their breaks because they had something in common. George's real name was Jorge Ramos da Silva. Only Paulina knew this. She kept her promise not to tell anyone, even years later, when a gay man would murder a Portuguese shoeshine boy and Paulina would see a newspaper photograph of George at the spaceship city hall, carrying a sign demanding the return of the death penalty for sexual deviants. She would wonder then what had happened to George, if he'd been forced to give up his dreams and become Jorge.

George was handsome, if a bit short, present and generous onstage, a reliable source of gossip about the Benny Hills offstage. He taught Paulina the lingo of the theatre:

what it meant to strike the set, what blocking was. Going off book meant you knew your lines, you didn't need to be prompted. Like Oliver and the other old men.

When Oliver complained about her to Little Ricky, it was George who came to tell her. Before he could get into the details, however, June had to be reminded who Oliver was. She sometimes confused him with Edgar. Paulina, too, had trouble correctly identifying the Benny Hills, and often relied on George for help. Archie and Reggie she could remember because they played June's accomplices in the bordello scenes, and because of the *Archie* comics. Reggie also stood out because of the turtle he'd once brought to rehearsal. June had threatened to leave because turtles carried diseases but Reggie insisted it was dead, poking it in the eye with his lit cigarette to prove his point.

"You're not strutting around with a tortoise under one arm like a schoolbook," Sir Jerome had told him.

"I'm a fisherman. It's more realistic."

Sir Jerome snorted.

"In a play that has a woman raised from the dead in her coffin?"

Denise, who played the resurrected woman in question, laughed her stage laugh at Reggie, even Little Ricky was laughing. Sir Jerome finally agreed to put Reggie's turtle in the scene, tucked away in a corner upstage. It stayed there until Reggie tripped over it during rehearsal.

"You know Oliver," George reminded June. "Steals the coffee creamers and sugar packets from the doughnut shop. Our most senior cast member."

"We should chop him in half and count his rings to make sure," said Denise.

Poor George had to share a dressing room with the Benny Hills but consoled himself by doing biting impressions of each. Now George imitated Oliver during their first table read when the old man had removed several coffee creamers from a plastic shopping bag and placed them in neat rows on the table before him. While waiting for his cue, he'd pulled the tab off one and downed the warm cream, throwing back his head as he did so.

"Ah yes," said June. "The gentleman with the creamers."

"He's not a fan of your accent," George told Paulina. "He doesn't think Shakespeare is for spics."

That word again. Where was her brother when she needed him? At that moment, in their apartment, sleeping until it was time for his night shift at the bread factory. He'd started the job around the same time Paulina had started rehearsals, reluctantly shaving off his beard for hygienic reasons imposed on him by his foreman. Without his beard he appeared even more vulnerable. Paulina worried his co-workers might goad him into a fight, but at least he got free bread.

George had arrived bearing the bad news just as Denise had begun braiding Paulina's hair. They were both going to wear their hair in a single braid pinned on top, Denise's idea of a classical hairstyle.

"What did Little Ricky say?" Denise asked George, her fingers combing Paulina's hair. Paulina felt a familiar pulse between her thighs.

"He said the play takes place in the Mediterranean so what does it matter? But that's not all. Oliver thinks she has the plague." George shifted excitedly on the edge of their shared make-up counter.

"What plague?" Paulina asked.

"*The* plague, as in bubonic. He says your hometown was hit by it. Val-something-or-other."

"Valparaíso?"

"Right. He said it's a port city full of rats and that cases of the plague have been reported."

"It's not true!"

Denise began rubbing her shoulders, trying to calm her. The resulting mix of righteous outrage and sensual pleasure was one that, in the future, Paulina would always associate with her brief theatrical career.

"What can I tell you? He says he looked it up at Metro Reference. He wants you quarantined."

Lucky George. None of the Benny Hills had divined his origins. What would they say if they knew that he, too, was a spic?

"Clearly, she doesn't have the plague," June said, taking her whistling kettle off her hot plate.

"Don't shoot the messenger. He doesn't want to be near her."

"So all's well that ends well," said Denise, smiling at Paulina in the mirror, her fingers moving again through her hair. Paulina's skin tingled in response.

"Ricky wanted to send Oliver home, but he wouldn't budge. He has his big scene today, raising Thaisa from the dead."

"Oh, God, I forgot it was today," said Denise, releasing Paulina's hair.

"That old fart doesn't think you have the plague, that's for sure," June said, pouring boiling water into four mugs.

"He can keep his hands to himself," Denise said, taking up Paulina's hair again. "When he has to lift me out of the coffin, you know, he's supposed to put his arms here, under my arms, but he's got suction cups for hands ..."

Paulina shivered with disgust at the thought of Oliver pawing Denise, or anyone else for that matter.

"I would rather have relations with Reggie's turtle," she said.

Everyone laughed, most importantly Denise.

"Reggie's been showing off the thing's undercarriage," said George. "He's so proud of how big it is you'd think it was his. If that's the male's equipment I don't want to see what God gave the female."

"Will I be fired?" Paulina asked. Oliver was the leader of the Benny Hills. Sir Jerome might take his criticism seriously. What was she doing, speaking Shakespeare's language?

Denise looked up from braiding Paulina's hair.

"Because of Oliver?"

"I doubt it," George said. June agreed.

"You've nothing to worry about, my dear. You're not going anywhere. You're wonderful, especially in your last scene."

She was talking about Marina's reunion scene with her parents. Paulina only had a few lines; George and Denise did most of the talking. But she got to deliver the play's closing line, *Thaisa was my mother, who did end / The minute I began,* as Denise laid a motherly hand on her head.

"How do you manage to cry like that? I can never cry during rehearsals."

"It just happens."

She pretended to shrug off Denise's compliment.

Secretly, though, Paulina was worried that if she kept it up, she'd have no tears left for opening night. Sir Jerome had confirmed this worry by taking her aside and suggesting she "rein it in" during rehearsals. He did not want her to spend herself. Another of Sir Jerome's strange expressions. Paulina imagined her tears as large, silver coins tumbling out of her body, like she was a piggy bank being shaken by a greedy child.

"I know what we'll do," Denise said, smiling at Paulina in the mirror. "We'll paint big sores all over your arms and scare those old shits."

Paulina smiled. She could barely keep her eyes open, it felt so good, Denise's hands raking her hair.

"All pranks must be saved for closing night," June said, handing round the mugs of hot, sweet tea.

"Is that what the union says?" George opened the white box he'd brought with him.

"Oh, lovely," June said, helping herself. According to her, the most important backstage equipment was a kettle and a hot plate, the only warm-up an actor needed was a mug of well-sugared Earl Grey, and something sweet, like custard tarts.

Denise accepted the tea but didn't touch her tart. She was saving it for later, she said. Paulina wished she could do the same instead of devouring not one, but two of the golden eggy treats.

～

The scene Paulina most dreaded rehearsing was with her suitor or "john" as Denise called the character played by Harold. Harold, now complaining about the air-conditioning he'd demanded, wore the same sweater every day to rehearsals. It had a big yellow stain on it that Denise said was a badge of honour earned either in the First World War or a hot dog-eating contest.

Sir Jerome had told Harold to be on all fives during this scene, a revolting if unlikely idea, Denise reassured Paulina, considering his age. Worse, he was to chase Paulina around the stage, trying to grope what Sir Jerome called her tender parts. Unfortunately, Harold turned out to be much faster than Paulina had expected. He could also nap with his eyes open, so perhaps he had superpowers. He was certainly a powerful pincher. When June saw Paulina's bruises, she told Little Ricky that if he didn't intervene she would file a complaint with the union. Little Ricky had reminded her that theirs was a non-union production, but he'd get Sir Jerome to talk to Harold.

At their next rehearsal, their last before dress, Harold kept a distance of several feet from Paulina. At first, Paulina stuck to the original blocking, running around the stage despite the fact that Harold was not chasing her. Frustrated, she changed course, chasing Harold while pleading for her virginity. By the end of the scene, she had Harold trapped in a corner upstage left, panting and sweating inside his filthy sweater.

Sir Jerome gave Paulina her first standing ovation. Even Little Ricky grinned into his binder. Harold, however, just frowned.

"We're opening tomorrow, it's too late to upset the apple cart."

"I think you're up to the task, Hal."

Sir Jerome's compliment seemed to further agitate Harold.

"It makes no sense. Why would she chase me while pleading for her chastity? And I'm still saying all that business about wanting to deflower her?"

"It works," said Little Ricky, usually silent during rehearsals. "This play is his weirdest and wildest. It's more modern this way."

"I think it's funny," Paulina said.

Sir Jerome told Little Ricky to note down the new blocking. Paulina's improvisation would stay. Harold could be buried alive in fallen apples for all she cared.

— 4. —

PAULINA WAS BACKSTAGE listening for her cue, gazing at the strips of glow tape on the floor when Oliver appeared beside her bearing a small cactus in a plastic green pot. Like all the men, he wore a white tunic with a rope belt, meant to signal antiquity. On George, the effect was noble, but on the Benny Hills, the rustic elegance of Ricky's Spartan design was lost. The Benny Hills had folds of loose, spotted skin and in Oliver's case, bushy white back hair that sprouted up the nape of his neck. At least the audience would be too far away to see his cracked, yellowed toenails hanging over the soles of his gladiator sandals.

Denise had shared her stage make-up with Paulina, showing her how to apply it. Paulina squeezed her lips together to keep her lipstick from smudging, Denise's trick, as Oliver pressed his cactus on her.

"To remind you of your country. Don't worry, it's not a tradition here, you needn't have got me anything."

"Thank you," Paulina said, placing her basket of artificial flowers on the floor so that she could take the small cactus from his shaking hands. It looked nothing like the cacti that flowered back home but it was an apology, she supposed, for Oliver accusing her of having the plague.

She'd forgotten all about his accusation in the excitement of opening night. A few hours earlier, as the three of them were making up their faces, Sir Jerome had entered the women's dressing room bearing bouquets. He had a few words for each of them, he said, leading them one at a time into the hallway where they could speak privately. Before his arrival, June had been snapping at Denise about the smell of her hairspray. The atmosphere was tense and pungent: sweat, hairspray, and a rubbery cosmetic aroma that made Paulina feel even worse than she already did. But after their meeting with Sir Jerome both women had returned to the dressing room serene and smiling.

At last, it was Paulina's turn. In the hallway, Sir Jerome put his hands on her shoulders. Without a word, he kissed her on the forehead, then let his hands wander down to her buttocks, squeezing first one, then the other, grunting into her ear as he did so, a grunt for each squeeze.

Paulina had returned to the dressing room dazed, to find June and Denise still at peace. Sir Jerome's good luck, break-a-leg, butt squeeze had done the trick. It had worked for her, too, distracting her from her mounting stage fright.

Waiting in the wings for her cue Paulina tried to control her trembling hands; her mouth was so dry she feared she wouldn't be able to speak, let alone plead for Marina's life. The warm-up exercises were not helping her stage fright. Denise had led her in these: running in place, massaging her jaw, blowing raspberries, while

June did her crossword puzzle, a mug of tea and cigarette at hand.

I am resolved, she heard Alfred say. Trembling but
resolved herself, Paulina stepped onto the stage and
began her speech. Not until she uttered the line, *to strew
thy green with flowers*, did she realize she was still holding Oliver's weedy little cactus. *The yellows, blues, / The
purple violets and marigolds* she was speaking of were in
the wings where she'd dumped them.

Paulina ran offstage, avoiding eye contact with a
stunned Little Ricky clutching his binder to his chest.
Picking up her basket, she rushed back onstage to drop
it at Alfred's feet. Then she bent down to retrieve the
flowers, shoving them back in the basket while reciting
her speech about carpeting the grave of her beloved
nurse with blossoms. Hearing herself speak these words,
she threw the flowers back down as if they'd burst into
flame. At least when she said, *The world to me is like a
whirring storm,* no one could dispute it. Instead of with-
drawing his dagger at the last minute, Alfred should
have plunged it into her heart. Dying onstage would at
least spare her from having to go on with the rest of the
play, from sweating miserably under the bright lights.

Coming offstage after her kidnapping by pirates
Paulina heard Sir Jerome telling Little Ricky that the
first night cock-up was out of the way, they could all
relax. She was about to rush off to the dressing room
when Sir Jerome stopped her with a hand on her head.
Such things happened all the time in the theatre, he
said. She was great, she would be great.

"Don't give up the ghost, dear girl," he said as he
embraced her, his hands above her waist this time.

Whatever that meant. At least she'd stopped crying. In the dressing room, June gave her a mug of tea while Denise touched up her make-up.

Things did improve, especially when Harold, playing the potentate bent on deflowering her, lowered his head to kiss Paulina's hand and lost his wig in the process. They both froze, Harold's wig at Paulina's feet, his expression pure helplessness. Paulina waited for him to speak his next line, to carry on with the scene, but he stayed silent, licking his lips like an agitated lizard. Without thinking, she bent down and retrieved his wig. Bowing, Paulina presented it to him like a crown while begging for his mercy and her chastity. The scene earned the biggest laugh of the evening.

"Good girl," Sir Jerome said, waiting for her in the wings. Beside him stood Harold, red-faced. Sir Jerome had his hand on Harold's shoulder, as if stopping him from leaping off a bridge.

Paulina's was not the only "cock-up" of opening night; Alfred often read the newspaper in the dressing room while waiting for his cues. In his last entrance of the night, he appeared onstage bearing his torch, reading glasses perched on his forehead. Only by biting her lower lip and avoiding eye contact with George was Paulina able to stop herself from laughing.

Best of all, she needn't have worried about "spending" herself before the final reunion scene. Paulina was still crying when the curtain came down.

The youngest cast member, she was the last to join in the final bow. The applause that greeted Paulina turned to laughter when Little Ricky appeared on stage to hand her the basket of flowers she'd forgotten at the start. Paulina laughed along with her audience, a full house, she'd heard Little Ricky say.

"Let's get pissed," Alfred said, as the final curtain descended.

In the dressing room, Denise's modesty deflated Paulina's high spirits. During rehearsals she'd looked forward to Denise walking around naked, shimmying in and out of her white tunic, but Denise changed behind the screen June had brought in, "for decency's sake." So did Paulina, grateful for the privacy it provided.

The opening night party took place on the stage, now cleared, or "struck," of the simple set, a series of large black boxes of various sizes, moved around by the cast during the darkness of scene changes like giant chess pieces, arranged to represent an altar, a throne, or a ship's deck.

Ernesto and the Weinribs had come to see her debut, and Valerie. Paulina was so infatuated with Denise that it didn't even bother her, Valerie arriving with a date.

Joseph was an American medical student, Black like Valerie but lighter-skinned, his eyes a deep blue. He bowed slightly when Valerie introduced them, as if meeting a legend of the stage.

"You were great," Valerie said, as they hugged. Paulina's heart was beating steadily, and she wasn't sweating anywhere unusual. Her fever, at least for Valerie, had broken.

Valerie wore a polka-dot dress, which fit her perfectly and made Paulina self-conscious about her own, yellow and full-skirted, bought second-hand in Kensington Market. Putting it on in the dressing room Paulina had noticed that the bodice was too big. June had done her best with safety pins but she felt silly, a little girl in her mother's cast-off.

"We'll be saying we knew you when," Ruth said.

Ernesto, between swigs of beer, admitted he had not understood a word of the play but he was sure Paulina had done well. He'd traded shifts with a colleague so he could attend her opening night.

"A new star is born," Nathan said. "What was that old guy's name? The one who lost his wig?"

He winked at Paulina. No one said anything about the cactus, which Paulina had given to June.

Paulina drank just enough beer to turn the evening into a blur of overlapping vignettes. People, many of them strangers, congratulated her on her performance, praising her skill at comedy but Sir Jerome, whenever he spotted Paulina, kept insisting that her future lay in tragedy.

— 5. —

PERICLES, WHILE NOT one of Shakespeare's best, still contained enough action to guarantee a worthwhile night at the theatre, at least according to one of the country's better drama critics. The performances ranged from competent (the Benny Hills) to outstanding (June, George, Denise, and Paulina). Denise he singled out for her grace and elegance. As for Paulina, there was something sad and ill-at-ease about this young actress, which meshed perfectly with her character, that of a girl adrift in a strange land. Her figure, petite and boyish, suggested a delightful purity, while Denise's figure, statuesque and sensual, lent vitality to her role. There was no mention of June's figure, only her face, which Francis Irwin said was as well-preserved as her talent.

To her relief, Irwin declared that Paulina's slight accent worked in her favour, enhancing her foreignness, appropriate to the role. He concluded his review by declaring Denise and Paulina welcome additions to the Canadian stage, although readers might better remember Miss Acosta as Ernesto Acosta's sister, the Chilean refugee who had suffered that brutal attack on the island ferry.

His review was accompanied by a photo of Denise in her coffin; the caption described her as, *ethereal*. A photographer had come to dress rehearsal and Sir Jerome had directed the cast to freeze during certain scenes. Most of the photos taken had been of Denise, including one of her and Paulina, as mother and daughter.

Paulina wished the paper would have used that photo but at least the critic had praised her and Denise in the same paragraph. It was almost a wedding announcement. Unbidden, Ruth bought Paulina several copies of the paper with the review and Paulina surprised them both by hugging her.

The next night, after another full house, Sir Jerome took Paulina aside, and gave her a small card.

"So many actors won't do television," he said. "But I think it would be a fine opportunity for you."

The producer was a friend of his; he'd been to the play on opening night and asked about Paulina. Her, not Denise. Onstage that night Paulina's tears were of secret joy, not rehearsed sorrow.

~

On closing night Paulina and Denise, using George as their intermediary, slipped Lorraine's pink pill into Oliver's flask. They were all disappointed when it had no effect on him. If anything, his performance improved. Paulina wondered if the drug had lost its potency after all that time inside that jar of Ruth's tea.

"I just wanted to teach him not to put his hands where they're not wanted," Denise said. George said that whatever drug it was, Oliver's heavy drinking had probably cancelled it out.

"Little Ricky says he's got a liver like Fort Knox."

Paulina was certain she would sob uncontrollably during that night's reunion with her parents, but she only managed a few hot tears. It was Denise and George who were sobbing this time, so much so that she, as Marina, had to console them.

In their dressing room, a fully recovered Denise daubed her cream blush on Paulina's arms. She patted Paulina's forehead with a damp cloth so it would look like she was sweating with fever, then led her into the men's dressing room.

"Oliver was right, she's got it! She has the plague!"

That was Paulina's cue to stagger forward, arms outstretched, displaying her sores. But Archie grabbed Paulina's arm and rubbed the sores off with tissue paper and cold cream while the Benny Hills just laughed.

George came in with an open bottle of champagne, followed by June, and everyone cheered.

"Easy on the booze," Oliver said, as George was filling Paulina's glass. "The kid's still under drinking age."

George filled her glass half-way, then raised his and toasted their prank, and Paulina's casting in *Prince of Cabbagetown*.

"You promised not to tell!"

She'd wanted to tell Denise when they were alone, but now she had to tell her, and the Benny Hills, about the card from the producer, the offer to play a small but pivotal part in the final episode of Canada's longest-running sitcom.

"You didn't even have to audition?"

Was Denise jealous?

"It's just one line. I said it over the phone."

"Just like that?"

"Yes."

The producer, a man named Bear Connors, had said he could tell she would photograph well and anyway, he didn't have the budget to test her for just one line. Hearing her say it would be enough. After Paulina had repeated her line a few times, he'd said the part was hers; her contract would be in the mail. Since she didn't belong to the union, she'd be paid below something called scale, but she wouldn't be underpaid, Bear Connors would see to that.

"Scale is what they give you when you belong to the union," June said. "It's like a minimum wage."

"So I will have less than the minimum?"

"It costs money to be in the union," June said. "More than you'll get for one line."

"What is the line?"

Everyone, not just Archie wanted to know, but Paulina had promised Bear Connors not to tell. It was in her contract.

"You're the queen of last lines," George said, and everyone laughed.

～

June drove Paulina, Denise, and George to Sir Jerome's home, a large apartment on the main floor of a large brick house north of the university. They were all drawn to the living room, to the large painting of two black horses in the snow.

"Is that a Colville?" Alfred asked, putting on his reading glasses.

Denise pulled Paulina into a narrow, photo-filled hallway.

"Sir Jerome is doing *Uncle Vanya* next," she said.

"How do you know?"

"He told me. I'm going to be Yelena and you're playing Sonya."

The sadness Paulina had been feeling over the loss of *Pericles* dissolved as she and Denise embraced, opposite a young Sir Jerome in fur cape and crown, gazing down at his sceptre.

Paulina's scalp was still tingling even after Denise released her and they rejoined the party. Denise was going to play her glamorous stepmother. Perhaps this time she would not be so modest about changing backstage. She looked so beautiful in her long, silky purple skirt, matching camisole and wide-brimmed hat, which Paulina recognized from the magazine pictorial, the hat that if worn while driving would cause the deaths of many innocent people.

They were so happy they even answered the call of the Benny Hills gathered at the bar in the far corner of the living room, mixing cocktails they promised would put hair on the girls' chests. Paulina took one sip, then sputtered and turned red. There was laughter and a spotted hand topped up her glass with more ginger ale.

Archie was playing the small piano near the fireplace. Oliver and Harold joined in, singing a song about having a bit of what you fancied because just a bit was best.

Paulina had just asked for a second drink when Sir Jerome appeared in her peripheral vision, followed by Denise. They disappeared down the hallway, probably to discuss *Uncle Vanya*.

"Easy on the soda," she told Oliver and he laughed, his arm around her.

"You're one of us now," he said.

"A Canadian?"

"Better than that. You're theatre people. The best people there are. We've got no flag, but plenty of songs."

He was right. These were her people; she'd found them at last. It was like riding the subway without stopping, this life in the theatre. Living in the moment, Valerie had called it. No, acting was better than that; you got to live someone else's moments, over and over, until they became your own.

Paulina was on her third cocktail, somehow sweeter than the previous ones, when Denise appeared beside her, clutching a tall glass of something brown. Paulina wanted to snatch it out of her hand and down it, prove to her and everyone that she could "handle" her liquor. Ernesto's sour, foamy beer had never made her feel like this.

"Are you alright?" Maybe Sir Jerome had told Denise to take Paulina home, that was why Denise looked so serious.

"I'm fine," Denise said, plucking a lit cigarette from George's mouth as he passed by.

"Come," she said, grabbing Paulina by the elbow. "To the bathroom. I've got something to tell you."

Paulina sat on the edge of Sir Jerome's bathtub while Denise leaned over the sink, her back to her, shoulder blades poking out from beneath her camisole. Had Denise lost weight? June was always after her to eat, she was too thin, what was wrong with young actresses these days?

"George is gay," Denise said as she rummaged through Sir Jerome's medicine cabinet.

"Gay?"

"Homosexual. I thought he might be in love with me. It happens with actors sometimes when they play at being in love on stage."

Denise said the words so easily, *gay, homosexual*, as if they held no power over her.

"What do you think?" Paulina asked, sweat blooming in the crease of one elbow.

"It's disgusting how some people behave. There was a woman on my street, she left her husband for another woman. Can you imagine?"

"No," said Paulina, who imagined something similar at least a dozen times a day.

"People still talk about her. But what else can you expect from the suburbs? They can't stand anyone who's different. It's very common among us artists."

The light in the bathroom, moments earlier too bright, was now not bright enough. Paulina sensed she must be careful, parse every word, gesture, inflection correctly. Instinct told her there was no room for misinterpretation. She pressed her palms against the smooth, cool edge of the tub.

"What is so common?" she asked, after what seemed hours.

"Sex," Denise said, taking a last draw of her cigarette, pitching the butt in Sir Jerome's toilet. "Artists have to experience everything, not just sex. Death, even. Yes, death. Otherwise we may as well be dead."

She laughed, a thin, high laugh. "It takes courage to be like George," she said, taking a bottle of pills from the medicine cabinet. "To be like me."

"Like me," Paulina said, more to herself than to Denise.

"Why be like the Ednas and Tims of this world? Those are my parents. They don't want me to act. Sir Jerome says to drink from every cup."

He did? As if to illustrate his point, Denise turned on the sink faucet, cupping the water in her hands. When she was done drinking, she slammed the medicine cabinet shut, then turned to face Paulina. The ends of her hair were wet, a single glistening strand between her reddened lips.

Raising herself from the bathtub ledge, Paulina walked over to Denise, approaching her like she might a deer. Gently, she removed the strand of hair from between her lips, her face over Denise's frail shoulder reflected back at her in the mirror. Her lips were parted, her skin was flushed, down to her throat. She heard her own voice, soft, low, saw the movement of her lips. *Sample all life offers us ... actors ... artists ... not the Edwards and Toms of this world ...*

Denise said nothing, just stared at her, eyes half-closed, arms dangling by her sides. Paulina took this for acquiescence and, closing her eyes, placed her mouth against Denise's. Denise did not respond but she didn't push Paulina away, either. Was this how women kissed? Mouths open, lips barely touching? Not the hard squashing of mouths like in movies. Not Lorraine's hard, dry kiss. The tip of her tongue was inside Denise's mouth, she could feel Denise's teeth, her tongue. For what seemed like a gloriously long time, she held Denise's hands (cold, was that normal?) her tongue fluttering inside her mouth like a moth beating its wings. The soft pulse between Paulina's thighs became a drumbeat guiding her as her tongue continued its gentle probing of Denise's mouth, who seemed to be responding, pitching forward, grasping Paulina's shoulders with both hands. Just as Paulina dared insert a finger under the strap of her camisole, Denise slumped forward, surprisingly heavy as she fell, nearly bringing Paulina down with her into Sir Jerome's bathtub.

Ricky and George were the first to respond to Paulina's screams, followed by Sir Jerome. The three picked Denise up and put her head under the tap. Denise moaned as the cold water poured over her.

"Her hat," Paulina said, but no one was listening. Denise's hat was in the bathtub, crumpled and wet.

"Put your finger down your throat," Ricky told Denise.

"I killed her," Paulina said as Denise was vomiting in the bathtub. Her mouth felt sore, battered. She rubbed her hand over it, as if trying to wipe it from her face.

"Take her to my bedroom," Sir Jerome said. "And get June."

The open pill bottles were on top of the toilet tank. How could Paulina have missed them? She brought them to the bedroom where Denise lay on Sir Jerome's bed, moaning softly. The room smelled sour.

"What is it?" George asked, as Sir Jerome examined the labels.

"Tylenol and some antibiotics I never finished."

"You're supposed to finish them," Oliver said. Behind him huddled the other Benny Hills.

"Could they hurt her?" George asked.

Ricky joined them, his usually pink face grey. "I called an ambulance," he said.

"I killed her," Paulina kept repeating but no one seemed to hear or care. June held Denise's hand and smoothed her wet hair, murmuring to her that she would be fine, she was brave, she was beautiful.

The ambulance attendants wrapped Denise in a red blanket and carried her off on a stretcher. June, George and Sir Jerome followed behind.

One of the Benny Hills gave Paulina a glass of water.

"I killed her," Paulina said, refusing it. She didn't deserve water, she deserved poison. Why should she live when beautiful Denise might be dead?

"How so?" asked Alfred, as if Paulina had discovered a new technique for going off book.

"The attendants said she'll be fine," Ricky said, in the same voice he used to announce it was five minutes to curtain. "Too much to drink, so she took an aspirin. It upset her stomach is all, but just to be sure, they've taken her to hospital. She was even talking to June."

"They tell you specifically at the pharmacy, you have to finish them," Oliver said, sniffing at the decanter he'd just opened.

Paulina leaned against the piano, tugging at the skirt of her yellow dress with both hands.

"I killed her, I killed Denise!"

"Kid's had too much to drink," Reggie said.

"She's not dead. Not even close," said Ricky, accepting a drink from Oliver.

Paulina moaned, wringing her hands like she did when she was Marina begging for her honour. She saw Denise before her, bundled up and carted away; she smelled the sour smell of her vomit; she felt the weight of Denise's body as she collapsed, no doubt from the shock of Paulina's hands so close to her breasts, for how long had she molested her unconscious body? She had crushed her! She was a monster!

Sobbing but still staying true to Sir Jerome's blocking, Paulina confessed her secret to the old men gathered around her.

A long pause, followed by a deep sigh and then an even deeper fart, which everyone, especially Paulina, pretended not to hear. Then the Benny Hills all began speaking at once, their words darting over her head.

"A kiss wouldn't kill her."

"They'll pump her stomach and she'll be good as new."

"Probably didn't even know what was going on. Too tight."

"Too thin, too. Can't hold her liquor."

"Then it is worse. I took advantage."

"You're not equipped to take advantage," Edgar told her.

A spirited cataloguing of the lesbians of stage and screen commenced.

"Tallulah Bankhead."

"Yes, but Tallulah played for both sides. So did Nazimova. They say she seduced Valentino's wife with a black marble dildo."

"Don't forget Marion Cartwright. I caught her and Joan backstage at the Dominion Drama Festival."

Marion Cartwright. The name sounded familiar but before Paulina could ask who she was, the Benny Hills had moved on.

"Garbo, too."

"Now they all want to be liberated. Everything out in the open."

"How ordinary."

"Was Tallulah ordinary? Was Garbo? Was Marion Cartwright?"

"Who was it who said, 'I don't care what they do, so long as they don't frighten the horses'?"

"Or was it 'involve the horses'?"

"Joan Bliss and Marion Cartwright, backstage at Stratford, not the Dominion. Last run-through for *A Winter's Tale*. Marion had Joan bent over her dressing table. Don't know how she did it, Joan had terrible back problems. She broke her hip last year falling off a ladder."

"Is Joan okay?" Reggie asked Alfred. "You go in for a broken hip, you never come out."

"That was Sir Jerome who saw them at the National," Ricky told Alfred. "You heard the damn story from him."

"Says the only one here who's never handled a boob in his life, Paulina included."

"Piss off, Alfie," Ricky said. "She's crying."

"So she is," Oliver said. "My dear, if at first you don't succeed, try, try again."

"It's not that," Paulina said. A new, terrible thought had presented itself to her.

"Sir Jerome said I will be Sonya but now he will give my part to someone else."

She blushed from the shame of such a confession. It was selfish to think Denise would even want to play her stepmother after Paulina had groped her. It was selfish to want to be close to Denise again, to spend whole days together in the theatre while at that moment Denise was in the hospital, fighting for her life.

Instead of admonishing her, the Benny Hills laughed; even Ricky smiled. She was not to worry, the part was hers. Who else but Paulina could play the sad yet stoic Sonya? She was to look on the bright side: being a young lesbian actress was not a bad thing, not at all. In fact, it was the most wonderful thing in the world, Oliver said, his arm around her. Paulina would have her choice of parts, and of choice parts.

ACT TWO:

THE MINUTE I BEGAN

— 1. —

THE SWEARING-IN ceremony turned out to be a mundane affair, not the stirring drama Paulina had anticipated. Had Sir Jerome directed, he would have changed the blocking so that the presiding judge delivered his short speech centre stage, not behind a desk, while the new citizens bowed as they pledged allegiance to their new country, its laws, and its Queen. There would be music, too, a stirring march, maybe even an appearance by the Queen herself, touching each naturalized head with her sceptre. The large conference room with its fluorescent lights and worn carpet would have pushed the limits of Little Ricky's ingenuity, however, especially the noisy air-conditioning that made it hard to hear the judge.

Paulina was grateful she'd chosen her grey wool dress for the occasion. It was too hot for the humid weather, but Pilar would have wanted her to look presentable, and it was freezing inside the sterile room. All around her the new Canadians, the men in short-sleeved dress shirts, the women in sleeveless dresses, shivered and complained in their own tongues.

Many of the new citizens wept during the ceremony but not Paulina, and definitely not her brother in his best suit, now too small for him. He had to wear the jacket open, and he couldn't get the pants zipped up, so he was wearing a new pair of slacks from the church, in a lighter shade of black that didn't match his jacket. Dry-eyed, he and Paulina pledged their obedience to country and Queen along with everyone else, as Nathan took their picture. Nathan, who had vouched for them so decisively that Paulina's encounters with immigration officials had been brief, mostly by phone; now she was one of the few Chilean Canadians in the country, a milestone so bittersweet all she and Ernesto could do was to shake Nathan's hand.

Back in the basement, Paulina took out the crumpled call sheet from *Pericles* which she kept tucked inside a copy of the newspaper with her review, the one that mentioned her and Denise in the same typed breath. As she'd done every night since the play had closed, she read out the names and phone numbers of the cast, from Acosta, Paulina to Waters, Harold, lingering on Denise. She'd survived the closing-night party; June had called the next day to tell her, and to ask Paulina to keep in touch. What did that mean, "keep in touch"? Did June expect her to call regularly, report on her activities? A strange, impersonal thing to say, *keep in touch*, when they'd all be seeing each other again for *Uncle Vanya*. June, Paulina decided, was just being nice. It was very Canadian of her. As a new Canadian, Paulina would have to learn to do the same.

Denise, however, did not seem to want to keep in touch and Paulina was too ashamed to call her. No matter how much she willed it, no matter how long she gazed at the red dot in the white box in that yellowing copy of *La Tercera*, Denise did not call or knock on her door.

~

"Ernesto told us. I can't get over it," Nathan said.

Her brother had just left to start his night shift at the bakery when Nathan and Ruth had come downstairs to congratulate her, knocking on the door that separated the basement apartment from their laundry room. Paulina was surprised that Ernesto had bothered telling them at all. He hadn't even congratulated her himself, just asked if this time she'd be properly paid.

"The last line in the last episode of *Prince of Cabbagetown*. From your mouth." Nathan stared at her mouth, as if expecting it to speak the line.

"We love the show," Ruth said. "And we love Tommy Lerner."

"The whole country loves him," Nathan said. "Would you do me a favour? When you see Lerner ask him to sign this."

Inside the envelope was a black-and-white photograph of two grinning boys in shorts and undershirts, arms around each other.

"That's Nathan's father," Ruth said. "On the left."

"The little guy next to him is Lerner. My dad discovered him. They went to high school together."

"Harbord Collegiate," Ruth said. "When do you see Mr. Lerner?"

"In two days," Paulina said.

Nathan nodded.

"Lerner should remember him. He discovered him."

"Tell her," Ruth said.

Paulina, realizing they were waiting to be invited inside, invited them in. She turned off the TV and turned on the overhead light, so they wouldn't know she'd been sitting in the growing darkness in shorts and a T-shirt, staring at "the idiot box."

Ruth insisted on serving the pound cake. She knew her way around, she told Paulina, refusing her offer of help. If it wasn't so hot she would have baked it herself, but the bakery on Harbord turned out decent cakes.

"You two sit down. Nathan will tell you how, if it wasn't for his father, Tommy Lerner would never have become famous."

"Your father is an actor?" Paulina asked Nathan.

"No. He wanted to be. He was in all the school plays. They were doing Shakespeare. *The Tempest*. My dad was Caliban and they needed someone for Ariel, the fairy part, and my dad said, what about Tòmas? For comic relief, I guess. He wasn't Tommy then, just this little pipsqueak from Lithuania. He barely spoke English; they called him the Litvak. My dad thought he'd be good, because of the funny accent he had back then. Didn't take him long to get rid of it."

Paulina felt a sudden kinship with Tòmas Lerner, the little Litvak.

"They said Tommy Lerner stole that show," Ruth said.

"I bet," Nathan said. "So did my dad. Thanks to him someone saw little Tommy and put him in that year's Christmas pageant at the Royal Alexandra."

"What happened to your father's acting career?"

"The Depression happened, that's what. Have you been watching the show? It's all reruns now."

"Yes," Paulina said. "It's funny. Tommy Lerner is funny."

"He's always been funny," Nathan said. "Right from the beginning. I'll tell you his life story, if you want. So you'll be prepared."

While Paulina picked at her cake, Nathan told her everything he said he knew about Tommy Lerner's career, beginning in the early 1950s, when he'd been famous for his nightclub act, particularly a bit he called *The Gassy Knight*. Wearing a full set of armour Tommy Lerner complained about going overboard on the roasted boar. Each time one of his maidens (volunteers from the audience, handpicked for their beauty) approached him to help remove a piece of his armour, Lerner would, as Nathan put it because ladies were present, "let one fly." No special effects were required; Tommy Lerner could produce these sounds at will. He performed this act in Montreal's burlesque houses, in upstate New York and once, just once, in New York City on live television. It had been a good time for Tommy Lerner; there was even talk of Hollywood. Unfortunately, on the night of the broadcast Tommy Lerner had been unable to produce his special sound effects. He complained about the boar, grimaced, clutched his armoured belly, but it wasn't the same. No laughs. Yet this failure, broadcast live across North America, endeared him to his countrymen, who were secretly delighted when one of their own failed stateside, Nathan said. Lerner soon became a staple of Canadian television, culminating in his casting as the *Prince of Cabbagetown*.

According to a recent profile in *Saturday Night*, Tommy Lerner could not enter a room without counting the number of people inside; he read his horoscope daily and had an astrologer draw up a chart for him on Rosh Hashanah, the Jewish New Year, Nathan explained. Decades of performing live, of never being sure what might make an audience laugh had made him superstitious. The producers of *Prince of Cabbagetown* were by

now accustomed to what they called his "quirks." Like
the olives and pickles he had to have in his dressing
room. These had to be an even number and in separate
dishes, never touching.

Paulina looked down at her plate. She was doing
something similar with the pound cake, eating the
golden-brown crust first, which she had to finish before
she could eat the yellow cake beneath. If any brown
crumbs got on the yellow cake, she had to pick them all
off with her fork before she could resume eating.

"First Sir Jerome Mason, now Tommy Lerner. You're
working with the greats, Paulina."

"Tommy Lerner is more famous," Ruth said, at last
serving herself. She ate her slice while leaning against
the sink.

Nathan said it was true, everyone knew and loved
Tommy Lerner. He entered their living rooms each week
at the same time, he was like family. Was it a coincidence, he asked Ruth, now that Paulina was a Canadian
citizen she'd been chosen to deliver the final line on
Canada's most beloved television comedy?

"We're going to watch it anyways," he said, leaning
toward Paulina. "So there's no harm telling us."

"I promised not to."

"Leave her alone, Nathan," Ruth said from the sink,
rinsing her plate.

Nathan shrugged.

"When you give the picture to Lerner, tell him it's
from Gordie's boy. His eldest."

"Break a leg," said Ruth, as they were leaving. She'd
washed and dried the plates and forks, refusing Paulina's
repeated offers to help.

— 2. —

TOMMY LERNER WAS seated at his make-up table smoking a cigar when the production assistant led Paulina inside. Paulina's first impression of him was not of his famous face, beloved for its comic plasticity, but of the belt of his terry cloth robe dangling obscenely between his hairy legs.

"They tell me you're Chicano," he said, after they'd been introduced. "I guess that's progress. I'm all for progress. Nathan Phillips, you know who he is?"

"Yes. He built the city hall."

"That's right. Toronto's first Jewish mayor. Tore down The Ward to build that ugly thing. You probably don't know about the old neighbourhood. Why would you? A lot of cramped streets where Blacks cut hair and the Jewish vaudevillians, the great ones, I'm talking Molly Picon, they came for the cheap Chinese restaurants. Tore it all down for that dump."

"It's very ugly," Paulina said. Tommy Lerner grunted.

"A real eyesore," he said, picking up his cigar.

Paulina was so pleased by this exchange that she almost forgot Nathan's photograph, the envelope under her arm.

"Where'd you get this?" Tommy Lerner asked after she'd given him the photo, the folds of his white robe parting dangerously as he shifted in his make-up chair, cigar between his teeth.

"Nathan Weinrib gave it to me, to give to you. He is Gordie's eldest son."

"Gordie Weinrib? He's still alive? How do you know him?"

"Nathan Weinrib is my brother's lawyer. We live in his house."

"You're kidding. And Gordie's still kicking?"

Paulina nodded. She assumed kicking meant alive.

Tommy Lerner fiddled with the belt of his robe and sighed. He put out his cigar and stared at the photograph.

"Poor Weinrib. Had to drop out of school and go to work, all his money going to his mother. I dropped out, too, but I ran away to New York. I left my widowed mother to starve."

"She starved?"

Tommy Lerner's eyes grew wet. The production assistant, a young, bearded man whose name Paulina had already forgotten, passed him a box of tissues.

"She survived, long enough to complain about the food in her nursing home. I heard old Gordie did all right, something in textiles. He begged me to take him to New York. Weinrib was good, you know, really good. He could sing and dance, he had great timing. I didn't want the competition. I told Weinrib, meet me in front of the Royal York. I was on the train to New York while poor Gordie was waiting for me. I knew he'd never go to New York on his own, he didn't have the kishkes."

Tommy Lerner looked up from the photograph, fixing his bloodshot eyes on Paulina for several uncomfortable seconds. "It's kismet, kid, you giving me this picture. I'm choosing my next move. I've got offers now that the show's ending. Big offers. And here you are, like an angel sent to guide me."

Paulina was wondering if kishkes and kismet were connected when, to the production assistant's astonishment, at least judging by his widening eyes, Tommy Lerner described his big offers to Paulina. The first was the role of a priest in a horror film, directed by a young Canadian and starring a former blue movie actress named Patty Cake.

"Blue movies are dirty movies," he explained. "Don't expect a sweet girl like you to know that."

Paulina blushed, which made Tommy Lerner chuckle as he described his second offer, to play a cop nearing retirement, a small part but a good director and an American production. There were other offers, he added, but these were beneath him and not worth mentioning. It was down to these two biggies but he couldn't make up his mind. Paulina would decide for him.

Why would he want her opinion? Not that it mattered, she would have to give it or risk offending him. Unless it was a trick question, and he was considering her for a role in one of those films, and he wanted her to guess which one?

Tommy Lerner told her to just go with her gut, whatever that meant. Paulina closed her eyes, playing the angel the legendary comic clearly wanted her to be. She counted to thirty, then opened her eyes and, exaggerating her accent for dramatic effect, told Tommy Lerner to take the horror film. It really did seem the best offer: they showed horror movies all the time at the theatre on Yonge Street, and the place was always packed. Thanks to Lorraine, she'd developed a fondness for the grotesque. It was fun to be frightened, and probably more fun to spurt fake blood and run after teenagers with an axe.

Paulina waited while Tommy Lerner considered her answer, her limbs heavy with the familiar need to please. At last, the star grunted as he lifted himself from his chair to hug her. He smelled of garlic and tobacco, but at least he did not reach for her buttocks like Sir Jerome.

"You're a doll," he said. They were so close she could count his nose hairs. Still, she liked him, so much that she would not tell Nathan about his hairpiece, which rested on the make-up table near the paper plates of olives and pickles.

"I'm glad it's you," Tommy Lerner said. "Giving the last line. A doll like you."

"Thank you, Mr. Lerner." She was blushing again, more deeply than when he'd told her about blue movies.

"Mr. Lerner's my father. Call me Tommy."

She didn't get the chance to call him either; the production assistant said it was time for her to go, Mr. Lerner was needed on set. Paulina was brought to another room, not as nice as Tommy Lerner's, and told to sit tight until her call.

The room also had a make-up counter, and an armchair with the stuffing sticking out of the seat. Paulina curled up in it, fighting to keep her eyes open, certainly the opposite of sitting tight, but she'd had to get up before dawn that day, and after a sleepless night. A car had been sent to her house to bring her to the set. It was exciting being ferried around like a movie star, even if it was an ordinary car, not a limousine, and she'd kept falling asleep in the backseat.

Ruth had told her that there really was a Cabbagetown, it was called that because of the Irish immigrants who'd settled in the city's east end and grown cabbages on their front lawns. But when she'd asked the driver, a tired-looking girl named Francine, she'd just laughed and said that the show was filmed in a studio outside the city, not in Cabbagetown. They filmed lots of shows there, she said.

The sun was just coming up when Francine brought her inside the L-shaped building with the aluminum siding. There were no other buildings on the street, just cars and vans.

The studio was where they filmed the interiors, Francine explained, looking for the assistant who would take Paulina off her hands. Paulina would deliver her line on this set, filmed in close up as she called to Tommy Lerner off-screen. They'd already filmed his part outside a real store in a real suburb, not Cabbagetown, but some place they could make up to look like it. Even the producer she'd spoken to over the phone wasn't there. Bear Connors was out with the first crew, filming scenes in the real-but-fake Cabbagetown. It was a pain to film outside a studio, Francine said. You had to close down streets and get permits, and the weather could be unpredictable.

Paulina felt stupid for believing that movies and TV shows were filmed in chronological order, for not knowing there were two crews filming different scenes simultaneously, in different locations and out of sequence.

Curled up in the armchair that smelled of sweat and cigarettes, Paulina tried to imagine what the last scene, her scene, might look like. In the opening credits, Tommy Lerner strolled the neighbourhood of which he was prince, waving to friends, helping an old woman across the street, nearly colliding with a kid on a bike, laughing and smiling all the while. Toward the end, he stopped at a grocery store. The grocer, unpacking boxes, tossed him an apple. A boy in a baseball cap caught it, biting into it as Tommy Lerner scowled at him. The grocer, laughing, now heaved an enormous head of cabbage at the star, throwing him comically off-balance, but Tommy Lerner righted himself, holding the vegetable above his head like a wrestling belt while a male voice crooned, *he's a prince alright, Prince of Cabbagetown.*

The very last scene of the series would repeat these opening credits. However, this time Tommy Lerner would attempt to bite into the cabbage, Paulina's cue to deliver her line, the last ever of the series:

"Hey mister, you gotta pay for that cabbage!"

Hearing this, Tommy Lerner would grin and throw her a quarter. That would be the last scene of Canada's longest-running sitcom, Tommy Lerner tossing a quarter to an off-camera Paulina.

Paulina had just dozed off when a woman barged into the room, lugging a large plastic box. She was there to do Paulina's make-up, not that she needed much. The woman sponged foundation on her face, curled her eyelashes, brushed her eyebrows with a toothbrush, and dabbed pink-beige gloss on her lips.

She was complimenting Paulina's complexion when another woman came in, bearing Paulina's costume. The two women debated the addition of a Montreal Expos baseball cap, finally agreeing that Paulina would look cuter with her hair in a ponytail and anyway, she was already wearing an Expos T-shirt under her denim overalls. It would be overkill, the costume lady said.

At last, the assistant came in, to bring her to the soundstage. High above her head, men adjusted spotlights while young women sprinted by her, clutching binders, leaping over cables without glancing down.

Paulina delivered her one line to the production assistant, standing in for Tommy Lerner.

"Give us some energy, okay? Punch up mister, and cabbage."

Paulina did her best for Frank, who'd introduced himself to her as the second director. He wore a leather jacket similar to those worn by her country's air force pilots.

Less than an hour later, Frank said he had what he wanted. She could go home. The assistant brought her back to the room to change into her clothes. Her cheque would be mailed to her next week, he told her. At least it would be more than her honorarium for *Pericles*. Maybe the less fun you had acting, the more you got paid.

When her taxi, paid for by the production, pulled up to her house Paulina saw that the lights were on "chez Weinrib," as George would say.

Nathan opened his door before she could knock. Too tired for "small talk," Paulina gave him the photograph.

"What does it say?" Ruth asked, looking over her husband's shoulder.

"It says he's an asshole, that's what it says."

"Didn't you ask him to sign it?"

"Yes," Paulina told Ruth. "He said he remembers him. He feels bad for going to New York without him."

Nathan looked doubtful.

"Asshole actors," he said as Ruth, smiling gently at Paulina, closed their door.

Paulina stood on their porch for a few moments, breathing in fresh air for the first time in over twelve hours.

— 3. —

SINCE HIS UNIVERSITY days Ernesto had yearned to join what he called the labouring classes, to savour solidarity with his fellow workers as they battled the "managerial class." But the bread factory workers were unionized, and the steward had warned Ernesto not to stir up trouble, they had no beef with management. Ernesto kept to himself, observing the workers as part of his informal study of Canadian society, waiting for a sign that they were ready to rise up against management, but it was slow in coming. Soon he was punching in and out unenthusiastically, completing his tasks so mechanically he sometimes forgot that those were his hands at work. The other employees found him standoffish, not lively like they expected Latin types to be. He didn't make any enemies at work, but he didn't make any friends, either.

Six nights of the week Ernesto mixed vats of emulsifiers and stabilizers. So accustomed was he to staying awake until dawn that he began hosting all-night parties on his night off. Around nine, the first of the exiles would arrive bearing beer and wine. By midnight, the basement would be full of Chileans smoking, eating, singing, and drinking. These parties came to be known as Ernesto's weekly peña, a morose version of those coffee houses back home where students and activists gathered to hear folk musicians, to eat and drink on the cheap. Ernesto even bought a fan, his first purchase of a household good, for much-needed air circulation in the cramped basement. A standing fan, more powerful than the one Nathan had provided, but not powerful enough to battle the smoky, humid air.

In Canada as in Chile, the women did the cooking and cleaning up. Wives and girlfriends brought their homemade empanadas and casseroles to the basement, heating them up and serving them to the men. Ernesto's latest girlfriend often stayed overnight, cleaning the apartment the next morning while Ernesto slept. Paulina never offered to help, slipping out of the apartment instead to spend her Saturday at a nearby record store where she could listen to new LPs through headphones.

The only draw was the food, and the small portion of wine she was permitted. At about ten each Friday night, Ernesto's current girlfriend would give Paulina a plate of food and a glass of generic cola mixed with red wine. A few of the women would ask her about school, which she hadn't attended in months. Valerie had called her at the Weinribs' after *Pericles* had closed, to ask if she would be back at school in the fall. Valerie would not be returning to ASPIRE, she was moving to New Jersey with Joseph. Paulina said she wasn't sure about school, and Valerie said that was fine, a year off might do her good.

Paulina soon invented a game for herself: how many monosyllabic answers could she give? Even with the challenges imposed on her by the Spanish language she managed well, at least well enough to send the women back to their men. She also mastered falling asleep to the sounds of laughter, music, and high-pitched arguments about the failure of Marxism in Chile, although the second-hand marijuana smoke may have played a part.

Mostly Paulina wanted to sleep, to hasten the coming of the next day when Little Ricky would finally call or drop by with her script for *Uncle Vanya*. Ernesto's people were not her people, they were depressing to be around. September 11 was just a few weeks away and they all dreaded marking the first anniversary of the coup in a foreign country. When not debating how best to observe this grim anniversary, Ernesto and his friends mostly speculated about a woman named Carmen Blanchet, one of the latest arrivals from Santiago. Had anyone seen her? Did anyone know where she was staying? Was it true she was in Toronto? They spoke of her as if she were famous, but her name meant nothing to Paulina.

Yet when Carmen Blanchet finally did appear in their basement one rainy night, Ernesto introduced her to his guests not as the famous Carmen, but as the sister of Mario Blanchet.

In the awed silence that followed, he told Paulina it was time for bed.

"But it's early." She hadn't even finished her glass of cola and wine. More importantly, she'd never seen a Chilean woman with such obvious disregard for femininity. Carmen Blanchet wore no make-up, no jewellery, her wet hair was short. She had on a man's blue-striped dress shirt and cut-offs. She was small-breasted but her legs were long, all the men were staring at them, the women, too.

"Don't argue with me."

"Let her stay," Patricio told Ernesto. "Let her find out what's going on."

To ensure her brother would not eject her from the room, Paulina, sitting cross-legged on the floor, began rolling perfect joints for her brother and his guests, a skill she'd honed while Ernesto was recovering from Douglas Watson's beating. Then, to her delight, the famous Carmen Blanchet sat down beside her, and offered to help.

"What is going on?" Paulina asked, passing Carmen the rolling papers.

"They mean my brother Mario," Carmen said, her voice soft and steady. "He was on the boat."

"What boat?" Was Mario a fisherman? Unlikely. Paulina could tell by her accent and complexion that like her, and the other exiles, Carmen belonged to her country's upper class.

"She means the prison ship anchored in the bay of Valparaíso," said Patricio, speaking slowly, like Paulina was an idiot.

"What prison ship?"

"It was after you and your brother left. And you wouldn't have noticed it, anyway."

Paulina would be sure to roll Patricio's joint loosely so that it unravelled as he smoked it.

She gave Carmen a tightly rolled one for her to smoke, noticing as she did so the dark spot on the white part of her left eye. Such spots were supposed to be the sign of evil, but Sister Teresa had said that was nonsense.

It felt like Carmen was speaking to her and her alone, telling Paulina about Mario, how as a union leader he'd been one of the first to be arrested, brought to the floating prison as soon as it was set up. Carmen spoke in a rush, as if in a hurry to get the words out of herself, her body:

"They did terrible things to people on that boat, just terrible, but Mario's suffering was unique. He had the bad luck to recognize one of his torturers, a man he'd once loved in secret. The guy was afraid my brother would expose him to the others. So to prove what a man he was he brutalized Mario, nearly killing him. Then at night he crawled into Mario's bed and begged his forgiveness. My brother had to stroke his hair, tell him that he forgave him, and the next day it would start all over again. One day the men brought a broomstick to his cell and hurt my brother so badly that even the doctor—they have a doctor there to make sure they torture just to the point of death and not beyond—even this doctor said it was too much, take him to the hospital. As soon as he was better, they sent him back to the boat. They used electrodes next, they nearly killed him, but this time instead of the hospital, they put him on a dinghy and let the sea take him. A prostitute working the dock found him and brought him to me. I'd been trying to find him for months, the police kept telling me they had no record of him, he didn't exist. Three days later he died in my arms."

Paulina's head ached as if it might split open. When Carmen was done, she burst into tears, for Mario, for Carmen. For herself.

What had happened to Mario could have happened to her.

Finally, Patricio broke the silence.

"At least now she knows."

"Shut up," said Ernesto.

Carmen was the last to leave the party that night, which ended early. She was leaving Toronto, she said as she embraced Paulina, she was going to Montreal, to join the exiles there. She raised her fist as she was leaving and Paulina, for the first time, raised hers.

— 4. —

YES, ANTON DESCRIBES Sonya as plain but the entire production will be transformed, as I am sure you will agree, by one part cast against type. Now when the good doctor rejects this blonde goddess the audience will want to know why. Can any man be so devoted to preserving Russia's forests? The whole rivalry with her stepmother Yelena will be transformed, too. And her powerful speech that closes the play, when she accepts her fate, her dull little life of work in the country, will be electric because the audience will truly feel her sacrifice, like a princess locking herself away in a tower.

Surely, Paulina could see that Denise was right, she should play Sonya? Sir Jerome would keep Paulina in mind for future productions, of course. She was a great actress, the best Marina he'd ever seen. Paulina was not to give up the ghost, he had plans for her, too.

That night Paulina tore the glossy photographs of Denise driving recklessly into long strips, the strips into confetti, flushing them down the toilet in handfuls, followed by her torn-up call sheet and Sir Jerome's letter, but not the review of her performance. That she was keeping, and not just because the toilet was getting sluggish. Maybe she'd do what Ruth had suggested and get it framed. After cutting out that photo of Denise.

Just when she most needed the escape that the theatre provided, it had been snatched away from her. But in his letter Sir Jerome had said he would keep her in mind for other roles. Unless Denise took those for herself, too.

It was late when Paulina, overheated, crawled into bed, her sheets and blanket crumpled on the floor. She closed her eyes and tried to sleep but something was buzzing in her ear.

Sitting up, she turned on her bedside lamp. It didn't take long for the mosquito to alight on her arm. Before it could feast she slapped it, a hard, stinging slap, snuffing out the parasite, hurting herself in the process.

～

"It's not my idea. Nathan wants us out. A trial separation, he calls it. He's going to live down here while Ruth stays upstairs."

Why wouldn't her brother just let her sleep? Since receiving Sir Jerome's letter all she wanted was sleep: a deep, dreamless sleep. But there were always dreams, they kept waking her up.

"Are you listening? We'll have to find an apartment. If you're not going back to school you have to work. There's electricity to pay, heat in the winter and the phone, we'll have to get our own, and furniture, a television, other things."

Alarmed, Paulina sat up. Huddling in the Weinribs' basement was one thing. But renting an apartment? Buying furniture? Enduring another winter? She'd already refused to go back to school. Ernesto had agreed she could take the high school equivalency exam when she was ready. But their own apartment?

"Patricio has a friend who works in a hotel. They need someone at reception. You speak good English, you'd be good at that. There's a union, I think, for hotel workers. You can join that."

"I'm an actress."

"And I'm your brother, and your guardian. Unless you plan to live by yourself?"

"Why not? I will be eighteen soon."

"It's not safe."

"I don't need your protection."

Ernesto pulled her out of bed by her legs, Paulina screaming at him to stop, he was hurting her. With an unpleasant thud she landed butt-first on the carpeted floor.

"Leave me alone, I don't need you."

"You don't need me. After I saved you from Guzmán." Ernesto was panting, his face pink and sweaty.

"What are you talking about?"

Ernesto turned on the bright, overhead light before pushing his way through the beaded curtain. When he returned, he was still sealing his joint with the tip of his tongue.

He lit up, inhaled deeply, then slumped down on the floor next to Paulina.

"It stinks," she said, waving a hand before her face, although she'd long grown accustomed to the smell.

"So do you. When was the last time you bathed?"

Paulina wasn't sure. She ran her fingers through her hair, then sniffed them. Her unwashed scalp smelled musky, like her mother's fur coat.

"After our little talk, you're going to shower." Ash from her brother's inexpertly rolled joint fell on the carpet as softly as snow. "All this because of a play."

"You said something about my godfather."

Ernesto leaned against the wall. There was a tear in his jeans above the knee, as if someone had slashed him with a machete. He'd been transferred to the day shift, so there were no more parties, but he still looked exhausted, hungover. For the first time Paulina noticed the two very fine lines on either side of his mouth, like those of a ventriloquist's dummy. As he spoke, he looked and sounded like a dummy, too, as if someone were moving his mouth and hands, speaking through him. Guzmán, he was saying. Guzmán had been at the stadium. That's where they'd brought him, after they'd picked him up at the cemetery.

"He saw me in a line-up. Guzmán made a big stink and they let me go. He drove me back home, insisted we have a little talk with Papa. It was all a mistake, my arrest, but he'd take care of everything. I would be safe, we all would. On one condition."

"What was the condition?"

Ernesto rubbed his forehead, above the eye that Douglas Watson had punched.

"That you marry Pío."

The pain of betrayal chose her lower belly, sinking its teeth there, not letting go. Pío Guzmán. He'd come calling a few times before the coup. Her father had ordered her to entertain him so she'd made him tea and listened to him talk about how better things would be when Allende was gone. His father was going to have an important role in the government, and Pío, too. On and on he droned, never asking any questions about her, what she thought about the chaos gripping their country, about Pilar having to line up for cooking oil and matches. It was like he was talking to himself.

Ernesto coughed, a deep cough originating in his chest. Only the best, strongest grass made you cough like that, she'd overheard him telling Patricio at the last peña.

When he spoke again, his voice was raspy.

"That fucking creep. Papa agreed, even after I told him about Pío's little visit to Santiago, right before the eleventh. He invited me out with his army buddies to some whorehouse. I was downstairs, talking to one of the girls, trying to find out more about her working conditions. We heard a scream, we ran upstairs. There was blood everywhere. The poor girl, he almost bit her finger off. He wouldn't let anyone call the doctor; he said he would come back and burn the place down if they did. Papa said it was my fault, bringing Pío to a place like that. I'd probably given him drugs, that was why he got violent."

Why don't you go and sit with Pío? Offer him some tea. You're cold, that's your problem. Why can't you smile?

"None of the good families would let Pío near their daughters. Guzmán needed Papa's help, he had big plans for the boy, but you can't go far in politics without a wife. We were fighting about it right until he died."

"I'm going to be sick."

"Put your head between your knees."

Paulina squatted on the floor, head between her legs. Ernesto stroked her hair.

"He wasn't a nice man," she said, looking down at the carpet.

"Papa?"

"He didn't love me."

The ground didn't open up, a bolt of lightening didn't strike her dead. She'd said what she'd known all her life, and nothing happened.

"Not everyone can afford to be nice," Ernesto said, helping her to sit up. "He had a hard life. He thought he was doing what was best for you. That you would be protected."

"So we can't go back, ever."

"No. Not for a long time. I humiliated Guzmán, and his son. Probably they don't blame you. They think I kidnapped you."

"And you were really in the stadium?"

"Barely. One night. I'm a fraud. Guzmán should have left me there."

"Why was he there?"

"Why do you think?"

"He is a torturer?"

"Of course not. He would never get his hands dirty. But someone has to be in charge."

"And Pío? He was the one on the boat, wasn't he? He killed Carmen's brother."

"I don't know. I hope not. If you ask him and his cronies, they'll say it's a war. A civil war, started by Marxist agitators. They'll say they're not murderers or torturers, they're protecting our freedom."

"But that's crazy! How does murdering Carmen's brother make us free?"

"It doesn't, it's not meant to. The military dictatorship is an illegitimate regime. You must never forget that, Paulina. They rule through fear."

A numbness crept over her. Before it took over, she had to know.

"It wasn't flowers, was it?"

Ernesto took a deep drag on his joint.

"It was a good story, you have to admit."

"Is he still our godfather?"

"No. We don't need him. What about this Tommy Lerner? Could he be your godfather? Would that make you a princess? Princess of cabbages?"

"Don't make fun of me."

"There's something else," Ernesto said. "The house. Guzmán moved into it. With Pío."

"But it's ours!"

"The lawyer sent me a letter, Guzmán took it over, after burying Papa."

All her letters to Pilar. Guzmán had probably got to them before Pilar could. He knew her address. He knew where to find her, her and her brother.

But Ernesto said not to worry. If Guzmán hadn't come by now, he wasn't coming.

"He'd rather take care of me on his own terms."

"You mean the stadium."

"He probably saw my photo in *La Tercera*. He must think that the people here will take care of me for him."

This time, Ernesto didn't object when she reached for what was left of his joint, even patting her on the back until her coughing fit subsided.

Paulina took another drag, then gave it back to him. She didn't feel any different. Just tired and angry and sad.

SEPTEMBER ARRIVED, BRINGING with it joyless anniversaries. The first anniversary of the coup on the eleventh, followed by the eighteenth and nineteenth of September, those two days of patriotic celebrations collectively known as the *dieciocho* and, unlike the eleventh, ignored by the exiles, who marked the day with a protest in front of the Chilean Embassy. Paulina wasn't at the protest, neither was Ernesto. He had to work.

Then September 28, the first anniversary of their arrival in Canada, a day the Weinribs had the good sense to ignore, just like Paulina and Ernesto. Not so her birthday the following month. The Weinribs insisted Paulina and her brother come upstairs for ginger ale and cheesecake, Paulina's new favourite, but their festivities were constantly interrupted by the doorbell ringing, Ruth rushing to the door to hand out candies, ask children about their costumes, chat up parents. Paulina got through the evening on Ernesto's promise to get her high, properly this time, but the grass just made her sleepy. Probably she'd built up a resistance to the drug, breathing in so much of it second-hand. Even more disappointing, Nathan still hadn't said anything about his promise to help her open a bank account when she turned eighteen.

Ernesto chose the next day, the Day of the Dead, to quit his job at the bread factory. A week later, he boarded a bus to Montreal, to stay with Carmen while he looked for an apartment. Paulina could call him there if she needed anything.

Ernesto had chosen Montreal because Carmen had told him it was cheaper, the people, if not the winters, warmer. They would be happy there, he said. Paulina was just glad that Carmen didn't have any friends working in hotels who could get her a job. Maybe in Montreal she could do something fun, like work in a clothing store or a record shop.

Just as Ernesto's bus was pulling into Kingston so that the passengers could relieve their bladders and stretch their legs, Nathan came downstairs to tell Paulina that his father was in a Florida hospital. Would she be okay on her own for a few days, a week at most? Paulina assured him she'd be fine. After all, she was an adult now. Eighteen years old! She couldn't wait for the Weinribs to leave, to be able to go to the bathroom without worrying about running into Ruth on her way to do laundry. But when night came without the familiar sounds of Weinrib family life, however fracturing, from upstairs, she felt more alone than ever, her stomach in knots.

Paulina climbed the carpeted stairs leading from the Weinrib laundry room to the Weinrib living room, as quietly as she could even though they were gone. She climbed the second staircase to Ruth and Nathan's bedroom, holding onto the banister like Alma Siqueiros in *The Face in the Window*, her sole horror film. There might be a murderer hiding in the Weinribs' bedroom, waiting for the hapless tenant in the basement to show her sorry face. But the bedroom was as silent as the rest of the house. Did Ruth and Nathan still sleep together? Was it against the law if you were going to separate?

Paulina identified what must have been Ruth's side of the bed by the stack of women's magazines on the night table. She tried to read the articles but didn't get past their titles: *Divorce: What Happens to the Children? Are Liberated Women Happier? The Once-a-Year Birth Control Pill: Your Questions, Answered*. Paulina looked at the pictures, trying to distract herself from her stomach-ache. She was too afraid to take her temperature and learn that she was sick, so she dipped a towel in cold water and put it to her forehead, closing her eyes but the sick, hot feeling wouldn't go away. She needed something stronger.

There were pills in Ruth's drawer, different kinds but all to be taken only when needed and never with alcohol. There were no pills in Nathan's bedside drawer, just boxes of suppositories. Pilar, too, trusted suppositories over oral medication, but she could never convince Paulina to try her preferred delivery method.

Pilar. She might never see Pilar again. For all Paulina knew she was dead. Or maybe General Guzmán had thrown her out of the house and she'd gone back home to her son, to her people. Maybe she was so happy to be back with her own family, she'd forgotten all about Paulina.

Paulina washed down one of Ruth's blue pills with some water, not sure what they were for, only that they were to be taken at night when needed. She made herself as comfortable as she could on Ruth's side of the bed. It was the first time she'd ever been sick alone; Pilar had always been there to care for her. Yet despite the prickly heat under her skin, Paulina slept deeply, untroubled for once by her dreams.

The next morning she felt better if weak. Probably she just needed to eat. In the kitchen she nibbled on scraps of food like a squirrel, then she climbed back upstairs to the bathroom, to soak in her first proper bath since she'd left Chile. She did not touch the soap or shampoo, however. That would be stealing, and besides, she didn't need it, not if the water was as hot as she could stand it. After her bath, she watched TV, helped herself to more scraps of food, then dozed a bit until she felt ready for bed and another one of Ruth's blue pills, the magic key to a dreamless night.

This was her routine for the next few days, until one morning after eating peanut butter from the jar (this was necessity, she told herself, not theft), she treated herself to a tour of Nathan Weinrib's study, starting with his closet.

On the top shelf, under a stack of files, she found the magazines, as easily as if they'd been calling to her. On their covers half-naked women pouted at her while the headlines promised to show her exactly what women deprived of men did when they thought they were alone.

That night Paulina slept without the help of Ruth's pills, deeply and peacefully. The next day she put the magazines away and went back down to the basement.

~

On her way to the powder room to brush her teeth, Paulina ran into Ruth. The Weinribs had returned late last night, she'd heard Nathan's car, followed by thuds and heavy footsteps. That morning she'd watched from the window as Hope waddled around the front yard, while Nathan raked the leaves that had littered the lawn in his absence.

Ruth was carrying her laundry basket. Killing two birds with one stone, she called it.

"I was just coming to get you," she said, stuffing clothes into the machine. "Ernesto's on the phone upstairs."

Paulina picked up the receiver in the hallway.

"Hello?"

"I found an apartment. Two bedrooms. Yours has a view of a park."

Montreal was beautiful, her brother said. He was already picking up some French. Did she remember any from school?

"Some."

"Good. It will help you find a job."

He sounded so confident. More than that. Happy. Ernesto was happy.

"I'm going to stay here another week or so. Do you mind? The landlord said I could paint. What colour do you want your room?"

"It doesn't matter."

"Yes, it does. It's your room."

"I don't know. White, I guess."

"Aren't you tired of white walls? What about green? Or purple?"

"Purple, then."

"Or green. Green is nice."

Carmen's roommates, he said, had painted their apartment in varying shades of green and purple. They, like everyone he'd met, were true comrades. Since arriving in Montreal, Ernesto had taken his wallet out exactly once. Wherever he went, as soon as they learned he was a Chilean exile, Carmen's friends fought each other to buy him food and beer and grass. Carmen said they did that for all the exiles.

Many of his new Canadian friends had also been political prisoners, rounded up during the October Crisis for no other reason than that they had long hair and played guitar outside in the park. Just like back home, Ernesto said. When he got back he would tell Paulina about that fall of 1970 when the French-Canadians had fought for their independence. Fought and lost, just like Ernesto and his comrades. Did Paulina know that they called themselves the Latin Americans of North America?

"No other people in Canada have been so oppressed. Besides the Indians, of course."

Paulina let him go on, talking more to himself than to her. None of his new friends worked, he let slip. They all shared whatever they had with each other. In the distance, watching over all this solidarity was a glowing crucifix atop Mount Royal, although here the Catholic Church had recently lost its hold over the people, following their relatively successful, Quiet Revolution.

It was surreal. It was Paradise. Paulina would love it. Last night, someone had brought a bottle of pisco to Carmen's apartment, smuggled into the country from Chile. Ernesto had filled the flask he'd brought with him from Valparaíso, he'd make them celebratory pisco sours when he got back. He'd had a few himself, last night.

"Some comrades were back from Cuba, we stayed up all night talking about agricultural cooperatives, how they've managed the sugar cane harvest and rotated the crops so that ..."

Ernesto was going on at length about soy and coffee crops when Paulina interrupted him.

"Ruth needs the phone."

"Say hello for me."

Paulina was about to trudge back downstairs when she saw Nathan. Hope was behind him, clutching his leg. Ruth came up the stairs with her empty laundry basket.

"Go with Mommy," Nathan said, but Hope was already toddling toward Ruth. "Daddy needs to talk to Paulina."

"You can help Mommy with lunch," Ruth said, taking her daughter's hand.

Nathan invited Paulina into his living room, the same living room where she'd stayed up late listening to his albums, sprawled on the same sofa where she now sat, hands in her lap, wondering if Nathan had somehow found out that she'd unearthed his dirty magazines.

Nathan, like Ruth, was tanned, although Ruth's nose was bright pink. It was hard to look him in the eye, knowing about his taste in magazines. Did Ruth know? Was that why they were getting a divorce?

"Look," Nathan said, leaning forward in his chair. "Ernesto told me he wants you to get a job, a regular job, and you don't like the idea. He wanted me to talk to you about it."

So that was it. Paulina didn't like her brother talking about her behind her back, but at least this wasn't about the magazines.

"He is in Montreal, looking for an apartment for us."

"Is that what you want? To move to Montreal?"

Did it matter? "I don't know."

"If you don't want to go, he shouldn't force you. You've moved around enough."

"I don't have to go?"

"You're eighteen. He's not your legal guardian anymore."

Nathan was right. It hadn't occurred to her that she was now in charge of herself, not her father, not her brother.

"I don't think you should go if you don't want to, and Ruth agrees. She says you need time to be with your feelings."

"My feelings?"

Nathan looked toward the kitchen, then back at Paulina.

"Ruth says that when you left Chile, everything was chaotic, you had to come here and adapt, go to school, start a new life. You couldn't allow yourself to really feel anything. But now you're more used to it here, you feel safe. So you can let yourself feel sad about everything you lost. If Ernesto makes you start over someplace new, you won't be able to feel your feelings."

"I don't feel sad. Not all the time."

Nathan smiled at her.

"That's because you're young. You're resilient. That's what Ruth says. Where there's life, there's hope."

Paulina could hear Ruth singing to her daughter in the kitchen, one of her nonsensical songs. Nathan was a fool to let her go. She was a good mother, full of unexpected kindness. Someone should tell him.

"You can stay here as long as you need to figure things out," Nathan said. "And don't worry about money.

You've got about five hundred from that fundraiser Helen organized. Ernesto did the right thing, letting me keep it locked away for you. Not because I didn't trust you. Ernesto's a good guy but he's what my dad would call a *schnorrer*, a dreamer. The coup interrupted his education, which is a shame, but for whatever reason he doesn't want to continue it here. He's a lost soul and until he figures himself out I don't think anyone should be giving him more than twenty bucks at a time."

"The money is mine?"

"All yours. What I suggest we do is get you your own account."

Nathan smiled at her. Five hundred dollars. So much more than her *Cabbagetown* money, which Ernesto had cashed for her. If Sir Jerome had asked, she would have given him every penny for *Uncle Vanya*. Too bad for him now.

"Am I rich?"

Nathan laughed.

"As my dad would say, you're comfortable. For now."

"How is your father?" Paulina asked, feeling ashamed of herself for forgetting why Nathan had gone away in the first place.

"Fine. He's pretty tough. Resilient, you could say."

Paulina returned his smile, heard herself accepting his offer to lunch with his family, upstairs in the kitchen. A first.

She wasn't hungry, but she would make herself eat. Her blood needed building up, as Pilar would say, for what lay ahead. For the first time, she had plans. Her own.

— 6. —

THE NEXT DAY Nathan brought Paulina to his bank to open her first chequing account. After she'd signed the papers and selected her cheques, the cheapest ones because Nathan said novelty cheques, while fun to look at were a waste of money, she returned to the basement. She was turning the blank pages of her first bankbook, roughly the same dimensions as the pocket-sized Book of Saints that Pilar kept in her apron, when Ruth knocked on her door, the one leading to the laundry room.

Her face was pink, but she was smiling. Something wonderful had happened, Ruth said, while Paulina was at the bank. She could hardly believe it.

"Tommy Lerner called for you. About a job, an audition for a kid's cartoon, he's the zookeeper, the animals talk and they need an alpaca. Isn't that fantastic? I mean, they need someone to play an alpaca. I told him you'd call him as soon as you got back."

Paulina had never seen Ruth so excited. Ruth even dialled the number for her, then passed her the receiver. Paulina was too dazed to share her excitement. It could all be Tommy Lerner's idea of a good joke. Who ever heard of a cartoon alpaca?

A young woman answered. Paulina asked to speak to Mr. Lerner.

"May I ask who is calling?"

"Miss Paulina de Acosta Zapatero."

Tommy Lerner's gruff voice came on the line.

"Weinrib's daughter-in-law told you? They had a lot of girls come in. Lucky for you they were all garbage. I can set something up for this week. You around?"

"Mr. Lerner, thank you so much . . ."

"The show's one of those educational deals to teach kids how we're all the same, Black, white, Jew, whatever. How boys can do girl things and girls can do boy things. You ask me that stuff is just confusing them. You raise kids to be open-minded enough, their brains fall out."

Animal Crackers had been on the air for a few months and was already a hit, he said, at least with the kiddie set. The producers had decided to add a new character, a girl alpaca. When he'd heard that the alpaca was native to South America, Tommy Lerner had thought of her.

"The money's the best part. All you have to do is show up to the recording studio, say your lines, no make-up, no costume, no futzing around. In and out. With this job you can afford to join the union. You know what that means? It means you'll get scale."

No more minimum wage. If she was comfortable before, she'd be floating now.

Of course, Paulina would have to audition. Someone would call her, Tommy Lerner said, to set up a time.

"Until then, stay away from drafts. Go to the library, look at some pictures of alpacas. Not that it matters, the part's yours."

Paulina, numb with joy and afraid of losing her precious voice, mumbled her thanks.

~

The audition took place in a brick building in the city's east end. Ruth, driving her there, said it had probably been a factory. A lot of the old industrial buildings were being renovated, she said, while Paulina pretended to listen.

The producers of *Animal Crackers* were a married couple Paulina thought could be twins. They were similarly dressed in white pants and sweaters, their identically feathered blond hair grazing their shoulders. The unisex look, it was called. Paulina liked it. It must be nice, not having to wear skirts and pantyhose, or suits and ties.

Hers had proven to be the most difficult part to cast, Ted Walsh told her, as he and his wife Susan were leading her to the recording booth. The space, so dim and hushed, reminded Paulina of the confessional where Pilar had once brought her to confess her sins when she was ten years old. Paulina had found it easier to let the priest do the heavy lifting, filling the silence with his suggestions: jealousy, deception, laziness, she'd taken them all on. Her father had been furious when she'd told him, threatening to put Pilar out on the street. His daughter had no sins to confess, she was a child.

What would he say now?

"Everyone who reads puts on this heavy accent," Ted told her, while he adjusted Paulina's microphone. Seated on a high stool, she felt exposed, though only her voice would be scrutinized.

"Like Carmen Miranda," said Susan, laughing.

"Which is not what we want. Would you like some water?"

"Yes, please."

"We loved you in *Prince of Cabbagetown*," Susan said.

Paulina's episode had aired while she was alone in the Weinribs' house. Her appearance had been brief but long enough for her to take note of her nose (too big) and her breasts (too negligible). The whole experience had been both thrilling and disappointing. The Weinribs said they were sorry they'd missed it. Ernesto must have missed it, too, otherwise he would have teased her about it.

"Anita's just arrived at the zoo from South America," Susan said, handing Paulina her script.

Paulina took a sip of water. What if she stammered? What if the words got stuck in her throat, her chest?

Susan crouched down beside her, her husband easing padded headphones over Paulina's ears.

"She knows that the world outside can be scary and confusing. That's what this scene is about. Is she going to be okay in this new place?"

"Need a few moments before we start?"

"No," Paulina told Ted, sitting up as straight as she could on her stool. "I'm ready."

She was ready, to make the words of a bewildered alpaca her own.

~

On her first day of recording Paulina was surprised to find out that June Fairfield was playing the zookeeper's wife. There was only time for a quick hug but June said they should catch up and soon, but not today, she was on her way to an audition. She didn't say anything about Denise. Not that Paulina wanted to talk or even think about her.

Recording her lines in the studio, sometimes alone, sometimes with the other voice actors (all of them Tommy Lerner's age or older, even the ones who did the children's voices), Paulina would wonder how the animators managed to sync her words to the movements of Anita Alpaca's wiggly mouth displayed on the screen before her. Like Paulina, Anita had long eyelashes, which she frequently batted to indicate impatience or coyness. A strand of blue beads encircled her long neck, her shaggy fur was grey and white. Tommy Lerner said she looked like a hairy camel with a Beatle haircut. Paulina had only seen an alpaca once on a school trip, but she reassured Ted and Susan that Anita was a believable rendition of what they assumed was Chile's national mascot.

Sister Teresa, it turned out, had been wrong; you could hear your own voice, if you wore special headphones. With Ted and Susan's guidance, Paulina developed Anita's voice, a higher-pitched version of her own, slightly breathy but cheerful, befitting, she believed, a creature used to the thin air of the Andes.

Over time Paulina came to love the recording studio, cushioned from the noise and light of the outside world. Not just the space, but her job. She was a working unionized actress, paid well for what never felt like work. Whenever she saw Tommy Lerner she tried to thank him for his gift but he wouldn't allow it. He owed her, he said. *Stigmata!* was promising to become a classic of the new genre of horror. Of course, the scandal of casting Patty Cake was working in the film's favour, generating excitement in the States, or so his agent said. Did Paulina have an agent? Why not?

So talent agents weren't only for blond goddesses like Denise.

"Go see Joyce," Tommy Lerner told her, that afternoon while they were waiting in the green room for their turn together in the studio. "Tell her I sent you. She'll take good care of you."

～

Joyce Shapiro had frizzy grey hair and large blue eyes under round glasses. Her desk was covered with papers and files, and she had a large black phone with many buttons. Paulina found her unkempt appearance and messy office reassuring. Joyce Shapiro must be very busy launching her clients' careers, too busy to clean her glasses or buy new pantyhose without runs.

At their first, rushed meeting in her downtown office, Joyce told Paulina not to worry, she'd arrange everything, beginning with headshots. She got on her phone, to schedule a photo shoot for Paulina, at a studio not far from where she recorded her lines for *Animal Crackers*.

"No time like the present," Joyce said, and Paulina agreed. There really was no time like this present.

Less than two weeks later, glossy black-and-white photographs of Paulina's face, expertly made up by the photographer's assistant, arrived at Joyce's office.

"Look at you! Those eyes! Like Joan Baez and Louise Brooks had a baby."

Joyce had instructed the assistant to cut Paulina's hair into a bob with thick bangs above her eyebrows. That was why she looked like Louise Brooks, whoever she was. Paulina liked her new haircut, June said it was very chic, but she barely recognized herself in the photos. Her skin was as pale as the surface of one of Pilar's blancmange puddings, her expression sweet and untroubled. Her eyes were ringed by tiny black spikes, her glossy lips slightly parted. It had been an awkward and trying experience, the photographer coaxing her to relax, lower her shoulders, turn her head in this direction, raise her chin, let her mouth fall open.

She was smiling in the photo Joyce eventually chose for her headshot because it showed her teeth, and everyone agreed Paulina had great teeth. There were other photos, too, of Paulina emoting, as the photographer called it. He'd recited scenarios to her, all involving a single, nameless man: the man of your dreams is telling you he loves you, now he's telling you he's been unfaithful, now he's pointing a gun at you, now he's dying in your arms. These would be sent to casting agents, proof that Paulina had emotional range.

Paulina thought she looked equally stupid in each of these photos, but Joyce was pleased, which was a relief; Paulina wouldn't have to pay for another session, even if the photographer had given her a discount because she was one of Joyce's "finds."

Photos settled, it was time for Paulina's resume.

"Any special talents?" Joyce asked, fingers poised above her electric typewriter.

"I can swim."

"Good. What about driving? Do you have your licence?"

"No."

"Get one. I know a guy, I'll give you his address. If you say I sent you he'll give you a discount."

When Joyce was done she read Paulina's one-page resume back to her. Her credible ethnicities outnumbered her acting credits. Paulina Acosta could play Italian, Greek, Portuguese, Mediterranean, Southern European, Gypsy, Mexican, Spanish, South American, Central American, Hispanic, Jewish, and American Indian. Her ages were twelve to twenty-five. Joyce added three pounds to what she guessed to be her weight, and a half inch to her approximated height. After much consideration, she dropped the *de* from de Acosta. Her name sounded better without it, Joyce said. Snappier.

Joyce did not promise to make her a star as Paulina had hoped. Instead, she promised to make her a working actor, one of the lucky few who earned a living by their craft. Paulina would never wait a table in her life, Joyce Shapiro said, opening a folder for her new client.

I am a working actor, Paulina told herself as she walked to the subway. Now all she needed was her own place, like Mary Richards in Minneapolis. Paulina never missed an episode of her new favourite show, tuning in mostly for Mary's apartment, on the top floor of a house, not the basement. Mary, who also worked in TV, would never live in a basement. Mary had better shag carpeting than Paulina, and a yellow chair by her wide windows, and she was never alone, people were always dropping by.

No one dropped by Paulina's basement. It was so lonely she kept making excuses to go upstairs and use the phone. It was pathetic. When Ernesto came back, she would tell him she was done living underground.

— 7. —

"I'm not in Montreal," Ernesto said.

Paulina had been about to dial the number for the lady who told you what time it was, when she heard Ernesto's voice, asking for Nathan. Instead he got her.

"Where are you?"

"In Cuba. Outside Havana. A small town, you don't know it."

"Why are you in Cuba?"

Cuba. That was where Lorraine's mother had discovered that Spanish-speakers were not to be trusted. Had Ernesto changed his mind, did he want them to move to Cuba now?

"I always planned to come here." He sounded irritated, as if Paulina should have known about his plans, when she was hearing about them for the first time.

Ernesto was so intent on visiting the island that he'd applied for a Canadian passport, as soon as he had his citizenship. He'd packed it with him when he'd left for Montreal. Carmen's friends were planning to volunteer on an agricultural cooperative, they didn't know when, but he was hoping it would be soon.

When they announced their trip, he was ready. The timing couldn't be better; Paulina was in the care of the

Weinribs, he could finally do his part after hiding like a coward for so long.

That first morning Ernesto, the only Latin American in his group, was invited to drive the new tractor. No one had driven it before, it was a gift from comrades in Remedios. A used vehicle but in good shape, his hosts said.

Ernesto had never driven a tractor before but he couldn't turn down the honour, and his new friends said it would be like driving a car. Still he was careful, driving slowly, a lovely field of soybeans in the distance. Just as he was beginning to feel at ease and in love with the Cuban countryside, he felt a strange vibration coming from the driver's seat. Probably some quirk of the old tractor. The rumbling continued, growing stronger, suddenly he was in pain, stabbed by tiny unseen knives in his buttocks and the backs of his thighs and his poor balls. He leapt out of the seat, the tractor continuing without him until it crashed into the barn. Ernesto, howling, ripped off his jeans, then his underpants. Rolling around half-naked on the field, he did not see the swarm of agitated bees emerging from the driver's seat.

Paulina's own driving lessons were going smoothly; her instructor expected her to pass the test on the first try. She could even parallel park. And here was Ernesto, crashing a tractor into a barn. But it wasn't because of his driving, he told Paulina.

"The tractor had been in a garage for a long time, the seat was all torn up. The bees were living inside the seat. The doctors said it's a good thing I'm not allergic to stings or I'd be dead."

It was too sad to be funny, too funny to be sad. Ernesto began detailing some of the observations he'd been able to make of Cuban society from his hospital bed but Paulina stopped him.

"What about the apartment you found?"

"It's too late, someone else took it. But we can find another one."

It wasn't the ideal time but it had to be done. Like pulling off a bandage, as Lorraine used to say.

"I'm not coming to Montreal. I'm staying here. In Toronto."

"With the Weinribs? You're going to live with them? Did Nathan agree to this?"

"No, not with the Weinribs. I'll find my own place to live. I have a job."

Voicing a cartoon alpaca sounded even more incredible than a tractor full of angry Cuban bees, but it was true, Paulina assured her brother.

"I'm making good money."

"You don't need money. You have the money Nathan's been holding for you. It's all yours."

Ernesto didn't want the money. It was Paulina's. For her education.

"Are you sure you don't need it?"

"Yes. I don't want you to be alone. It's not safe. And no one will rent an apartment to a foreign girl. They rent to families or to men, but not to single girls."

"They rented to the Toronto Girl Problems."

"What are you talking about?"

"Nothing. Nathan said there are plenty of people who will rent to me."

"Nathan is going to help you find a place?"

The idea seemed to reassure her brother so before hanging up, Paulina said yes, of course, Nathan would help her. It wasn't exactly a lie; she knew he would help her if she asked. But Nathan, on the verge of divorce, must have his own problems. She would manage without him.

~

When not at the recording studio Paulina spent much of her free time at a nearby public library where she could consult the newspapers for free. Late one afternoon, taking a break from Apartments to Rent, she finally turned her attention to the card catalogue, her initial reason for coming to the library. Specifically, she looked up the cards filed under the letter, "L." She didn't expect to find the word, but there it was, typed and almost ordinary, on card after card: Lesbians-Fiction. Lesbians-Motherhood. Lesbians-Musicians. Lesbians-Poetry. Lesbians-Psychiatry. Lesbians-Religion. Lesbians-Women's Liberation.

She did not expect to find the books either, but they were there, too. Fiction was less extensive than psychiatry and religion, so she took a few novels down from the shelves, not sure what to do with them. No one noticed or tried to stop her, even when, seated at a small table in a quiet corner, she studied the names of their borrowers, written by hand on the cards tucked inside the paper pockets glued to the back covers.

The books she would read later. First, Paulina wanted to meet the women who had dared take them out.

Borrowing a pen and some paper from the librarian, Paulina wrote down the names of the most recent borrowers. Then she got up and asked the librarian for the city directory.

By the time the library was closing, Paulina had collected nine names and addresses. For five of these she'd found more than one listing in the directory, but not for Sylvia D. Lewis, the first name on her list. Whoever she was, she was as good a place as any to start. Paulina would find her tomorrow.

~

Paulina had never been this far north on Bathurst Street. Before arriving at Sylvia D. Lewis's home, the bus went over a bridge, and Paulina could see a portion of the city's ravine below. The main, winding path was littered with dead leaves, but there were a few people down there, walking dogs, jogging. It must be nice, Paulina thought, living so close to such contained wilderness. She missed her long walks back home, daydreaming as she ventured farther and farther from her house.

Sylvia's home turned out to be a brick apartment building. Sylvia D. Lewis lived in apartment 604, according to the directory inside the lobby. Paulina was wondering if she should press the button beside the name when a man appeared. Under almost any other circumstance, his thick neck and giant hands would have terrified her. But this man carried a mop and bucket, not a knife or a gun.

"You here for apartment?" he asked when he saw her.

Paulina, afraid the man would figure out what she was up to, said she was. Yes, she was the girl who had called earlier, about the apartment.

The man sized her up, in one long but not unfriendly look.

"You gymnast? I coach in Hungary. Girls all look like you. Even when old. They have baby, they snap like branch."

Paulina nodded. Yes, a gymnast, that's what she was.

The man looked impressed.

"For you gymnast, I have one-bedroom, very nice, fourth floor."

That wouldn't do.

"Do you have one on the sixth floor?"

"Sixth floor, I have two-bedroom. You want to see?"

"Yes, please."

The vacant apartment was directly across the hall from Sylvia D. Lewis in 604. Paulina did her best to play the part of prospective tenant, nodding as the man showed her the freshly varnished floor, the freshly painted walls, the all-new appliances. The small kitchen was to the left of the apartment door, opposite the living room. Down a narrow hallway was a bathroom, flanked by two bedrooms.

"Two girls living here before," the man said.

Paulina followed him into the bathroom and watched him flush the toilet, then run the water in the sink and the bathtub. He showed her the radiators, insisting Paulina touch one to feel its faint heat.

"Nice view," the man said. Paulina followed him into the kitchen where he showed her the small window through which she could see the tops of trees, their branches nearly bare.

The rent was beyond the budget Nathan had helped her work out and she was supposed to save money for those long periods of unemployment Joyce kept warning her about. Dry spells, she called them.

"Nice neighbours," the man said. "Quiet."

He opened the apartment door as if to prove his point. It was quiet, except for a humming noise that might have been the elevator.

"Who lives there?" Paulina asked, pointing to the apartment across from hers.

"Very nice girl. Nurse. Old people home."

A nurse. Sylvia D. Lewis was a nurse. Paulina had imagined a singer, accustomed to late nights in smoky bars.

"How old is she?"

The man did not seem surprised by her question.

"Twenty-nine," he said. "Beautiful girl. Too beautiful to live alone. I tell her, find boyfriend while young. She say she not interested. And you?"

"I don't have a boyfriend, either," Paulina said, her face warm.

"No, how old you are?"

"Eighteen."

When she'd finally told him she was moving out, Nathan had offered to serve as her guarantor. Paulina added his name, occupation, and address to the lease. Her hand trembled as she wrote.

"I am Mr. Hirsch," the man said, as if by signing the lease she'd earned the right to his name.

Her move-in date was December 1, less than two weeks away. As she walked to the bus stop Paulina told herself that she didn't have to come back, she hadn't left a deposit. She could pretend it had all never happened.

She was back the next day. As she was giving Mr. Hirsch her cheque, a young woman appeared in the lobby, wearing a long, dark coat, carrying several overstuffed tote bags. Under the coat, she wore light green pants and a matching smock.

"You have new neighbour," Mr. Hirsch said to the woman. "Right across from you."

Sylvia D. Lewis smiled at Paulina as she opened her mailbox.

"Welcome to the building," she said, still smiling as she stuffed several envelopes into one of her tote bags.

"Long day?" Mr. Hirsch asked.

"No longer than usual."

"No time for fun, eh?" Mr. Hirsch asked, pressing the elevator button for Sylvia.

She can't be almost thirty, Paulina thought. She looks the same age as me.

"If you ever need anything, just knock," Sylvia called to Paulina as the elevator doors were closing.

Paulina nodded, raising her arm to wave back at Sylvia but it was too late. She let her arm drop down by her side, still seeing Sylvia's lovely wide face, the dimples when she smiled, the animated, generous mouth.

"No family here, all in Nova Scotia," Mr. Hirsch said. "Good people, they come visit just once, mother, father, brothers. All good people."

"Yes," Paulina said, as if she had met them and found them to be good, too.

"You have people like that in Chile?"

"Good people?"

Mr. Hirsch smiled.

"Blacks," he said. "You have Blacks in Chile?"

"Not really," Paulina said.

"Some people don't rent to them. We rent to foreigners, why not them?"

Paulina nodded, not sure what to say. Was she to congratulate Mr. Hirsch for renting, as he put it, to all kinds?

"Mailbox key," Mr. Hirsch said. "I give you now. Right next to Sylvia. Maybe if you go away she take your mail for you."

"Or if she goes?"

"She never go, not even vacation. Poor girl. Too pretty to be alone."

Paulina wondered just how pretty one had to be, to be considered too pretty to be alone.

Mr. Hirsch gave her more keys, one to the building, another to the garage.

"This for yours."

Paulina added her apartment key to the ring. It glittered like a wedding band.

— 8. —

RUTH TOOK PAULINA to a warehouse outside the city, which promised deep discounts on furniture and household goods. Paulina chose a sofa, a bed, a small kitchen table and two chairs, a night table, and a dresser. At Ruth's urging, she added a coffee table and a loveseat. For entertaining, she said. Ruth also helped her find towels, bed linens, dishes, glassware, cutlery, cookware.

At the checkout Paulina looked down at her purchases, the smaller items that did not require delivery, and saw that she had just put together her own trousseau. Some of her friends in Chile had linens and dishes set aside by mothers and grandmothers, waiting for their wedding day. Now Paulina had her own things, small and big, including a white sofa Ruth had tried to talk her out of but Paulina wouldn't budge.

She'd spent too much money on headshots and driving lessons, and she'd have to pay for movers, too. Luckily, the store offered a payment plan. On the store clerk's recommendation, Paulina changed her initial order of a twin bed to a double. Better for restless sleepers, the woman said. Paulina wasn't sure how restless she was, but Mary Richards probably had a double bed, too.

On the drive back, Ruth told Paulina about the dorm room she'd once shared at the University of Toronto, how her roommate had become engaged and left school in the middle of the fall semester, leaving Ruth alone in their room with its large leaded windows and solid old furnishings. To date, this had been her only experience of living alone and to her surprise, she'd relished it. She'd loved the mornings best, drinking the coffee she brewed for herself in her room, looking out at the quad from her windows.

"Like Mary Richards," Paulina said, and Ruth laughed.

Paulina could just leave her packages in her car, Ruth said, since she was moving out soon.

"Come on in. Nathan has something for you."

It was her mother's fur coat, still inside its garment bag, along with a sheet of instructions for proper home storage.

"How can I thank you?"

She didn't just mean the coat. Without Nathan's signature on her lease and his intercession on her behalf with Bell Canada, she would never be moving into her own apartment, with her own phone line, too. And she'd thanked him by lying to him, that she'd chosen a two-bedroom because she planned to rent the second bedroom to another girl.

"It was nothing," Nathan said. "Wear it in good health."

Holding back tears, Paulina accepted the coat, not that she would ever wear it. Her mother's fur would have kept Paulina warm in Canada, but no one her age wore coats like it, and she'd always feared damaging it. No, it would remain in its protective bag, at the back of her closet.

Paulina was certain someone would stop her on her moving day, as Héctor Torres had stopped Alma Siqueiros's marriage to Raúl Flores in *The Bride Wore Red*, bursting into the church to proclaim that she was pregnant with his dead brother's child. Someone knew, someone had to know her motivations for choosing this apartment with its superfluous bedroom in this neighbourhood, a long bus and streetcar ride from the recording studio. But should anyone object, she would show them her lease, that document she'd signed stipulating that she would indeed live across the hall from Sylvia D. Lewis for the next twelve months, so long as she kept her pledge not to interfere with her fellow renters' enjoyment of the premises.

~

Two weeks after moving in Paulina invited June over for tea, eager to show off her apartment to someone, anyone, now that she was unpacked and settled in. There was really no one else she could invite. Tommy Lerner? He didn't seem like the tea type. Her agent was too busy. She could have invited the Weinribs but she hadn't spoken to them since the day after her move, when they'd called to see if she'd recovered from the ordeal of moving. A short, awkward conversation had followed. No, there was no one else but June.

That morning Paulina cleaned her apartment for the first time since moving in. Over the past few days, the place had revealed its quirks to her. The toilet was full of mysterious, stubborn rust stains. When she washed her dishes in the kitchen, the water sometimes would gurgle up from the bathtub drain, vomiting bits of onionskin, tea leaves, and in one horrifying instant, slivers of fish skin from her first effort at cooking herself a proper meal. Did Sylvia also scrape kitchen garbage from her bathtub?

Paulina did not bother to clean the second, empty bedroom. She kept its door closed, only opening it in her dreams where she discovered a whole other apartment in need of cleaning.

Besides cleaning, she'd done her best to decorate, hanging up old movie posters she'd bought at a garage sale in the neighbourhood, already framed by their original owner. She did not hang up the framed review of *Pericles* Ruth had given her as a housewarming present, because of the picture of Denise. It was in her hallway closet, along with her new hammer, nails, and screwdriver.

"You look exhausted," June said as Paulina took her coat, to hang on her brand-new coatrack.

"I've been cleaning."

"You could hire someone."

"To live here?"

"What? No, a charwoman. I have someone come every week, I can give you her number. She's from Italy, doesn't speak much English but she's very good. Poor woman has five children and who knows how many grandchildren, she could use more work."

Paulina took down Elena's phone number, knowing she wouldn't call. She felt sorry for Elena, but she did not want some older woman poking around her apartment, her life.

"Is that Myrna Loy?" June asked, walking toward the wall for a closer look at the poster.

"I remember seeing *The Thin Man* with my uncle. He worshipped William Powell."

Paulina invited June to sit down on the white sofa, as she placed the tea tray on her coffee table. June needn't worry about spills, she told her. The sofa had a special coating that repelled stains.

Paulina sat beside her. As she was pouring their tea, June asked her if she'd heard the latest about Denise.

"No," Paulina said. She'd been hoping to get some news of Denise from June, perhaps that she'd gotten fat and no one would hire her.

"You didn't see her in *Uncle Vanya*?"

"No."

Something in Paulina's stomach seized up, rolled over, and died. Of course, June knew about her pawing of the semi-conscious Denise. Why hadn't she realized this during their time together in the recording studio, the gently inquisitive way June looked at her?

"I thought she was very good. Of course, I only saw the play once. Sir Jerome did her a great favour giving her that part, it was the least he could do. Now she's off to Stratford to play Ophelia. I really thought you were the one, my dear, but then ... well, it's nothing to do with you, what happened."

June laid a papery-looking hand on Paulina's denim-clad thigh.

"You mustn't take it personally. I may be at Stratford myself this summer. Have you thought of it for yourself? Wonderful place for young actors."

Paulina nodded. What was nothing to do with her?

"The girl's not a total dodo," June said, pouring herself more cream from Paulina's new pitcher. "She's got herself engaged to a lawyer. A good insurance policy although I wonder what will happen if Hollywood comes calling?"

The white tea set Paulina had picked out now looked cheap, like a toy for children's pretend tea parties. As soon as June left she would smash it with her hammer.

"Poor girl," June said. "Was it distressing for you, what happened with Denise? At the closing night party?"

"I was worried for her," Paulina said, avoiding June's gaze.

"We all were. It was a stupid thing to do."

"She was sad." Was she? Denise at the sink, her lips pressed together. No, Denise had been angry, not sad.

"I don't mean Denise. She didn't do anything. Jerome. I was so disappointed in him. Such a cliché. The famous director seducing the ingénue. 'Taking liberties,' we used to say."

"Liberty?"

"You didn't know? He chose the party to break it off with her. So devastating for a young actress."

Denise and Sir Jerome? He was so old, was it even possible?

June patted her mouth with one of Paulina's cloth napkins, a stiff white rectangle she'd chosen to match her ugly tea things.

"It will be so much easier for you," she said.

"What do you mean?"

"I mean, there's no danger of you falling in love."

"But I want to fall in love."

June pulled Paulina to her so she could cry on her peach-coloured, woolly shoulder, her spiky brooch, a rhinestone-encrusted flower, dangerously close to Paulina's eye.

All around her people loved, married, grew old together while Paulina's desires remained theatrical, eccentric, defiant. The ordinary love she craved was beyond her reach. The most she could hope for, based on those novels from the library, was to join some all-women's commune out in the country where she'd wear men's work clothes and perform manual labour.

"But my dear, think how lucky you are. If you had some dreadful office job and everyone there knew, too ..."

Paulina looked up from June's shoulder.

June was still smiling at her, her hands on Paulina's shoulders. There was a softness now in her face, the flesh under her chin had become slack.

"Ours is a small world. We're not New York or Los Angeles, we all know each other, we talk. But you're hardly alone. You must know that."

"Even Tommy Lerner?"

"I'm not sure if Tommy knows, his head is so far up his own arse. But everyone else, Ted and Susan, and the cast. Everyone thinks you're very brave."

"Why? What did I do?"

"It takes courage to be true to yourself."

Paulina felt robbed, cheated somehow. But of what?

"You've nothing to worry about. There's no judgement. Ted and Susan are quite liberal. It's your life, to live as you wish."

June hugged her again as she was leaving. The fur collar of her wool coat tickled Paulina's cheek.

"You'll do fine," June kept telling her.

"How do you know?" Paulina asked, almost wailing.

"Because you're adorable." June kissed the tip of Paulina's nose, just as Sylvia opened her apartment door.

When the elevator arrived, June turned and waved at Paulina. Paulina waved back, watching Sylvia follow June inside the elevator.

"Goodbye, Mrs. Fairfield," Paulina cried out, desperate to communicate that June was not her lover but it was too late, the doors were closing, Sylvia probably hadn't heard her.

— 9. —

SHE SHOULD HAVE been grateful, but Paulina began to dread Joyce's phone calls. Time to wash and style her hair, a waste of time, since it would be ruined as soon as she pulled on her woolen hat. Time to sit in a waiting room with the other girls, all of them eager to chat about their favourite topic: the scarcity of acting jobs. The worst was recognizing them from past auditions, having to acknowledge that she, too, hadn't booked the last job.

Paulina quickly learned to bring a book with her—not one of her lesbian novels, but the one June had loaned her: *An Actor Prepares*. But then some girl would look over her shoulder. *Stanislavski? I love him. Isn't he the best?* Like the Russian master was their favourite Beatle.

After that, there was no stopping them. Who's your agent? Really? Lucky you. But their expressions were not congratulatory. They were sizing her up, sizing each other up, before going inside that room to be sized up themselves.

How could these backhanded girls be her people? They all said her English was excellent, her accent barely noticeable and so charming, too, it shouldn't stand in the way of her career like it had for so many other girls they knew. Paulina didn't tell them she wasn't desperate like they were, she had *Animal Crackers*. Not that they gave her a chance; after their pointed questioning had run its course, they recited their resumes in loud voices, as if projecting to a theatre balcony. Famous actors in American productions always turned out to be so much nicer than you could imagine. Directors were always so impressed that they gave them extra lines. Yet it was so difficult, this business. So difficult knowing what casting agents wanted. No wonder so many girls just gave up and got married. Did she know, they even had a friend with an agent as well-known as Joyce Shapiro who'd spent years auditioning but, in the end, just didn't have the right look. *She just wasn't right.* That was what they said when they didn't cast you: *you just weren't right.* Why, Paulina wondered, didn't they just say you were wrong?

Less than two weeks before Christmas, Joyce called her with good news: Paulina had got a callback for a part on a popular mystery series. She might be right, after all.

Almost as soon as she hung up, Paulina got another call, from Ernesto in Montreal. He was still despondent over Pinochet declaring himself President, officially dissolving the junta that had pledged to rotate the presidency between the four military men until elections were called. Hoping a joke would lift his spirits, Paulina compared Pinochet's decision to John Lennon leaving the Beatles, enraging Ernesto. She was frivolous, stupid, she didn't understand the significance of what Pinochet had done. For nearly an hour, he continued his tirade, while she vowed that the next time he called collect she would not accept the charges.

~

In the waiting room at the callback, Paulina scrutinized her competition. Who looked the most like a defecting Romanian table tennis champion? Not these fair-haired, large-breasted girls, that was for sure.

Entering the audition room, Paulina knew that this time, she was really "right." She read her lines to the camera with what she thought was a convincing Eastern European accent, but it became hard to focus with the producer's increasingly jerky movements from under the table. She was about to ask him if he required medical assistance when the man emerged from behind the table, pants down, some purplish thing in his hand that at first she mistook for a wounded appendage.

Paulina pretended not to notice him violently masturbating onto her headshot. When she was done begging not to be deported she thanked the man, now zipping up his pants, for considering her for the role, then fled the room.

Paulina stood outside the door for what seemed like hours, the other girls staring at her, then she was outside. Her coat was in her arms, but she couldn't feel the cold, only the panic that seized her as she descended the steps to the subway. Those other girls. She had to warn them. She ran back up the stairs, then back down again, pausing by the turnstiles until someone pushed her out of the way.

Then she was outside her apartment door, emitting a short, shocked scream.

Paulina shut her door, just as Sylvia's opened.

"Everything okay?"

"Yes," Paulina said, her legs trembling. "Thank you."

"Are you sure?" Sylvia asked, now stepping out into the hallway. A cat appeared behind her, stretching its front paws and yawning.

"A mouse," Paulina said. "There is a mouse in my apartment. Or a rat."

"Probably a mouse," Sylvia said, smiling her lovely smile. "This building is full of them. Management won't do anything except put a few traps in the basement. Cleo keeps them away from me but I've seen a few down in the laundry room. I always scream, too."

Paulina nodded, following Sylvia's gaze to her skirt. Had that man dirtied her during the audition? No, the brown corduroy was clean.

"I love your skirt," Sylvia said. "The buttons are great."

"Thank you. I like your pyjamas." Sylvia was petite, only slightly taller than Paulina, but womanly, with the hips and breasts Paulina still wanted for herself.

"Don't feel bad about freaking out. I'm terrified of mice, too. But not Cleo."

The cat was pacing back and forth in front of Paulina's door, her tail high and twitching, making chirping sounds. Sylvia laughed, a warm, friendly laugh.

"You have a cat," Paulina said, as if she'd never heard Sylvia calling the animal by name whenever it ran out into the hallway, had never seen her returning to her apartment with the calico squirming in her arms.

"She's never caught one before but she goes nuts when she hears them scratching inside the walls. I can't guarantee anything, but do you want to borrow her?"

Paulina unlocked her door. Her hands were steady now.

"Come to my place," Sylvia said as Cleo slipped purposely into Paulina's apartment, a cat on a mission. "I'll make us coffee while we wait. It might get ugly in there."

~

Sylvia's apartment was a sensible bachelor with a foldout sofa bed and modest kitchenette. Unlike Paulina, she had bookshelves and plants. Instead of movie posters, she'd put up a few framed paintings of seascapes. Paulina remembered Mr. Hirsch saying she was from Nova Scotia. So she and Sylvia had both grown up by the sea.

A shaggy, multihued rug separated the kitchenette from the living room. The tablecloth bore the words, *Bon appétit*, repeated in red against a white background.

"Mr. Hirsch says you're a gymnast? Was that woman who came to see you your coach?"

Paulina felt her cheeks grow warm.

"I'm an actress. I just told him that to impress him."

"All this time I thought you left early for practice. An actress! You must meet a lot of famous people."

"No. Just Tommy Lerner."

"Tommy Lerner is pretty famous. Mr. Hirsch told me you're only eighteen, you're from Chile. And here you are, a movie star."

Sylvia smiled at her as she poured their coffee into cups inscribed with the names of hospitals. Paulina's said St. Michael's Hospital.

"What about you? Mr. Hirsch says you are a nurse?"

So many questions to ask, she was bursting with them. She would have to control herself. She would not think of the producer, not now, not of his bald spot as he lowered his head to watch himself ejaculate onto her headshot, the stuff cloudy, dribbling, not clear and harmless like egg white. She would not think of the girls waiting their turn, of what he might do to them. She would ask Sylvia questions, all day and into the night if she let her.

"I'm with an agency right now. My plan is to work at an ICU. Intensive care unit. They keep offering me jobs doing administration but I don't believe in Plan B. I get bounced around different hospitals, but lately I've been working at a nursing home."

Did this rigidity also apply to Sylvia's personal life? Paulina had always thought of lesbianism as a sort of Plan B. Was Sylvia really a lesbian? How could she be sure?

"I'm off work today," Sylvia said, staring down into her mug, this one from Sunnybrook Medical Centre. "That's why I'm still in my pyjamas."

"Have you ever seen a dead person?" Paulina heard herself ask. But Sylvia didn't seem disturbed or even surprised.

"Yes. I was an intern then, in urgent care. They had a special ward set up, there were so many women. Some younger than me, but some older than my mother."

"How did they die?" What had killed all these women in Toronto, and why hadn't she heard of this plague?

"I guess it doesn't happen in your country. Some of them used knitting needles, or they sprayed Lysol in their wombs. That was a popular one. A few threw themselves down the stairs. Most paid for back-alley abortions and got infections and died. It's still happening now. If you can't prove you need an abortion to save your life, what can you do?"

"It happens in my country, too."

"I guess it happens almost everywhere," Sylvia said, as she brought their mugs to her kitchen sink.

"Why don't we check on Cleo?"

In the hallway Paulina unlocked her door, stepping aside for Sylvia to enter first.

"Yikes," Sylvia said.

"What is it?"

"I'm not sure you should see this," she said, standing in Paulina's doorway, blocking her view.

"Why? What is it?"

"Let's just say Cleo took care of it."

The cat was at Sylvia's feet, purring. Sylvia bent down and picked her up. Paulina stepped forward and there was the mouse on her living room floor, decapitated, tiny spine sticking out of its mangled body. "She's tasted blood," Sylvia said, scratching Cleo's chin. "She'll never be the same."

Paulina was so happy and relieved she kissed Cleo on the head. Sylvia, laughing, brought the cat back to her apartment, returning with a pair of tongs. Paulina had already put on her oven mitts, a housewarming gift from June. She picked up the dead mouse with Sylvia's tongs, depositing it in the small plastic bag Sylvia had been thoughtful enough to bring. Together, they tossed the bag down the garbage chute, Paulina still wearing the oven mitts, the two of them listening to the small, echoing thump the creature made on its way down.

Paulina heard herself asking Sylvia if she would like to go for a walk in the section of ravine near their building, the ravine where Lorraine had planned to hide out if falsely accused of murder.

A walk in a ravine in December. Like normal people do.

Sylvia said she'd get dressed and meet her in the lobby. Paulina went back to her apartment, rushing to the bathroom. Splashing cold water on her face, she realized she was still wearing her skirt and blouse, robin's-egg blue, from her audition. She changed out of them, tossing the clothes into the second bedroom, and shutting the door. Tomorrow she'd take them to the dry cleaners.

— 10. —

THERE WERE NOT many people in the ravine, just a few stray, determined joggers. Still, they walked on until they were on a new, rougher path, leading them deeper into the woods where the sounds of the city couldn't reach them, where they could be alone.

The sky was grey; a mist hovered over the tops of the trees. The path they were walking on was pewter-coloured, the ground strewn with wet leaves. The trees and bushes were unlike any Paulina had ever seen. One tree was bare except for its uppermost branches, which still held a scattering of leaves, brown and heart-shaped. They passed some bushes, bare branches tipped with tiny white puffs or cones the colour of old blood. It was, in its own way, as unearthly as the geysers Paulina had once visited on a school trip, a moonscape of boiling, steaming puddles in the Andean plateau. As the sun rose, Indian children had come out to play soccer, unfazed by altitude sickness.

Sylvia suggested they rest their feet, sit for a spell on the fallen tree trunk that was deeper in the woods.

"Look at that." Sylvia pointed to a nearby tree. Its trunk was infested with mushrooms, half-moons stuck to one side like tiny spaceships that had crashed into the bark. Another tree had just one of these mushrooms stuck in its trunk, a large half-disc. That must be the mothership, Paulina thought, staring at it.

"I love the ravine," Sylvia was saying. "You should see it in the summer, it's like a different place. And October when the leaves change colour and in spring, too. It's never the same, it's always changing. Even in the dead of winter, it's full of life."

Paulina clung to Sylvia's words, but it was no use, she was being pulled back into the conference room with the producer, seeing again his erect penis, her first and hopefully last one, an ugly mushroom she couldn't banish from her memory. How could she ever audition again, what would she say to Joyce?

She made it to a bush just in time, Sylvia behind her, saying something about a nasty stomach virus making the rounds of the city.

"It's not that."

From a cold, high place Paulina heard herself telling Sylvia what had happened that morning. When she was done, Sylvia was silent for so long that Paulina began apologizing for telling her but Sylvia stopped her.

"I've never made it with a Black chick before," she said, staring at the dead leaves stuck to the ground before them. "That's what he told me. A paediatric surgeon. We were in line at the cafeteria. He wanted to know if it was true, if Black girls could fuck all night. He whispered it in my ear."

"What did you do?"

"I was in shock. I went and sat with the other nurses and ate my soup. I could still feel his hot breath in my ear all day."

"Did you see him again?"

"He would wink at me in the hallway. But I was only there for a few weeks. It hasn't happened anywhere else since, but I'm always afraid some doctor will try something and then what can I do? I have patients asking me how long I've been in Canada. My family's been here for centuries and they compliment me on getting rid of my Jamaican accent."

So she wasn't alone. Sylvia had to deal with it, too.

From inside her coat pocket Sylvia produced a flask.

"Something to keep us warm," she said, taking a sip, then passing it to Paulina.

Paulina drank the burning liquid, forcing herself to swallow. Then she laughed. The idea was so crazy she had to laugh.

"What if I get the part?"

"I guess you'll have to see his freaky ass again."

"But I don't want to see a freaky ass ever again."

This was too much for Sylvia. With her mittened hand, she gently pulled Paulina toward her. "What planet are you from?"

"Planet Chile."

Hands, ungloved and unmittened, found their clumsy way inside coats, under sweaters, to brush against nipples as hard as acorns. Paulina cried out in surprised pleasure when Sylvia bit her neck. Her body convulsed, her mind went deliriously empty. There was mud on their jeans. Leaves plastered to their boots. A smell like smoke in Paulina's nostrils. Another smell, more intimate, rose from them both. They held each other's bare hands, warming them.

"I am a virgin," Paulina said, as she plucked a dead leaf from Sylvia's curly hair.

"I am not," Sylvia said, mocking her solemn tone.

"What is it like?"

"If you mean with a man, the first time was lousy. The second time too. I didn't wait around to see if it got better."

"I may die a virgin."

"Not if I have anything to do with it."

Paulina kissed the palm of Sylvia's hand.

"Live with me," she said.

"Are you serious? I was thinking maybe we could spend Christmas together, but you want me to move in?"

"It's a two-bedroom."

"Just like that? What if we hate each other after a month?"

"We will love each other more after another month."

"Let's go home then," Sylvia whispered, hotly, in Paulina's ear.

ACT THREE:

THE HOME FOR WAYWARD DAUGHTERS

— 1. —

Paulina gave herself to the end of January to "come clean" (an expression she'd picked up during an audition for a cop show) but then in mid-January Sylvia got a terrible, lingering cold, which she gave to Paulina, and then it was Valentine's Day, her first as a woman in love. Sylvia gave her a potted African violet and she couldn't tell her, not until the romance of that day had faded, at least a week, she reckoned.

So long as Paulina told her before the first of March, but then Sylvia was so busy during those days leading up to her move across the hallway, with extra shifts at the nursing home and finding a buyer for Paulina's white sofa, not to mention selling her own furniture, that it seemed cruel to add to her stress. Finally, the male graduate student taking over Sylvia's apartment agreed to buy most of her furniture, though for less than what she was asking. No one, however, responded to Sylvia's notice about Paulina's sofa, so they were stuck with it.

Paulina was prepared to tell her on moving day, but then Sylvia dropped a box of her books on her foot, a sign, Paulina decided, that it wasn't such a big deal if Sylvia didn't know the truth about how they'd met. Books had brought them together, together and happy, although sometimes Sylvia fretted over the gap in their ages, usually after sex in Paulina's double bed. Sylvia's first lesbian relationship had been with an older woman, although the gap between herself and Irene was not so wide, six years, not the decade (eleven years, Paulina would silently correct) between her and Paulina, who lay silently, letting Sylvia sort things out, knowing she'd conclude, as she always did, that Paulina was an old soul, having endured so much, the prospect of a forced marriage to a brute, her father's betrayal followed by his sudden death, the rush to flee her home. The coup, that tragedy that had befallen her country, her godfather's complicity. Exile in a cold country, living in a stranger's basement with her brother. No, Paulina was not like most girls her age, circumstances had forced her to grow up much faster, that was why she was so mature, so insightful.

Was she? Sylvia had given up her apartment, cancelled her phone, packed up all her belongings, spent her days off painting Paulina's walls a warm shade of yellow, and for what? To live with a deceitful, cowardly child. Yet the only way she could prove to Sylvia that she wasn't deceitful, wasn't a child—the jury was still out on the cowardly part—was by telling her the truth. They couldn't start their life together with a lie hanging over them, so Paulina chose one of Sylvia's rare days off to finally come clean.

It was raining that morning, a welcome, appropriately cleansing April rain they could smell through the open kitchen window. They were cuddled up on Paulina's impractical white sofa drinking tea, Paulina being extra careful not to spill on the upholstery. They'd been living together for a little over a month, long enough for Paulina to realize she never wanted to live alone again. The only wrinkle was the unspoken truth of how they'd met in the first place.

"Please don't be mad."

Not the best beginning, but she had to start somewhere. Sylvia's expression became serious, she even took her feet off the coffee table—hers, a solid dark wood, not Paulina's, which was in the second, still-unused bedroom, along with Sylvia's duplicate kitchen utensils and the other, extraneous items Sylvia planned to sell so they could turn the room into their study—and turned to face Paulina.

Paulina began with the bit about looking up Lesbian in the card catalogue, how she hadn't expected to find the word there, neatly typed, let alone so many lesbian-themed books. How she'd started with the names of the most recent borrowers of each book, beginning with Fiction.

"I looked up your address first," she said, so that Sylvia would know she was special. "Mr. Hirsch thought I was looking for an apartment. He showed me this one, across the hall from you."

Paulina meant this as proof that she and Sylvia were destined to be together but Sylvia just stared at her, in the same penetrating way the nuns at school would inspect the girls, watching for the unfocused gaze, flushed cheeks and swollen legs that betrayed a secret pregnancy.

"You signed a lease on a two-bedroom because of me?"

Paulina felt her face go red, red enough for a nun to pull her aside and tug at her waistband.

"You think I am crazy," she said, intending it to be a question, not a statement.

"I don't think you're crazy," Sylvia said. "Impulsive, definitely. What were you thinking?"

"I don't know. It just happened."

"Renting an apartment doesn't just happen. And all because of a book? A book I didn't even finish. That I just happened to take out from that library because it was near the hospital where I used to work. Crazy."

She was angry, but she wasn't in their bedroom packing a suitcase, like women did on television and in the movies after fighting with their husbands.

"So if you hadn't found me, you would have just tracked down the next woman?"

This hadn't occurred to her, but Sylvia was right. Paulina would have just kept working her way through her list of lesbian book borrowers. She might be living with some other library user now, if Mr. Hirsch hadn't appeared in the lobby and assumed she was there to look at apartments. What had she been thinking? It was crazy. She was crazy, and Sylvia knew it, and who in their right mind would live with a crazy girl?

"I didn't look up any other women," Paulina said. "Just you. I knew it was you. It was destiny."

A lie, but a modest one. A nice one.

"How is looking up someone's address in a phone book destiny?"

Sylvia was being playful, but she had a point. She was so smart, smarter than Paulina, smarter than anyone she'd ever known. She'd even explained Paulina's own body to her, insisting she squat over a mirror with a flashlight and feel her cervix, which either felt like a hard ball or her earlobe, depending on where she was in her cycle.

"Sometimes destiny must be pushed," Paulina finally responded.

Sylvia grinned at her. Maybe this would become something else to tease her about, like the posters from the old movies Sylvia had never heard of, now sharing wall space with Sylvia's framed seascapes, painted by her favourite auntie Gloria.

"Did you get that from a fortune cookie?"

"It was in the book you took out," Paulina said, another lie. But Sylvia laughed, just like she'd hoped she would, pulling Paulina down on top of her. Paulina reached for her thick hair, its soft, reassuring weight.

"Just don't lie to me again, okay?"

Paulina, inhaling the warm, musky scent of Sylvia's hair, promised she would never lie to her again, not as long as she lived.

"Are all you South Americans so impulsive and romantic?" Sylvia asked, helping Paulina out of her jeans.

Paulina, not wanting to ruin the moment, told her that yes, it was in her blood, South Americans would do anything for love. Except for Pinochet, of course, but Sylvia, head between Paulina's knees, had moved on, and so had Paulina.

— 2. —

THE NEXT DAY brought a phone bill with Nathan Weinrib's name listed at the top. When she saw it, Sylvia said their phone number should be in their names only, or at least hers. As far as the phone and utility companies were concerned, however, Paulina was still too young to be trusted to pay her bills on time, not without a guarantor. It wasn't fair, she told Sylvia:

"I always pay on time. They should just put my name."

"Well, they won't, and I don't like having some strange man's name on our bills."

"I can introduce you."

"That's not the point. It's all in his name, the bills, even the lease. That means it's all his. You told me he's getting a divorce. He might decide this place would be perfect for his new bachelor life. And who cares if the phone and hydro people think I live here alone? It doesn't change anything."

Paulina, also tired of seeing Nathan Weinrib's name on her bills, had to agree. In her case, his name was a guilty reminder of her failed promise to keep in touch. She should at least call, she owed him that much, but too much time had passed, it would feel strange and anyway, he already belonged to her past, her life before Sylvia Deborah Lewis.

Mr. Hirsch, like everyone in the building, assumed that she and Sylvia were just roommates. That Sylvia was a nurse made her seem like a big sister, nothing more, so Mr. Hirsch transferred the lease to Sylvia's name without question. It was a start, Sylvia said.

~

Alone in the elevator or laundry room, she and Sylvia might hold hands, even kiss, breaking apart if they heard someone approaching. They went further in the darkness of movie theatres; they were all over each other in the wooded corners of the ravine, but that was the extent of it. There were too many strikes against them, Sylvia said. First, she was Black and Paulina was a foreigner, and then there was the age gap. Without make-up, which she never wore, Paulina could easily pass for twelve. People, specifically white people, would think Sylvia was Paulina's nanny, and if Sylvia kissed her full on the mouth while they were waiting for the Bathurst bus they might call the police. Sylvia had heard enough stories about lesbians arrested while leaving their own bars and coffee shops, dragged to police stations, subjected to cavity searches, locked up overnight with prostitutes and drunks. One day things would change, but until then, they had to be careful.

Paulina didn't like to admit it, but the stolen kisses and caresses turned her on. They were in the closet, a terrible place to live, according to Sylvia's books, the ones Paulina read while Sylvia was at work. It felt like a betrayal of the gay liberation movement she was learning about, touching herself while she recalled Sylvia emerging sleek and wet from their local public pool. It was too thrilling, pretending this goddess was a stranger, that she wasn't on intimate terms with those heavy breasts inside the red swimsuit.

No, no one could know, not nice Mr. Hirsch, not their neighbours, not the lifeguard at the pool Sylvia suspected was also a lesbian, not Nathan Weinrib, and definitely not Paulina's brother, in the dark in Montreal.

~

Thanks to Paulina's agent it soon became even easier to hide, to pretend they were each living alone in the same apartment. The answering machine was Joyce's suggestion, that way she wouldn't miss any more calls about last-minute auditions, or that second callback for the table tennis champion part. Paulina had been relieved she'd missed that one. The machine would also save Paulina from worrying that Sylvia might answer the phone if her brother ever called her, not that he did. To save him the embarrassment of calling collect, Paulina called him once a week, when Sylvia was at work and she didn't have an audition or lines to record in the studio, those long days when she couldn't wait for Sylvia to come home and make her laugh, make her come alive. She felt so bleak, so hollowed-out, she might as well call her brother and listen to him talk to her like he was on the radio, transmitting his declarations that any day now their people would rise up, their country was not some banana republic ruled by caudillos, but a proud democracy.

Exiled Chileans all over the world were forming secret cells to topple Pinochet, or so he proclaimed. Paulina
assumed this was yet another marijuana-tinged fantasy,
like her brother's insistence that some exiles had even returned to Chile and were now living in secluded villages
under assumed names, preparing to continue the strug-
gle. A year, two at the most, then she and Ernesto and
all the exiles would be home, justice would be restored.

Ojalá, Paulina would respond. *Ojalá*, I wish, I hope,
I pray. A corruption, she remembered Sister Teresa saying, of the Arabic *O, Allah*, from when the Moors had
conquered Spain. But Paulina doubted any god could
help them, Muslim or Catholic.

To Paulina, and hopefully no one else, Ernesto proclaimed himself a resistance fighter in absentia, ready to
take up arms when the time came. Until then, he would
live in his barely furnished bachelor's apartment, on the
top floor of a triplex owned by an elderly Jewish couple
who reduced his rent in exchange for his services on the
Sabbath. From Friday to Saturday, starting and ending
at sundown, he shopped for them, shovelled their steps,
turned their lights on and off, as well as their appliances.
In return, Mrs. Rosenblatt brought him containers of
Jewish delicacies, and their daughter was teaching him
French and English, in addition to the Yiddish he was
picking up. Pinochet, he once told Paulina, didn't have
the *kishkes* to call a referendum and legitimize his rule.

"You sound like Tommy Lerner."

"Who is Tommy Lerner?"

During these calls, Paulina would tease Cleo with a
shoelace, the receiver stuck between her ear and her
shoulder, while her brother boasted of how he scraped

together a living, translating the poems and manifestoes of Quebec separatists into Spanish. He considered himself a separatist, an allegiance he hid from his landlords, along with the newly arrived exiles he invited to sleep on his floor so he could pump them for intelligence. Back home, he'd learned, people had lost all sense of solidarity. Most were happy to forget the coup, so long as Pinochet kept his promise to make Chile the economic jaguar of Latin America, with colour TV sets and washing machines for all. Paulina, recalling how Pilar had done their laundry by hand while she listened to the radio, didn't think this was such a bad thing, but she kept this to herself.

Chileans could only move forward, Ernesto said, by letting go of their delusions. For too long they'd believed they were the superior sort of South American:

"We are the English of South America, nothing like the Peruvians and Bolivians we conquered in war, no, we are cultured, we don't live in jungles, we are a land of poets, even our music is serious, no one dances the samba to the pan flute. It's all bullshit. How are we better than our neighbours? We have more priests than fleas, just like them."

Not once during these marathon calls did he show any interest in her. As far as he knew, Paulina was living alone in that cold, unremarkable city where he'd been called a spic and beaten to a pulp, a city he had no intention of ever seeing again, not even to visit his sister. Not that she wanted him to visit and disrupt her life with Sylvia, but he could at least ask her how she filled her hours, as Pilar used to say. Or watch an episode of *Animal Crackers* and tell her she was great in it, like everyone did. At least he never asked Paulina about her love life; all he talked about was himself.

Before hanging up, Paulina would promise to visit, when she wasn't so busy with the show. And she was busy; inside the recording studio confessional, she'd discovered a talent for mimicry, or what Ted and Susan called her vocal flexibility. They'd given her other roles to voice, mostly those of the children, boys and girls, who visited the zoo. This meant more money, and more time in her favourite place, after her apartment.

Thankfully, Ernesto never pushed her to keep her promise, even before Christmas, so she was free to spend it with Sylvia, but still. Did he think she spent the holidays alone? He probably thought she'd gone to the Weinribs. Just because he'd stopped observing all holidays except for the anniversary of the coup, didn't mean she had.

Now thanks to this marvellous new machine she wouldn't have to worry about Sylvia answering should Ernesto ever call. Better he believed she lived alone than to have to lie and say Sylvia was just a roommate. Anyway, Sylvia also feared Paulina picking up at the wrong time, so Paulina never answered her own phone, letting the machine screen their callers, weeding out Sylvia's relatives, the occasional heavy-breathing pervert. Joyce was right; the machine, while expensive, was a godsend.

— 3. —

ON HER FREE evenings Sylvia brought Paulina to the old Victorian house northeast of Yonge and Bloor that everyone called The Home for Wayward Daughters. A group of women, known as the Elders, had pooled their money to buy the place. It was meant to be the headquarters for a new feminist collective, the name of which was still being debated, so for the time being everyone just called it The Home.

The feminists Paulina met at The Home were nothing like the glamorous, forbidding Helen Koenigsman. Once, she'd overheard a woman in overalls and little else refer to Paulina's former benefactress as an armchair activist, writing her newspaper column from her chic apartment, supported by a rich and powerful husband. Another, older woman countered that Helen Koenigsman had opened the door for women like themselves, that she gave large sums to the right people. People like Paulina, who still had a good chunk of the money the Koenigsmans had raised for her, but she kept this to herself, not that she would have been able to interject, as yet another furious debate was now underway. Only Sylvia knew about the money and like Ernesto, she expected Paulina to use it for university.

Paulina and Sylvia attended the dances and concerts the women organized, as fundraisers for their renovations. The rooms, many of which did not have doors, or if they did, doors that would not close properly, were full of old, mismatched furniture bought at garage sales. The women, particularly the Elders, were becoming self-taught electricians, carpenters, floor sanders, and plumbers. Bit by bit the old house was becoming more liveable, but it was always lively, thanks to the stereo in the main room, or parlour, as everyone called it. From the blackened gas range in the kitchen came plates of food, happily not always vegetarian, to be eaten off paper plates.

Being with women and women only, a first, thrilled Paulina—less so the endless, often contradictory debates. Even though she was doing her best to get through Sylvia's books, she was afraid to ask questions, let alone share an opinion. Probably no one expected a high school dropout to have much to say. Sylvia had accepted her explanation that exile had come between Paulina and her high-school diploma, if not her driver's licence. When the time was right, she would go back to school but Paulina knew she would never set foot in a classroom again, not one full of snotty teenagers, like her and Lorraine.

Yet Sylvia, well-educated, was also silent during these debates. In her case, she was waiting for the women to address class and race. It was hard, she said, being the only Black woman at The Home, but equally hard on those evenings when another Black woman showed up and everyone expected Sylvia to gravitate toward her or worse, to already know her. When she talked like that Paulina would feel guilty for sometimes wondering if Sylvia and Valerie might have been friends.

They were all white women, but Sylvia did like the Elders, especially Deirdre Zeldin. Paulina liked her, too. They'd first met Deirdre at a fundraiser for a legal defence fund for lesbian mothers, those women who'd lost custody of children to ex-husbands because a judge had deemed them unfit. Deirdre's protruding blue eyes and thinning eyebrows were probably the result of a thyroid condition, Sylvia said. Paulina wondered if this condition also explained her nervous energy. Even seated and silent she seemed in constant motion. Yet when she spoke her voice was soft and low, seductive even. To Paulina, she was larger than life, like all great actors were supposed to be. Like she herself wanted to be.

~

One warm June night during a potluck dinner to raise funds for a new roof, Deirdre Zeldin rushed into the parlour. There was just enough champagne for everyone, she said, popping the cork, laughing. She was about to pour some into Paulina's glass when Sylvia stopped her:

"What if there's a police raid?"

"I will be nineteen in October."

"And you look thirteen."

"If the pigs show up we'll hustle her outside," Deirdre told Sylvia, pouring Paulina a glass, but only a quarter full. "Let her celebrate."

"What are we celebrating?" Paulina asked. The champagne tasted fresh and sharp, better than what she'd been served after *Pericles* had closed.

"Dr. Henry Morgentaler has been acquitted of all charges," Deirdre said, joining her and Sylvia on the floor, where they were sitting on cushions. The parlour, used for meetings, did not have a sofa, just a few chairs and a lot of floor cushions.

"The abortion doctor?" Paulina remembered his name from the news. She and Sylvia sometimes watched before bed, although Sylvia usually dozed off a few minutes in.

The very same, Deirdre said.

"They put him in prison, in solitary confinement. Him, a Holocaust survivor. Barbaric."

Dr. Morgentaler had been charged with the crime of providing abortions to any woman who came to his clinic without, as Bernadette, one of the other Elders said, making her go through "the whole sorry, patriarchal song-and-dance" of having to convince male doctors her life was in danger.

"It's almost like they don't want women to have abortions," Hannah said. She was Bernadette's partner.

"That's why I used to make my appointment for one before getting laid," said Sophie. She was Hannah's former partner. Sylvia said some of the women at The Home treated relationships like a game of musical chairs.

"Deirdre was in the first abortion caravan," Sylvia told Paulina. "They drove across the country, took over the House of Commons."

"I drove the car with the coffin on top. The papers called us shrill abortion promoters. Everyone else called us hussies."

The champagne must have brought it on, this memory, so sudden and painful that Paulina had to close her eyes.

"I knew a girl," she said.

"We all did," Sylvia said, stroking her hair. "That's the problem."

"What was her name?" Deirdre asked.

"Marcela."

Paulina put down her celebratory champagne and began to tell Marcela's story, the story she'd kept like a secret. In a way, it was her secret, too.

~

Pilar said that if Paulina ever got into trouble she would brew her a special herbal concoction, but lots of girls drank their housekeeper's teas and were still sent away, or worse. Girls like Marcela.

It hurt to remember it, how Paulina had wanted Inez for her best friend, but while she was waiting Inez had chosen Flor and Marcela was the only one left. You couldn't be in the group for long if you didn't have a best friend, so they became Paulina and Marcela. Not that they had much in common. Marcela was as baby-crazy as the other girls, stopping in the middle of the street whenever she spotted a baby carriage. Paulina had to stand awkwardly beside her while she cooed and tickled the poor creature, who didn't know Marcela from a can of condensed milk.

Babies held no special allure for Paulina. Not because her own mother had died after giving birth to her—her father and even Pilar had told her she'd died of measles, not childbirth—no, the whole, bloody prospect terrified her. Anyway, babies were boring, she made the mistake of finally telling Marcela.

Marcela had smiled at her, a smug, hateful smile. There was something wrong with her, she'd said. Paulina wasn't a normal woman; she should see a doctor.

That night, Paulina prayed for Marcela to die in childbirth. Instead, she got a boyfriend. Where do they get virgin wool, Diego had asked Paulina when Marcela introduced them. From the fastest sheep, Paulina had said before he could. She thought he might hit her, his face got so red. Marcela just giggled, throwing her arms around him. Paulina was glad when, a few months later, a sobbing Marcela told her that Diego's father was sending him away to a boarding school in Europe, lest he be corrupted by Allende's Marxist Chile.

Despite her heartbreak, Marcela seemed to be always eating, and when she wasn't, she was licking her fingers, brushing crumbs from her skirt. The other girls began calling her *la china*, the Chinese, because her face was so swollen her eyes looked half-closed. They all made fun of her, Paulina included, right up till the day the coup closed the schools.

Paulina forgot about fat Marcela, probably would never have thought of her again but then one morning she saw Marcela's mother in the line for cooking oil, her thick black hair now sparse and white.

"Poor woman," Pilar said as they walked past. "That girl was her only child."

Some girls waited until it was too late to do anything about their condition, hoping no one would notice how far along they were. Then they became desperate, Pilar said. They went to doctors who weren't really doctors, but butchers.

"Is that what happened to Marcela?" Paulina asked, but Pilar wouldn't tell her, no matter how many times she asked.

"She died," Bernadette said. Sylvia said the Elders did not "mince their words."

"Poor kid," said Hannah.

"I should have helped her," Paulina said.

"How?" asked Sophie.

"You couldn't have done anything to help her," Deirdre said, as Sylvia wiped away Paulina's tears with her sleeve. "But there are a lot of other women you can help now."

— 4. —

At seven each morning Sylvia put on her new eye mask, inserted a pair of foam earplugs into her ears, and joined Paulina in bed, falling into a deep sleep that lasted until late in the afternoon. Their bedroom door had to be kept open, otherwise Cleo would scratch and meow to be let in and out, waking her up. Sylvia was not to be woken.

Around nine Paulina would get out of bed. Afraid of waking Sylvia, she moved about the apartment as if underwater or on the moon, slowly opening drawers and cabinets, not flushing the toilet, keeping the volume on the TV barely audible, like she had when her brother was working the night shift at the bread factory. She couldn't even turn on the standing fan, no matter how hot it was, because Sylvia said she could hear it, even from the bedroom.

From three to five each afternoon Paulina had Sylvia to herself, barring an audition or a recording session. When she was awake, Sylvia talked about her work and little else. The surprising amount of paperwork. The sometimes tedious, always anxious monitoring of patients. It was hard, she said, not knowing what they needed, if she was even helping them. Paulina imagined a ward full of pod people, but Sylvia said it wasn't creepy or scary, her patients were in artificial comas so that their hearts could heal.

Sylvia had landed what she called her dream job, tending to patients in the intensive cardiac care unit of the city's largest hospital, not long after she and Paulina had started volunteering at The Home. For the first few months of her dream job Sylvia had to work, perhaps appropriately, the night shift, leaving her no free time, let alone the energy to write MPs, but it was better than the nursing home. On her last day Mrs. Brandt had accused her of stealing the cotton balls that came in her pill bottles, insisting the home's director search Sylvia's purse in front of her. It wasn't the first time Mrs. Mendes had gone through the motions of searching for some supposedly stolen treasure, a broken watch or dried-out pen that always turned up later, clogging a toilet or gathering dust under a bed. But it would be the last, for Sylvia.

If not for The Home, Paulina would have willingly gone into an artificial coma herself, so lonely was she with only two hours of Sylvia a day. Because she worked part-time for the city's board of education, Deirdre wasn't always at her office at The Home but it didn't matter, Paulina stuffed envelopes just the same, to the sounds of hammering and laughter. The house was always full of women, and soon she was invited to share their meals, even help with the renovations, tearing out rotting floorboards, priming and painting baseboards, touching up the crown moulding that was a much-loved feature of the house.

Over the summer and into the fall, Paulina became so busy with *Animal Crackers*, auditions, and The Home, that she sometimes forgot Sylvia, ministering to her pod people across town.

~

After a month of letter-writing Deirdre said she was ready to petition. Paulina was pleased; getting people to sign something felt more active, more urgent, although at first she was too nervous to approach anyone, hanging back as Deirdre flagged down a man in a business suit. Paulina was certain he'd balk, maybe call for the police, but he signed, as did most people. Most but not all. When this happened Deirdre would hurry Paulina down Yonge Street, pretending not to hear the shouting at their backs. Time for a much-deserved break, she'd say. They'd get doughnuts or ice cream, and while they ate Deirdre would tell her that while it might not feel like it, they were making the world safer for women.

Soon Paulina could spot the body language of those hostile to their cause, although some people surprised her, like the hairy man in the white undershirt who called them ladies and told them to keep fighting the good fight.

She was so busy that she almost forgot the second anniversary of the coup, but not Ernesto. When she called him that night he told her about his new girl-friend, yet another university student he'd met at the park on yet another of those Sunday afternoons he spent listening to the drummers, sharing their dope. Maude practised numerology, and she'd crunched the numbers for him. Democracy would return to Chile in time for next year's anniversary of the coup.

"Ojalá," Paulina said. They made their usual noises about Paulina visiting before saying goodbye.

~

One day while they were canvassing Deirdre asked Paulina if she had time to come to her office after they were done. She had something important to show her. Paulina wondered if this might be a present, to thank her for volunteering. Deirdre was like that, she thought. Generous, and genuinely interested in her, so much so that Paulina almost looked forward to some stranger accusing them of promoting infanticide, so they could hasten to the nearest coffee shop and talk. The last time this had happened she'd told Deirdre about dropping out of school—for Sir Jerome Mason and Shakespeare —and how afraid she was to return to the classroom. Deirdre reassured Paulina that she could get her diploma without going to school. When she was ready, of course. Paulina agreed to let the idea marinate, as Deirdre put it.

Maybe Deirdre had some textbooks in her office for her. Paulina was still marinating, but there was no harm in accepting them.

"I can't stay too long," she told her. "I have an audition at three."

"We'll get you there on time," Deirdre said. "What's the audition for?"

"A commercial, for a sports equipment store. They want girls to skateboard."

"Can you skateboard?"

"No, but it doesn't matter. I won't get it anyway."

As they walked to The Home, Paulina told Deirdre about her dry spell. It was normal, Joyce kept saying. At least Paulina had *Animal Crackers*. But it was depressing, getting so many auditions, even callbacks, but not booking anything. Was there something wrong with her?

"Maybe you want it too much," Deirdre said. "Next time, walk into the room like you don't care, like you're just meeting a friend."

"I'll try," Paulina said but she doubted she could pull it off. How was she supposed to breeze into the room when she still worried about encountering another pervert producer who wouldn't even cast her in the role? So far she'd been lucky, her auditions had been brief failures, very professional, *thank you for coming in, we'll be in touch with Joyce*. She hadn't had to defend her person, as Sir Jerome would say, with the small kitchen knife she kept in her tote bag. But it was too awful, being rejected for bit parts, mostly maids and housekeepers, largely silent young women who worked with their hands and spoke only a few lines.

Deirdre's office, still doorless, always looked like it had been ransacked by movie detectives. Strange, then, that she kept her filing cabinet locked. Paulina watched as Deirdre unlocked the bottom drawer, carefully sliding it out.

"Voila," she said, placing the object wrapped in brown paper on the desk beside her typewriter.

"I think it's time you met the Del-Em 1971. I picked her up a while ago, in California."

Deirdre unwrapped what turned out to be an ordinary glass jar, but then Paulina saw the two tubes attached to the lid, like long, curling straws. It reminded her of Pilar's gourd for drinking maté, which came with a metal straw to filter out the leaves as you drank. Paulina found the taste too weedy, but Pilar said it was better for you than coffee. Was this some ceremonial beverage, to commemorate her activism?

Deirdre lifted up the longer of the two clear plastic tubes, like the tendril of some fragile plant.

"This part's the cannula. A medical straw, to extract fluid. The cannula goes inside the uterus, and then you pump the syringe, this part here, and it goes through the tube and into the jar. Now that abortion's legal in the States it's not used as much. But we could use it here."

"Does it hurt?"

It had to be agonizing, but Deirdre said it wasn't painful, just uncomfortable. And much safer than a wire hanger or any of the other methods desperate women used to terminate unwanted pregnancies.

"I saw it demonstrated at Berkeley, all you need are two pairs of hands. Officially, it's called a Menstrual Extractor. Unofficially, they call it the lunch-hour abortion, you can have it done and be back at work that afternoon. Providing it's early enough in a pregnancy. It's a short window but it works."

No more relying on male doctors; they could do it themselves. They should print up posters, Deirdre said, promising women a chicken in every pot, a Del-Em in every bathroom.

They were easy to make, too; they could set up a Del-Em factory, hand them out at Christmas.

To Paulina, the device looked handcrafted but sturdy, made with love and ingenuity, she was sure of it, like the oranges Sylvia pierced with cloves to put in her ham stock, the vibrant quilts the Elders tacked to the walls of The Home to disguise water stains.

"I've been getting the word out," Deirdre said, wrapping up the Del-Em. "I was thinking maybe you could give a talk in Spanish. Here at The Home? We could invite women, immigrants, refugees, who might not know they have options."

That day Paulina left Deirdre's office with the phone number for the Centre for Spanish-Speaking Peoples. She couldn't wait to tell Sylvia about the Del-Em, so excited that she was tempted to skip her audition and catch Sylvia before she left for work, but Joyce would be angry and she was eager to see if Deirdre was right about acting like she didn't care if she got the part. Anyway, tomorrow was Sylvia's day off. She could tell her then.

~

"No fucking way."

"But Deirdre says it's safe, and so easy a child could operate it."

Paulina was sounding like a child herself, but she couldn't help it, not when Sylvia was actually forbidding her from laying hands on any and all abortion devices:

"I don't care what Deirdre says, there's always a risk of infection."

Their kitchen smelled of fish and salt. Slabs of whitened cod were in a pan on the counter, getting soft and slippery. Sylvia said the secret was to keep the salt cod in water long enough for it to start swimming.

"They used it in America and no one died."

Sylvia said she couldn't care less what they did in America.

"It's illegal and if something goes wrong, who do you think they'll go after, the white Canadians, or you?"

She rinsed her hands, then led Paulina out of the kitchen to the sofa where they had their serious talks. First, though, she stroked Paulina's hair with fingers that still smelled of cod. Paulina would have to wash and style her already washed and styled hair for tomorrow's audition. Joyce said it wasn't the lead but still a big part, in what she called a slasher flick, but that didn't mean Paulina should show up smelling like a fish market, not if she was going to follow Deirdre's advice and walk into the room like she was between two amusing errands and thought it might be a gas, to quote Deirdre, pretending to be the ghost of an Indian priestess back to avenge her people. She'd tried it at yesterday's audition and it had worked, sort of. Joyce said they wanted someone sporty but they'd keep her in mind for their next ad campaign.

"I don't want you getting into trouble, Polly. Stay behind the scenes. Leave that thing to Deirdre."

"She asked me to give a talk, in Spanish. At The Home. I'm going to tell them about the Del-Em."

"Please tell me you didn't advertise it as such."

"No. Deirdre said to just say it's about women's health. Anyway, it's just a jar. If the police come we will tell them we are making jam."

Paulina braced herself for more probing and forbidding, but Sylvia was smiling.

"Alright then. Sing them a song about that thing if you want, just don't go near it when it's in action. When's your talk?"

"It's in the evening," Paulina said. "When you're working."

Cleo jumped up on the sofa, curling up between them. Sylvia rubbed her chin, Paulina her belly, Cleo chirping and purring.

"Things will be better when I'm on the day shift. We'll spend more time together. We'll learn to play tennis, like I promised."

"It's been forever," Paulina said.

"Only a few months more, Polly."

For a moment Paulina thought Sylvia might rub her chin, too, but instead she kissed her on the forehead before returning to the kitchen.

From the sofa Paulina offered to peel the potatoes but Sylvia said not to bother. It took Paulina forever and she risked slicing off a finger.

— 5. —

PAULINA ARRIVED AT The Home that wet evening in early October to find the parlour full of Spanish speakers, like an all-woman version of one of Ernesto's basement peñas. She was so distracted that she nearly collided with Deirdre carrying a kitchen stool into the room. Paulina helped her bring in more chairs until there was just Deirdre's office chair, which they rolled in and gave to one of the older women. She sat on it, purse in her lap, like she had an appointment with her child's principal or a bank manager.

Deirdre ushered Paulina into the hallway, as more women were filing into the parlour.

"They were told it started at six, not seven. The woman at the centre got the time wrong. I tried to explain that you'd be here at six-thirty. Can you start now? There must be at least thirty women here."

Deirdre was positively vibrating, hands flying, sparse eyebrows twitching. Paulina was buzzing, too. She followed Deirdre back inside the parlour, the women turning to look at Deirdre, not her. They probably thought they were here to listen to the giant white woman tell them about birth control, not the scrawny bird-like creature in the black and red checked jumper, red tights, and turtleneck. Why had she dressed like a schoolgirl, and not a grown woman like Deirdre in her velvet skirt and patchwork blouse?

Paulina was halfway through the crowded room when a woman jogged over to her, beaming.

"Paulina? I'm Luisa. We spoke over the phone?"

So the director of the Centre was here, too. She was looking forward to the talk, she told Paulina, in Spanish. All the women were Spanish-speaking, some Chilean, but also Colombian, Ecuadorian, Argentinean, Uruguayan. What in his sociology days Ernesto would have called a good cross-section of South American subjects.

Paulina had never been so nervous, not backstage during *Pericles*, not at any audition. As she walked past the women now watching her, no doubt wondering what this child was doing here, she tried and failed to summon the light, off-hand attitude she now channelled for auditions. By the time she reached the defunct fireplace where Deirdre had set up a podium she was trembling, and there was a bitter taste in her mouth, like she'd been sucking on pennies.

Deirdre, leaning in the doorway, gave her the thumbs-up.

Paulina looked out at her audience. For days she'd agonized over how best to introduce her topic, finally settling on five words that pleased even Sylvia, five words that, Deirdre had joked, would separate the men from the boys:

"Welcome to the abortion underground," she said, in Spanish.

A few gasps, some nervous laughter, but no one ran out of the room in horror, even when Deirdre placed the Del-Em on the podium next to Paulina's index cards.

~

Deirdre had warned Paulina that these talks usually turned into what she called rap sessions. Women were eager to finally share their stories, even the shyest among them and so, when Paulina was done explaining the restrictive, time-consuming process of obtaining an abortion in Canada, she wasn't surprised when the silent women erupted in chatter. Neither was Deirdre, who passed Paulina the stripped and bleached tree branch used at The Home as a talking stick.

If only she understood Spanish, Deirdre said. Maybe Paulina could tell her what she'd missed when Deirdre drove her home.

Paulina passed the stick to the older woman seated in Deirdre's office chair, who needed no instructions for its use. On her feet, stick in one hand, purse in the other, she spoke of her closest childhood friend dying of cancer in their Colombian village:

"Her husband, a real macho, wouldn't let a doctor examine her breast until it was too late."

"It happens all the time," said another, older woman as she reached for the stick. "Even if their husbands allow it, women are either too embarrassed, or they don't know to ask for such exams."

"I grew up learning more about the anatomy of a chicken than my own body," said another woman, this one middle-aged. Stick in hand, she told them she'd had her first child, a stillbirth, at age fifteen.

The younger women were even more open, sharing horror stories of illegal abortions, theirs and those of friends and relatives. The money saved for school or begged from a boyfriend or relative, now in the dirty hands of some stranger. The men who took advantage, the perverts who kept underpants as souvenirs. The table still bloodied from the last woman. Women providers were not much better, they all agreed. Some were just ignorant, selling overpriced herbs that sickened but didn't work. Some cursed their patients even as they performed the abortion. Others butchered you so badly you could never have children again.

"She said she did me a favour," said one tearful woman, whose abortionist had sterilized her without telling her. That such carnage had occurred in a city as sophisticated as Buenos Aires shocked Paulina. What horrors had Marcela endured, up in the hills of Valparaíso?

Deirdre whispered to Paulina that the subway was about to close, she should wrap things up. Had they been talking for that long? Still standing behind her podium, Paulina could have listened all night, but she relayed Deirdre's message to the women. They thanked her before hurrying out the door, all except one woman, silently approaching the podium Paulina had been using as a shield of sorts, a flimsy barrier against the pain and sorrow the women exhaled into the very air.

The woman wore an ugly brown jacket that was too big for her, perhaps a cast-off from the same church where Paulina had reluctantly selected her first winter jacket. As if in defiance of having to wear something no one would pay good money for, the woman had matched her nail polish to her lipstick, a hard, cherry-red.

Stammering, her face pink, Gladys told Paulina how she hadn't had a period since fleeing Santiago. Last week, a volunteer had taken her to a doctor, who'd confirmed her worst fear.

"My husband doesn't know," she said, dabbing her eyes with her glove.

Paulina guessed she was in her thirties. By Chilean standards she should have at least two children by now, but Gladys had never been pregnant before, the doctors had told her she couldn't have children. Yet here she was.

"Is it too late for me?"

Paulina was about to translate but Deirdre's expression told her it wasn't necessary.

"Ask her when her last period was," she said.

When Paulina told her, Deirdre lit a cigarette. It felt like they were bank robbers in a movie, plotting who would drive the runaway car.

"It's still early enough," Deirdre said, exhaling smoke. "But she shouldn't wait. We can do it now if she wants."

"I have money," Gladys said, in Spanish.

Deirdre, noticing her open purse, told Paulina to tell Gladys that buttons were available for ten cents.

Paulina gave Gladys a *Wages for Domestic Workers* button. Deirdre, smiling, took her dime, then led them both upstairs.

~

They had just settled Gladys on the sofa in Hannah's office, the only one with a door, a homemade quilt draped over her lower body, when she grabbed Paulina's arm.

"What is it?" Deirdre asked. "Has she changed her mind?"

"She wants us to know what happened, why she doesn't want the baby."

The blood was pounding in Paulina's ears as she looked down at Gladys's pale face. Whenever someone mentioned a woman prisoner of the regime, the exiles at Ernesto's peñas would exchange looks, conversation would cease. No one dared say what everyone was thinking. Women, like Carmen's brother Mario, were subject to an additional form of torture that no one had wanted to acknowledge.

But Deirdre said it didn't matter why she was there:

"Tell her there's no such thing as a bad abortion or a good abortion. She doesn't want to continue with her pregnancy, that's all we need to know."

Paulina looked down into Gladys's terrified, teary face.

"We don't need to know why," she told her in Spanish.

Gladys closed her eyes and loosened her grip on the blanket, pulled up to her chin, like a child afraid of nightmares.

Deirdre pulled on a pair of latex gloves, as did Paulina, though hers were too big. Not that she really needed them; to her relief Deirdre would insert the cannula inside Gladys, hold it in place while Paulina pumped the syringe.

Deirdre pushed up the quilt, revealing Gladys's naked, lower half. She showed Gladys her speculum.

"It looks like a duck," Paulina said in Spanish, hoping a joke might help her relax. Gladys smiled faintly, then closed her eyes.

"Tell her I'm inserting the cannula," Deirdre said, but Paulina could tell by the way Gladys's body had stiffened that she already knew.

"Does it hurt?" Paulina asked.

"It feels strange," Gladys said, eyes still closed.

It was go-time, Deirdre said, her expression grim. Paulina began pumping the syringe, afraid nothing would happen, that she wasn't strong enough, that she might somehow hurt Gladys, but then she saw the tube fill with a dark red fluid, down the tube and into the jar, so she kept pumping, trying to steady her hands, imagining it was Marcela lying stiff on the sofa, it was Marcela's life she was saving, Marcela's future she was protecting.

She'd anticipated a smell, of something intimate and exposed, but the room smelled the same as all the other rooms in the house, of paint and sanded wood.

"Is it working?" Gladys asked, eyes now open.

"We're almost there," Deirdre said.

Deirdre held on to her end while Paulina pumped, it seemed like they would be there forever, and Gladys hadn't moved or made a sound in what seemed an alarmingly long time, but then the blood slowed until it stopped and Deirdre said they were done, it was over, she was taking out the tube.

Deirdre looked at her watch.

"Not even twenty minutes."

It had felt like hours, but Deirdre was right. She took the jar from Paulina and left for the bathroom.

Gladys sat up, the colour returned to her face. Paulina was about to ask her if she needed water when Gladys, in a small voice, asked Paulina to pray with her.

Paulina had not prayed since leaving Chile, and school. Like Sylvia she no longer believed, but she followed Gladys's lead and crossed herself, the two women holding hands as Gladys led them in the Lord's Prayer.

— 6. —

THEY WERE PUTTING on their boots when the phone rang. They let the machine pick up, but then Paulina heard her brother's voice asking if she was home, he had to speak to her, it was important. Probably calling because he'd realized he'd missed her birthday, which she'd celebrated at a Halloween party at The Home while Sylvia was at work. Paulina had borrowed Sylvia's scrubs for a costume, and Deirdre had surprised her with a chocolate cake with nineteen blazing candles. Make a wish, she'd said, and Paulina, blowing hard, wished for Sylvia to finally be transferred to the day shift.

Paulina turned off the machine, picked up the receiver, about to tell Ernesto not to worry about her birthday, she was on her way out, to save his money, she'd call him later, when she heard him say Guzmán was dead. No *hello, how are you*, just, *our godfather is dead, at last, the old bastard is dead. He's been dead for months.*

"He died?" Paulina could not imagine her godfather old and frail, let alone dying.

"A massive stroke while watching his horses race at the track. Of course, the papers say he went peacefully in his bed, surrounded by loved ones, not shouting at a horse in Santiago."

"What are you talking about? How do you know all this?"

"From Manuel. He's here, in Montreal."

"Where is Pilar? Is she in Canada?"

Already she was thinking she would ask Ted and Susan if she could record her scenes in advance, tell Joyce she'd be gone for a few weeks, unless Pilar came to Toronto, but then where would Sylvia go?

"Paulita. I'm sorry."

Cancer, her brother said. It had spread so fast, no doctor could help her.

"Paulina," her brother kept saying. "Listen to me. Manuel is here. He made it here."

She listened in numb silence as Ernesto told her all that had happened after they'd left, filling in those blank months. How Pilar had stayed at the house to work for Guzmán, how Manuel had showed up one night, how they'd pretended he was the gardener.

How Manuel had turned Pío into a drug addict.

The man who would have been Paulina's husband liked to unwind from torturing prisoners with a joint or two. Sensing an opportunity, Manuel started plying him with their father's painkillers, which Pilar had stashed in her hut, eventually introducing him to heroin, procured from his dock-worker friends:

"When Manuel told them who it was for, they gave it to him for free."

With their godfather dead, Pío had sold their father's house, used the money for more drugs.

"Manuel says he's in Peru, lost in the jungle, out of his mind on drugs."

"Are you sure?"

"You can ask him yourself, when you see him."

"He's coming to Toronto?"

"Why would he do that? When you come here. There's a lot to do, but we're not alone. So far there's five of us going back. Felipe, you'll meet him, he's forging our papers, his father was a notary."

From Santiago they'd drive north to San Pedro, where someone had a cousin who ran a hotel and could give them jobs. They'd start an underground cell that would go unnoticed in the world's driest desert, joining the network of clandestine activists chipping away at the regime, illegitimate and bound to fall.

When it was safe, they would visit their father's grave, seek out their mother's people, kept from them by their father.

"Is everything okay?" Sylvia asked, watching Paulina slowly hang up the receiver. "You look like someone's died."

"Yes," Paulina said, waiting for the room to come back into focus.

"Yes, everything's okay, or yes someone's died? Polly?"

At last the room was taking on its familiar shapes. Paulina got up, put on her jacket. Sylvia held her by her waist.

"Tell me what he said."

It all came out in a numb rush. When she was done, Sylvia said they were staying home. Paulina was in shock.

"Please," Paulina said. "I can't stay here. I want to go."

"Are you sure?"

"Yes. Please. Tonight you do not work. Let's go."

Sylvia got up and put on her coat. Her mother's fur.

The coat, so wrong on Paulina, fit Sylvia perfectly. Like it had been made for her.

~

They were leaving with their Christmas tree, or festive sapling, as Sylvia called it, when Paulina heard her name shouted from across the parking lot where vendors were selling wreaths and children's mittens.

In her rush to pretend that nothing had happened and everything was normal, Paulina had forgotten how close the Christmas market was to the Centre for Spanish-Speaking Peoples.

"We had a language class," Gladys told Paulina when she reached her, red-cheeked and panting. "We came here to practise our English."

"And buy gifts," said one of the other women, also in Spanish. Paulina recognized her as the older woman whose best friend had died of breast cancer.

Pilar. Had the same cancer taken her, too? Had she, too, avoided the doctor until it was too late, out of shame?

A flurry of introductions followed, each woman kissing Paulina and Sylvia on the cheek, in shifting configurations. Gladys and Sylvia were the last to embrace.

"Paulina saved my life," Gladys told Sylvia, in English. "Has saved my life?"

"I think either tense is fine," Sylvia said, her smile frozen.

"Thank Jesus for the Del-Em," said one of the women, pointing to the Portuguese church ahead of them.

The women, laughing, rushed off, to buy Christmas wreaths, they said.

At first Paulina thought Sylvia might not be upset, the way she just stood silently, fiddling with the ends of her scarf, looking off in the direction of the laughing women. She would keep her anger to herself, she wouldn't want to upset Paulina, still reeling from Ernesto's news.

But then Sylvia turned to face her, blinking as if trying not to cry, her mouth hanging open. It was worse than anything she could say, that look, or so Paulina believed, until Sylvia grabbed her by the arm and pulled her back inside the rows of Christmas trees.

"How stupid are you?"

"You're hurting me."

"You think you can go around performing illegal abortions? What happens when you get caught? That girl could have died. She could have gone septic and died. You lied to me."

"It's safe," Paulina said, her wisp of a voice lost among the trees. "You see her, she is fine."

"You don't know what's safe. There is always, always, a risk of infection. And what if one of those women tells the police you're performing illegal abortions?"

"They will not. They are afraid of police. All police."

"They should be. I could kill you for being so stupid."

"Then kill me."

Paulina was sobbing, loud enough for someone to hear, not that anyone could hear her over the stupid Christmas music. Sylvia was crying, too, saying it was her fault for accepting the night shift; she was either at work or sleeping, she wasn't around to keep Paulina, too young to know better, out of trouble. Paulina who was just a teenager, not the old soul she'd thought she was, but reckless, flighty. As if to prove her right, Paulina took flight. She almost ran into a tree, then she was swerving to avoid shoppers as she ran past the stalls, Gladys and the other women a blur in her peripheral vision, their voices drowned out by Christmas music and her pounding heart.

~

Inside the apartment the living-room light was on, and there was a note from Sylvia on the coffee table: *you have a message.*

Probably her brother, furious with her for hanging up on him. She pressed the button, bracing herself; instead, it was Joyce, apologizing for calling so late but she had good news. Paulina had booked *Crooked Prairie*. It meant a month in freezing Saskatchewan, but the shoot was mostly indoors, except for that scene of Paulina's character running through the snow, chasing the horny teenagers she'd been haunting. She was not to worry; Joyce would make sure she didn't freeze to death on set. She'd give her all the details when she signed her contract. Paulina would have to grow out her hair, lose the Louise Brooks bangs, but if there wasn't enough time, she could wear a wig. It was a low-budget production, but they could spring for her hair.

Through the bedroom door, left open just enough for Cleo, Paulina could hear Sylvia's strangled snoring.

Lying facedown on the sofa, still tasting the coffee she'd been drinking at the doughnut shop near their apartment, Paulina pressed her face into the cushions, again and again, but it was hopeless. Try as she might, she couldn't stop herself coming up for air.

— 7. —

TED AND SUSAN said it was good timing—*Animal Crackers* was pausing production so they could work on a new project. Paulina hoped there might be a part in it for her, but she knew better than to ask. If they wanted her, they could call her agent.

June said the role, Paulina's first in a movie, was the start of something big.

"We'll be saying we knew you then."

Ruth had said the same when she'd come to the opening night of *Pericles*. Why did people say that? What did it mean?

"You know me now," Paulina said, but June thought she was joking, and gave her another heavily perfumed hug.

Tommy Lerner gave her a more pungent hug, and some advice:

"Making a movie's not like coming here, recording a few lines, and leaving. There's a lot of sitting on your tush, waiting for the crew to set up."

Paulina, recalling the tedium of *Prince of Cabbagetown*, looked around the pokey, windowless room where she'd waited for her turn in the recording studio, the sofa where Tommy Lerner liked to nap, and fart, the sagging armchair where June drank tea and did her puzzles.

"I'll get my high school diploma," she said.

June said that was a wonderful idea. Even Tommy Lerner, so proud of dropping out of high school during the Depression to support himself, grunted his approval.

She would study on set, do her homework between takes. Maybe knowing that she was finally getting her diploma would make Sylvia feel better about her going to Saskatchewan. She was still angry with Paulina for waiting nearly two weeks to tell her about the shoot.

"Are you taking the Del-Em with you out west?" she'd asked.

For weeks she'd been making bitter jokes about the device. When Paulina said they should finally decorate their tree, Sylvia said sure, did Paulina have any abortifacients she'd like to use as ornaments? But she was the first to put a present under the tree, a small box with a red ribbon and silver wrapping. Paulina tried wrapping Sylvia's gift so that she wouldn't guess what it was, but it was hard to disguise two tennis rackets.

Every time Sylvia made a joke about the Del-Em, Paulina would remember Gladys, how happy she'd looked at the Christmas market. Sylvia kept pushing her to say she regretted it, that it had been a stupid mistake, but Paulina refused. Sylvia would never understand, just like she couldn't understand why Paulina felt so sad about the death of her despotic godfather and her aging housekeeper. Sylvia said she just couldn't "get her head around it."

One afternoon when Sylvia was drinking coffee before her shift, lecturing Paulina yet again about the dangers of blood poisoning, Paulina, without thinking, blurted out that Gladys had been raped.

"In Chile?"

Paulina nodded. She didn't need to say anything more, Sylvia's imagination would supply the dark, filthy cell, the soldiers, the rifles, even Gladys's screams. Just as other Canadians had supplied what her brother called the gory details when they learned that she and Ernesto had fled Chile, assuming they'd been tortured, that they feared for their lives. Which they had, but for other, unimaginable reasons.

For all Paulina knew it was the truth, if not Gladys's, then some other woman's. Maybe even Marcela. It made her sick, remembering how often Marcela had sworn to wait until marriage. Diego hadn't looked like the waiting type, but still she hoped she was wrong, that Marcela had at least given herself willingly and lovingly. As Paulina had.

～

One evening Paulina left her apartment for the corner store and a package of Oreos, or so she'd thought but then she was boarding the Bathurst bus going south, getting off at Bathurst Station, wondering as she was walking east on Bloor just how it was that so many people could be so important to you, then disappear. People like Valerie and Helen Koenigsman, Denise Francis and Sir Jerome and George Woods. Robin at the church! And Pilar. Above all, Pilar.

The entrance to her old apartment had at last been cleared of paint cans and electrical cords, but no one seemed to be living there or maybe they weren't home.

Paulina walked over to the same spot where General Guzmán, or more likely his Canadian twin, had bent down to pick up after his dog. Looking across her old street she saw Ruth in the living-room window, carrying a houseplant. When Nathan appeared beside her Paulina expected him to caress her belly like men in the movies did, but he kissed her on the cheek instead.

So their trial separation had been just that, a trial. Walking up the street to the subway in the falling snow, Paulina vowed to call on them when she was back, bearing a gift for the new baby. Ernesto could pay for half. She'd tell her brother their good news when she called him that night.

~

"I can't go with you," Paulina said. No *hello, how are you*, just, *I'm not going*.

"It's safe," Ernesto said. "Didn't you get my messages? Pio's probably dead, too, from an overdose. It's safe. And no one will know who we are."

"It still won't be safe for me."

She let her words hang in the air, hoping they would do the work for her. *Don't make me say it*, she silently told her brother. *Don't make me say it over the phone, that it's not safe for me because in that country, in our country, I am a crime.*

"Are you sure?"

She knew he didn't mean, *are you sure you don't want to come home?* He meant, *are you sure you are a lesbian?*

"Yes, I'm sure."

"Okay," Ernesto said, breaking their long-distance silence. "But come here anyway. Manuel wants to see you, he has your things, Pilar kept them for you. She always felt bad about pushing you out of the house. Manuel, too."

"They saved my life."

Pilar wouldn't like it, Paulina crying so much the receiver was stuck to her ear. *If you keep crying like that, girl, you'll be nothing but a lump of dried salt.*

"I'll come to Montreal," she said, between sobs. "For Christmas."

"Good. Carmen will be happy to see you. She's coming back with us, to Chile. I was going to tell you when you got here. We're engaged."

"That's wonderful. A woman your age at last."

"Ha ha."

Paulina wanted to tell her brother not to go, how did he know it was safe, but instead she said she was looking forward to seeing him again, to spending Christmas together.

"Me, too. I am sorry, leaving you alone for so long."

I'm not alone, Paulina wanted to say, but the truth was that lately she felt alone all the time, even with Sylvia. Especially with Sylvia.

— 8. —

THEY WERE WAITING in the lobby when Mr. Hirsch walked by, lugging a small, plastic Christmas tree.

"Merry Christmas," he said. "But not so merry, when good tenants leave."

"Not for two months," Sylvia said.

"Good," Mr. Hirsch said, grinning. "I tear up letter of notice."

Sylvia managed to return his smile, but not Paulina.

"I need a place closer to work," she said.

"And you?" Mr. Hirsch pointed to Paulina. "What excuse you have?"

"She wants to move downtown," Sylvia said. "Where the action is."

She winked at Paulina.

"Two good tenants gone," Mr. Hirsch said.

When the taxi pulled up Sylvia came outside with Paulina, even though she'd forgotten her coat upstairs. Paulina watched the driver dump her mother's suitcase in his trunk, thinking she should tell him its contents were fragile, but then Sylvia would get suspicious.

"I'll be back in a week," she told Sylvia, who looked like she was about to cry, and if she started, there would be no end of crying for them both.

"And then you leave for Saskatchewan."

While she was gone, Sylvia would be circling ads for apartments to rent, for both of them. They would help each other move, get settled. We're not straights, Sylvia kept reminding Paulina, and herself. We'll always be in each other's lives, we'll share custody of Cleo, we'll see each other at The Home. They would always know each other, be known to each other. That was why Paulina was wearing the thin gold bracelet Sylvia had given her for Christmas, why Paulina insisted Sylvia keep her mother's fur coat.

Paulina was getting in the taxi when Sylvia stopped her:

"Say it one more time."

Paulina smiled.

"Saskatchewan," she said, or tried to say, but it came out a lisping mess.

Sylvia laughed, then they were waving at each other like lovers in a war movie as the taxi pulled away.

~

Distracted by the presence of a police officer inside the terminal, Paulina swung her suitcase too sharply, bumping it against a table set up between the entrance and a row of padded seats with what looked to Paulina like mailboxes attached to the tops of the armrests.

Quickly, so as not to draw attention, she gently shook the suitcase, listening for the sounds of broken glass, not that she needed to worry, she'd done as Deirdre had suggested, wrapping each glass jar in her clothing, her socks and underwear and T-shirts. At first, Deirdre had refused to let Paulina pay for the jars and other medical supplies they needed, but Paulina had insisted. She couldn't think of a better use of those funds raised for her benefit and there was still plenty left over for their next round of deliveries.

Reassured that her cargo was intact, Paulina turned her attention to the pile of brochures she'd knocked off the table. Probably Jehovah's Witnesses or some other religious garbage, but she bent down to pick them up all the same, apologizing to whoever was behind the table. She was returning the brochures when a hand reached across the table and grabbed her sleeve.

"Paulina?"

She'd straightened her frizzy hair and her face had grown into her long chin but it didn't matter, she could have sprouted wings, Paulina would have known her anywhere.

"What are you doing here?" Lorraine asked. "Stupid question. You're taking a bus. Where are you going?"

"To Montreal, to see my brother. He lives there now. What about you?"

"I'm with a group that helps runaways. We get them a place to sleep, food, whatever they need, without making them accept Jesus Christ as their lord and saviour."

"That's fantastic. Maybe I can help? But I am not back for a month."

"That doesn't matter, we always need volunteers. Back from Montreal?"

"No, from Sas—out west. I am in a movie. A horror movie. I play a ghost."

Lorraine laughed, grabbing Paulina's forearm like she used to when she whispered "lezzy" in her ear.

"I knew you'd make it one day. That's why I was such an asshole to you. I was jealous. You were my first kiss, you know."

So she'd remembered, after all this time.

"You were my first kiss, too."

"Oh, no, you poor thing. I was such a pain. I just wanted to be special, to stand out. Like you did. The headshrinkers were right, I just wanted attention. I said a lot of crazy shit, did a lot of crazy shit, too. Telling people my old dad was a draft dodger! I hope you forgot it?"

"Yes. I only remember the kiss. And the Crunchie."

Lorraine smiled at her from across her table. They may as well have been alone, not in this crowded, overheated bus terminal that smelled of sweat and snow. Paulina had been wrong, those first weeks in Toronto. There was a rain smell, and a snow smell, she could smell them both on Sylvia when she came home. Sylvia. It hurt to think of her.

There was paper all around them but Lorraine wrote her number on Paulina's arm, just below the crease of her elbow. Arm tingling, Paulina inscribed her number on Lorraine's arm, in the same hidden spot. Then they hugged goodbye, Paulina promising herself she'd write out Lorraine's number on a piece of paper as soon as she was on the bus, otherwise she risked sweating it off.

On her way to the platform Paulina saw that the mailboxes attached to the seats were, of all things, little TV sets. She turned around, eager to say something clever to Lorraine about these space-age marvels, but it was too noisy, so she waved at her. Lorraine waved back, then blew her an extravagant kiss, like a beauty queen being driven past her admirers. Paulina returned the gesture, laughing aloud as she hurried to catch her bus, her mother's suitcase secure in her hand.

Acknowledgements

Thank you to everyone at Guernica Editions, including Michael Mirolla for his patient stewardship, Julie Roorda for her equally patient editing, David Moratto for the striking cover image and design, and Anna van Valkenberg, for help getting the word out (so to speak). It seems only fitting that my novel has found a home with a publisher whose motto is, "No borders. No limits."

I would also like to thank my first readers for being so generous and thoughtful: authors Paul Ross and Mary-Lou Zeitoun, friends Kathleen Mullin and Zoë Constantinides. Thanks, too, to Gibraltar Point Centre for the Arts for that view of Toronto from the other shore, and your wonderful staff.

This is a work of fiction, inspired by historical events and personal encounters. Above all, I wished to pay tribute to the consolations of coincidence, that sense of interconnectedness that surprises and instructs. I have been fortunate enough to work and live in two countries that are not my own, Chile and France. The first inspired this novel; the second took me to the town of Nîmes and a restaurant, now closed, called El Rinconcito. A mural on the wall told the story of Héctor Herrera. I am indebted to his story, and those of so many others.

I am also indebted to, among others: Becki Ross's *The House that Jill Built: A Lesbian Nation in Formation*, Liz Millward's *Making a Scene: Lesbians and Community Across Canada, 1964-1984*, and Eduardo Galeano's *The Book of Embraces*.

The poem on page 104 is the first stanza of "Song of the Dead Girls", from *A Gabriela Mistral Reader*, translated by Maria Giachetti and edited by Marjorie Agosin.

Lastly, this one's for The Bro.

About the Author

This is Rebecca Păpucaru's first novel. *The Panic Room*, her first book, was awarded the 2018 Canadian Jewish Literary Award for Poetry and was also a finalist for the A.M. Klein Prize for Poetry and longlisted for the Gerald Lampert Memorial Award. Her short story "Yentas" won *The Malahat Review*'s 2020 Novella Prize. Her work has also appeared in *I Found It at the Movies: An Anthology of Film Poems* (Guernica Editions, 2014), *The Best Canadian Poetry in English* (2010), and numerous Canadian journals. You can find her at: @rebeccapapucaruwriter.

Printed by Imprimerie Gauvin
Gatineau, Québec